The Vortex Winder

Books by Duncan Smith

The Vortex Winder

The Maelstrom Ascendant

Cultown

Conquest By Concept

The Tightarse Tuesday Book Club

The Vast and the Spurious

Hammer and Heat

Music Albums

Vortex Winder

The Maelstrom Ascendant

Cultown

Waves Upon Waves

Website – www.vortexwinder.com

The Vortex Winder

Duncan Smith

Alfadex Books

Second Edition, Published by Alfadex Books, Sydney, 2023.
Copyright © Duncan Smith 2023, 2012.

A CIP catalogue record for this book is available from the
National Library of Australia.
ISBN 978-0-9872228-0-0
1. Fiction 2. Music 3. Philosophy

Cover design by Cornelia F. Wiesemüller.
Lighthouse XIII band – www.vortexwinder.com

Alfadex Books orders and information - email: matthew.
alfadex@gmail.com

Introduction

The Vortex Winder first came out in 2012. The sequel, *The Maelstrom Ascendant* followed in 2015. Nearly a decade later, both books have been revised for a second edition.

It is hard to classify these books by genre. Should they go under thriller? Fantasy? Psychological drama?

I prefer to simply call *The Vortex Winder* 'a modern fairytale' due to the mix of real and supernatural parts, and the theme of an innocent making his way in the world.

The Maelstrom Ascendant is darker, 'a Jekyll and Hyde story set in the corrupt world of showbiz.'

The books are also unusual because they come with music albums by my rock band, Lighthouse XIII. The album *Vortex Winder* goes with Book One. As for Book Two, it has two albums – *The Maelstrom Ascendant* and *Waves Upon Waves*.

You don't have to hear the music to appreciate the book. Each stands alone – but for those who are interested, the albums are on iTunes, Amazon, Spotify, and YouTube.

Duncan Smith
September, 2023

Duncan Smith is the guitarist and songwriter with the rock band Lighthouse XIII, whose albums include *Waves Upon Waves, Vortex Winder, The Maelstrom Ascendant,* and *Cultown.*

He is the author of *Cultown, The Maelstrom Ascendant, Conquest By Concept,* and *The Tightarse Tuesday Book Club.*

Part One

1 - Iolango

Some life changing moments happen by mistake. For example, a friend of mine met her future husband when he dialled a wrong number and she answered the phone. Now, why would that happen? Whether it's fate, luck, or a ricochet in God's random plan, who knows? Yet when it comes to life's big moments, the last place I expected one was in the hotel toilets at a heavy metal show. Who could have guessed an act of compassion for a drowning cockroach would lead so far?

Now stop right there - and don't make that face. Yes, I too wish this story had a more glamorous start. If only it had begun at a jazz concert at one of those Paris restaurants you have to book a year in advance, it would have been much more convenient for me. But it didn't, and I'm obliged to present the facts as they happened.

The show was at the Excelsior Hotel in Surry Hills, Sydney. The band 'Nevermore' was playing that night and I was warming up with a couple of drinks. My rigorous preparation for the show had begun on the bus trip in. I'd sipped discreetly from a beer bottle, without attracting the interest of the bored, balding bus driver whose life had slumped to the depths of working on Saturday night. How could he do it? Personally, I can't stand working when other people are enjoying themselves around me. Like the time picking up glasses in that north shore nightclub a few years ago. Never again.

The bus stopped and I got off in Surry Hills, an inner city suburb once frequented by street gangs but now semi-respectable. Not knowing where to find the hotel, I asked some young guys in black t-shirts for directions. Judging by their attire, they were going to the same place as me. They gave me the brush off, which was odd, but then I saw it from their side.

Here I was, alone in a Surry Hills backstreet, clutching a bottle of beer in a brown paper bag, with the first flush of my youth somewhere over the rainbow. It seemed the lads took me for some kind of unsavoury character, and didn't identify me as one of their own. It was a sobering thought.

Brushing off the slight, I simply followed their general tracks and before long the Excelsior Hotel loomed up before me. There were many more black-shirted rogues spilling out into the street before the show. Through force of habit, I scanned the various displays of band allegiance on the t-shirts. It was all quite predictable, with the usual clues to personality. A few conservative Megadeths and Slayers. Some more recent fare like Opeth and Arch Enemy. A faded, retro Metallica from the Justice tour. An inappropriate AC/DC. Great band for sure, but not really the right genre tonight. Then there were a few pretentious underground types wearing the shirts of bands no one's ever heard of. It seems a bit contradictory putting your arcane knowledge on show like that.

Inside the hotel, the support band was thundering through its last few songs. I decided they weren't worthy of going deaf for, and headed off to the gents to relieve myself. The toilets weren't yet crowded. It wasn't like the chaos at one of the big rock shows, where you almost have to take a ticket to line up. At the moment, the toilets were almost empty, with no queue for the trough.

Metal fans are a mixed bag, but my impression from twenty years of attending shows is that they're a decent bunch on the whole. There's also that sense of family, so that no matter what your outside story - whether you're a plumber or a pilot or an accountant - once you put on that black t-shirt, you're a brother. This view may be somewhat idealised, and it only took a few weeks exposure to the Blabbermouth website to realise that the metal scene, like most subcultures, contains the usual cross section of intellectuals to idiots. Still, you get that anywhere, don't you?

In the Excelsior Hotel toilets that night, I ran into a couple of the idiots, and was disgusted by the casual cruelty on display. As I reached the urinal trough, I glanced down to observe a large cockroach all at sea, struggling between dry icebergs, floating in a sea of flush, and - most disturbing of all - being callously pissed on by a couple of sniggering young guys. The poor creature was floundering desperately, and its prospects of escape were grim. Even if it could somehow escape from its watery peril, it would still be trapped in the stark surrounds of the men's toilet, a windowless prison soon to be invaded by hordes of stampeding drunken giants in black t-shirts, as soon as the support band finished its set.

I found myself appalled by the pissers' cruelty. There was no need for this weak act of inter species bullying. A drowning cockroach was an easy target, but it would be nice to take these two to an African wildlife reserve and see if they were tough enough to piss on some passing lions. I was almost as appalled to see one of the guys wearing a Guns and Roses shirt. In the 21st century, there was no call for that. G'n'R were a great rock band in the early nineties before imploding under the weight of their own egos and drug-fuelled dysfunction. They'd blown the chance to create an immense body of work by trying to be rock stars rather than musicians.

When it comes to animal relations, I'm no vegetarian, so my hands are not clean. These hands are bloodied, and I know it. Yet the guilt I sometimes feel isn't strong enough for me to change my ways. In all honesty, I was no braver in the present situation. Though disgusted, I didn't wade in throwing heroic punches at the urinators. I winced internally, but wasn't bold enough to rescue the drowning insect. In the macho atmosphere of a metal gig, I didn't want to be thought soft, or someone who sticks his hands into piss filled urinals.

The next moment, however, the two urinators left and returned to the hotel, and for once there was hardly anyone in the bathroom. Just a couple of guys behind me at the wash basins. The poor cockroach was still struggling, more feebly now, as it faced its liquid doom. There would be no escape for that wretched creature. Unless I did something very simple.

Impulsively seizing a decent sized wad of toilet paper, I stooped down and wrapped it round the wet insect before heading for the exit. There was hardly anyone around, apart from a big guy standing by the door. I glanced up anxiously as I passed, hoping he'd not seen my act of rescue. In this glance, I took in a Morbid Angel t-shirt and was surprised by the look of extreme malice its owner shot at me. I brushed past him, moved through the hotel crowd, and emerged into the cool night air.

Behind the hotel was an empty beer garden with a few trees and plants round the edges. Unfolding the wad of toilet paper, I dumped the cockroach onto some dirt at the base of one of the trees. It crawled weakly away to safety.

Now that I was alone in the beer garden, I pulled out a cigarette and lit it. I never smoke, except after a few beers. I'd have to hurry. It would soon be time for Nevermore's pulverising musical attack. I took a few quick puffs, nervous in case the band started without me. There would still be a fair bit of jockeying for position in the crowd before the band's entrance, yet I was by now a veteran of moving through densely packed crowds at gigs. There are two rules. One: keep moving, don't lose any momentum you've built up. And two: let someone else do the work. Find someone who's already blazing a trail through the crowd, and simply follow through in their wake when they've done the hard yards for you.

There's nothing like the start of a rock show. Those first moments when the house lights dim, the stage lights go on, and the crowd roars when the band appears. The mighty manifestation of a great musical entity is always a climax. With a sudden sense of urgency I turned to walk back into the hotel – only to be interrupted by a voice behind me.

'Wait.'

I'd been sure the beer garden was empty, and turned around in surprise. A man was sitting at one of the tables. Some old homeless guy, it appeared. I ignored him and turned away. Who cared about him, when Nevermore were about to come on? But again he called on me to wait.

He was dressed in a drab brown suit which looked way too warm for the time of year, so it was no surprise to see him perspiring freely. Even his clothes looked a little damp. And he was close enough for me to notice his choice of cologne left a lot to be desired. It seemed that *eau d' Urine* was scent of the month in *Homeless Guys Weekly*. What a disgusting, smelly wino! Yet basic manners forced me to acknowledge him.

'What is it, mate? I've got to go.'

'Let me thank you first. We need to talk.'

The comment made no sense, and there was nothing this guy could possibly offer me. Nevermore would be on stage any minute, so I was about to turn on my heel for the last time when something odd happened. The perspiration so visible on the man's face seemed to dry up right in front of my eyes, and more dramatically, the drab brown suit changed colour. It lightened to tan, morphed into gold, evolved through red and green, before finally settling into a dull luminescent blue. The odour of his 'cologne' also receded, and I was standing in front of a handsome man in a blue robe.

'That doesn't usually take so long,' the man said, 'but I was exhausted. Without you, it wouldn't have happened at all.'

In my twenties, I'd taken LSD once or twice, and for a moment I thought I was having a flashback. Yet in spite of what had just happened - and this should give some idea of the single-mindedness of the metal fan - my only concern was the need to go in and get a good spot for Nevermore! So if this guy thought I was going to stand by while he drew me into a long winded conversation, he was mistaken. I still didn't know who he was, and I didn't much care.

'Good trick,' I said. 'Whatever you did, very impressive, but I've really got to go. So whatever you want to say, you've got about ten seconds.'

'You don't know who I am?'

'No idea. Never seen you before.'

'Until tonight, when you saved my life.'

I was starting to get it. The guy was a religious freak. He was about to convert me, then ask me to deposit ten thousand dollars into a Nigerian bank account.

'I am in your debt,' he continued. 'Through my long and hazardous lifetime, I have faced many perils and sometimes wondered how I would finally meet my end. But to come to such a dire fate as nearly occurred would have made me a tragic laughing stock. Which was exactly what Elijinx intended.'

'Who?'

'Elijinx, my mortal enemy. We passed him on the way out.'

'Out of where?'

In hindsight, I'm ashamed of my slow-wittedness.

'You're in a hurry, so I'll get to the point. My name is Iolango. Elijinx and I are shape shifters. We live in the shadows of your world, the nocturnal realms. We change our form to blend into the patterns of your planet.'

'Change your form - what, change your clothes like you did just now?'

'More than that. We can change our bodies too.'

'Change your face?'

'Easily - and our sex or race. All that was mastered aeons ago. There's more than that. We have gone far beyond identification with any one species. We enjoy the myriad creature forms in this world.'

'Meaning what - you can change into animals too?

'We can and we do.'

'Really? That's great, but I'm still not giving you any money, OK? I'm broke, so forget it.'

'We have no need for money. That's for you humans. But if we ever do need it, there is no problem getting it.'

'Speaking of getting it, can you get to the point? Nevermore's about to start.'

'Very well - two points. First, we can, as you say, turn into animals. And second, you saved my life tonight. Understand?'

I shrugged and glanced at the hotel, then looked back at Iolango.

'To save time, I'll take the express route and bypass the skeptical inquiry stage. So tell me, do you and your pals ever turn into birds, or even insects?'

'We do indeed - as I did today.'

'Are you trying to say you're that goddamned cockroach I fished out of the piss trough tonight?'

'Yes, and thank you for saving my life.'

Iolango extended his hand to shake. I reached out my own, then quickly retracted it. Who knew what I was really shaking hands with?

'So you people are some kind of magicians?'

'Magic is only a word. It is technology really. Clarke's magic, to use the words of one of your own kind.'

'Oh yeah, I've heard that one. "Any sufficiently advanced technology is indistinguishable from magic." Arthur C. Clarke.'

7

'Exactly. Anyhow, Elijinx and I have feuded for longer than I can remember, and tonight he nearly brought me to an ignominious end. I would have been the laughing stock of our race. It was Elijinx who changed me into the cockroach and dumped me in the trough. I couldn't break the charm while he was in the room. Watch out for him, by the way. You've made a foe there.'

'My friend's enemy is my enemy?'

'He is now. Watch your back - and your front and your sides. Especially your sides. He's very cunning.'

'You mean that guy in the Morbid Angel t-shirt is Elij-whatsisname? I'll keep an eye out for him then.'

'He won't look like that next time though, will he?'

'Oh yeah, of course.'

'But you may still have an inkling. Look for the shadow behind the smile. A certain malevolence which can't be hidden by change of form.'

'What about you? Will I bump into you again?'

'More than likely. But I've a gift for you, a gift that will offer some protection on your travels.'

'I'm not going anywhere, am I?'

'It's up to you. You're stuck in a rut. Give yourself the gift of freedom. Go and do something different, have some adventures. And take this, it will help you.'

Iolango handed me a small rectangular device. It looked like some kind of phone but was only the size of a playing card.

'That's the Vortex Winder. It will give you special powers, a different one every week or so. Then you must use them as best you can.'

'Thanks, I'm sure. Very good of you. Now I hate to be rude, but I've got to GO! Nevermore is about to start.'

'OK. Go and start your travels. Your random, surprising adventures. My people do not have a monopoly on shape shifting.'

That was the last thing I heard before I ran back to the hotel. I made it inside just in time to find a prime spot to see Nevermore's opening song, 'Enemies of Reality.' Brilliant!

2

Thug Repellent

I woke the next day tired from the excesses of the night before. But I had enjoyed those excesses in moderation, and was in a good mood. What a great show it had been from Nevermore. Jeff Loomis was a sorcerer on guitar, and Warrel Dane could actually sing, such a novelty after so many cookie monster vocalists in extreme metal.

I remembered the whole cockroach incident with disbelief. What had I really seen? A guy whose clothes had changed colour, which could be some kind of conjuring trick. As for the tale of shape shifting and the deadly foe, he probably told that to any passing stranger in the pub for a laugh. Yet there was the 'Vortex Winder' lying on the floor beside my bed. I turned it on to see if anything happened. The screen lit up with a message.

You are now the owner of a VW12, which grants one special power each week. For best results, wait seven days for the Vortex Winder to attune itself to your psyche. This will help it choose powers most suited to your needs. It is wise not to use your device before then. If you cannot heed this advice, activate your Vortex Winder and it will randomly select a power from those on file.

Patience was never my strength, and as I did not yet take the Vortex Winder at all seriously, I turned it on at once. Under the heading 'Power of the Week' were the words 'the Unforked Tongue' with a short description. It seemed the 'Unforked

Tongue' was a kind of truth serum. *'All those with whom you converse will be compelled to speak truth.'* That sounded like a useful power to have, but it was bound to lead to trouble. Wondering what else was on offer, I pressed the skip button.

The next power was 'Rhyme Master' which was apparently *'the ability to speak in perfect rhyming couplets.'* Huh? What am I, a rapper? I don't think so. I pressed skip again.

The third power was called 'Thug Repellent.' I'd heard of slug repellent. It was for plants in the garden, a defence system against slow moving, slimy predators. But Thug Repellent? The message explained.

> *Useful in today's high stress world. Suitable for road rage, office bullying, drunks, and miscellaneous thuggery. If under attack, point device at aggressor. Effective for ten minutes.*

That was all. It didn't make much sense. So, I'm getting mugged in New York and I turn on the Vortex Winder. What then - the cops are going to show up? Superman? Iolango and hordes of avenging angels? It seemed pretty silly, so again I pressed skip - but this time nothing happened. The screen was stuck on Thug Repellent. The Vortex Winder had either become fed up with my rejection of its randomly picked magic powers, or the skip button could only be used twice. What a pity. I should have stayed with the power of the Unforked Tongue and found out what my friends and associates really thought of me.

Oh well, I supposed I'd better carry this thing so it could 'attune itself to my psyche.' I slipped it into my pocket, left my flat in Coogee, and walked out to buy bread and coffee. It was a peaceful Sunday morning and nothing could spoil it.

Or so I thought, until my ears were assaulted by a barrage of barks from the black dog at number nine. Again, just like every other time. It was one of the smaller, yappy breeds which never shuts up. I was growing tired of this four legged moron coming on like the King's protector with its oafish, unnecessary attacks. It snarled at me viciously from behind the safety of its owner's front fence.

'Oh, shut up,' I chastised. 'I'm allowed to walk down the street. Go get a real job guarding Hades or something.'

The impertinence of my reply goaded the mutt to further frenzies. It must be annoying half the street by now.

'That's enough,' I snapped. I pulled the Vortex Winder out of my pocket and stood just out of range of the dog's yapping jaws. 'That's it, pal, I'm activating the Thug Repellent. You're for it now. You're in big trouble.'

I was only messing around, but I made a big show of holding the Vortex Winder up and pointing it in his direction. Then something odd happened. The dog sort of... froze in mid-bark. Its jaws were still wide open, but both its bite and bark were now out of action. It just stood there with a bewildered look on its face, and some drool dribbling pathetically out the side of its mouth.

In a flash, I reverted to my mood of last night, when I'd entertained the idea Iolango might be telling the truth about the cockroach and the shape shifting and the rest of it. As I stood in front of the immobilized canine thug, I could see no other explanation but that the magic did work and it was all true. How bizarre.

I cleared off before the dog's owner came out to investigate the sudden silence. By the time I came back from the shop it was nearly ten minutes later, and I waited nervously to see if the spell had worn off, for I didn't want the poor creature to suffer any harm. To my relief, the dog unfroze and regained movement in front of my eyes. 'No hard feelings,' I said, as my former aggressor slunk off, clearly terrified.

After that, I made sure I took the Vortex Winder on my trip to Canberra, just in case. I'd promised an old friend to help with her apartment. She was overseas, so I was going to drop in, make sure the place was clean, and return bond to the tenant who was moving out.

It was more of an excuse for a drive and a couple of days away in a city I think is quite underrated. Some people say Canberra feels sterile because it was specially designed by an architect in the 1930s to be Australia's capital, but that's one reason I like it. It has a clean, orderly feel, like one of those 'moon base' space cities you used to find in science fiction books. So much better than most of the world's cities which have sprung up 'organically' into urban slums of human spontaneity. There are plenty of those around, and you can have them.

One such is a place called Queanbeyan, a smallish town on the outskirts of Canberra. It was here that the Thug Repellent had its second outing. I was due to pass through the place on my way to Canberra itself. Queanbeyan is quite pretty but has some rough spots, and its fair share of hoons and outlaws. Strangely enough, I was about to be lectured on a finer point of the law by one of those very hoons.

There I was, driving through Queanbeyan, with nothing more on my mind than getting a spicy bowl of Laksa from the Malaysian place in the main street. A few blocks away, I stopped for petrol, then turned onto the highway. It was a six lane road, three of them going the same way I was. In the inside lane, some cars were waiting at the traffic lights. I assumed they'd be going straight ahead or right when the lights changed. I entered the outside lane so I could turn left, and my car was at the very front of the queue.

How great to be able to have Laksa, I thought. The conveniences of the modern world shouldn't be taken for granted. To be able to order almost any kind of food on a daily basis was a real luxury. Lost in the thought, I hardly noticed the sound of a car horn just behind me. I turned left when the lights changed, drove up to the main street and parked the car. Immediately, there was a screech of brakes, and an old Ford pulled up at my rear. To my surprise, a burly, goateed guy in a flannelette shirt got out and was soon standing in front of me. He was red faced with fury and almost seemed to have steam coming out his ears. Why, I had no idea, but apparently was about to find out.

'Do you have a problem with breaking the law?' Mr Goatee asked.

'I'm sorry?' I said, playing for time, trying to process this sudden jolt of hostility intruding into my world.

'Don't you know it's an offence to turn left from a feeder-lane?'

'Oh, you mean the lane coming out of the petrol station. I thought that was the lane I *had* to take to go left at the lights. I didn't know that. How long's that been a law here?'

'Only about four hundred years.'

It seemed prudent to remark that in this case, such a law must have pre-dated not only the invention of the automobile, but the settlement of Australia by Europeans. Presumably, the law had been in operation when the road was still a patch of dusty outback during Aboriginal times. Yet before pointing this out, it might be wise to apply the old Thug Repellent. I picked up the Vortex Winder and held it close to my assailant, which was easy given that he was right in my face. Having done that, I pretended to be grateful.

'It's an offence to turn left from a feeder lane. Well, what do you know? You learn something every day. Thanks for telling me.'

'So don't do it again, you idiot.'

'Ok, I stand corrected. Just one question though. Are you a cop?'

'Eh?'

'I said, are you a cop? An officer of the law?'

'What's that got to do with it?'

'So you're *not* a cop. That puts a different light on the matter. In fact, now I know you're not a cop, but a concerned citizen who's decided to inform me of this arcane traffic law, I suggest that the optimum solution is as follows. Go home and check your spam email folder until you find an offer for a penis enlargement kit. Order it at once, and when it arrives, use it every day until you're able to auto-fellate. Then, when you've managed to achieve full satisfaction, come back and see me with some more of your views.'

The fist came fast. Indeed it came a lot faster than the penis enlargement kit would probably have come in the mail. It came fast and violently, and it stopped about two inches from my nose. Mr Goatee reacted with shock. It was as if the air was a bowl of wet cement which had suddenly set around his fist. He pulled vainly trying to free it, but his arm remained absurdly stuck in mid air.

'Please, enough of this police brutality,' I remarked, before correcting myself. 'Oh that's right, you're not a cop. You're just a standard issue bully with a big mouth.'

'What have you done?'

'Nothing. I was just minding my own business, until you decided to attack me because you were angry I was ahead of you at the traffic lights. Don't worry, it will wear off in about ten minutes, so you can go home and beat up your wife, or whatever it is you do on a Sunday night.'

I got in my car and drove off. This Thug Repellent was really cool. I hoped I wouldn't need it anymore. Then again, I almost hoped I would. And as it happened, it was just a few days later that it got another airing. In hindsight, I've a theory that the Thug Repellent also acted as an attractant, but that's another story. On Thursday night, back in Sydney, I paid a visit to the Coogee Bay Hotel.

There was no real reason to visit, I was just at a loose end and dropped in for a game of pool. I put a two dollar coin on the side of the pool table to reserve a game. There were already several coins ahead of it in the queue. As there would be a wait, a good time killer was always the CD juke box. I pressed the buttons which flipped over a stack of CDs to show what was on offer.

It wasn't a bad selection. Mainstream stuff, nothing too left field, but at least it was albums. Not like the old fifties style juke boxes which only had seven inch vinyl singles. At least with the albums, you could slip in a few obscure album tracks. There was even some heavier material. Again, fairly mainstream, top sellers, but that's what you get on a juke box. There was Metallica's black album. AC/DC's black album... almost identical covers, in fact. What next - *Smell the Glove* by Spinal Tap? And who'd have thought, I mused, AC/DC's *Back in Black* the second biggest selling album of all time, according to a recent report. That was a surprise. They could hardly get a song played on the radio, when they started out. They had to go overseas to make it big at home. That's Australia for you. Actually, that's human nature for you. Pathetic!

What else? *Deepest Purple*, one of the umpteen Deep Purple compilation albums. And, surprisingly, Iron Maiden's *Live After Death*. Iron Maiden, eh, the only band in the world with more live albums than studio LPs. Or so it seemed.

By the way, I hope I can be forgiven my little free association raves on music. Those who don't like them can skip ahead.

Going back to Deep Purple, I chose the song 'Burn' from the David Coverdale era. It was probably their best song. The funny thing was that when Ian Gillan rejoined the band, he refused to sing any of the Coverdale songs. This reflected poorly on Gillan. After all, Coverdale had to sing the old Gillan-era songs when he was there. Why shouldn't Gillan return the favour? Ego and arrogance, the usual story. So, from then on, all the Deep Purple fans missed out on hearing their best song at live shows. It's the same as when Sammy Hagar joined Van Halen, he hardly sang any of the David Lee Roth songs. Bloody singers. Egomaniacs, the lot of them.

I was drifting off into a reverie, and almost forgot I was in the pub until a white ball crashed into a triangle of coloureds behind me. I took a seat by the pool table to wait for my game. Suddenly, an AC/DC song came on the jukebox. It was one of the Brian Johnson songs, but it wasn't off *Back in Black*. I couldn't place it until the chorus came on. 'She's got you by the balls,' sang Brian over and over again. Ah that's right, I remembered the title now. It was indeed 'She's Got You By the Balls' itself.

Now that I heard it again, it wasn't such a bad song. Some of the Brian Johnson tracks were quite overlooked. They should put out a new live album, with no Bon Scott songs and nothing off *Back in Black*. Just some of the more obscure album tracks from the Brian Johnson era. That would be cool. Same as if Slayer put out a live album with nothing from before *Divine Intervention*. That would shut up all the 'nothing-good-since-Seasons' dickheads who posted on Blabbermouth.net. I shook my head sadly at the waste of my talent. Why wasn't I some kind of creative consultant to bands, so they could get the benefit of all my great ideas? No one ever listened to me.

I drifted off further into my musical daydream, and only half noticed the actions of a couple of people at a nearby table. The second chorus of 'She's Got You By the Balls' had come on, and some guy in a denim jacket was acting out the song lyrics in front of a young woman, while laughing raucously. He didn't seem to realise the song was a purely metaphorical tale of a young prostitute's emotional and financial hold over a sex crazed CEO. Failing to grasp the intellectual dimensions of the lyrics, the guy was clutching at his own groin area through his pants, and grinning like he'd made a phenomenally witty joke. Whether the young woman with him was his girlfriend, or just some stranger he was trying to impress, I couldn't tell. I watched him with mild interest and stronger distaste, and wondered if the girl was amused. Yet I was mostly still toying with the thought of the Slayer live album.

Suddenly the crotch-grabber looked around and saw me watching him. The broad smile vanished, and a face of thunder appeared. It was as if he'd caught me as a peeping Tom looking into his bedroom while he made love to his fiancée.

The oaf walked over to me and scowled into my face. Here we go again, I thought, another cretin. He connected with a strangely gentle head butt to my forehead. It was if he was performing the first step in a ritual, yet wanted me to throw the first punch so he could claim not to have been the aggressor.

Time for the old Thug Repellent. I quickly pointed the Vortex Winder at him, then asked, 'AC/DC fan are you, mate?'

The ball grabber only scowled, then uttered the immortal words.

'What are you looking at?'

Yes, he really said it. It was like he was reading off a script.

'What am I looking at?' I replied. 'I'll tell you. I'm looking at you, kid. You're irresistible. The rugged exterior, the rough hewn, bawdy charm. The aura of simmering violence masking a tender heart of gold.'

The full head butt came like a reflex. The air set like jelly. The familiar facial expression appeared - shock, bewilderment,

fear mixed with rage - and all attached to the frozen head butt.
I continued to speak.

'You want to know what I'm looking at. I'm looking at an
idiot who can't go out and have a good night without ruining
someone else's. I came here for a game of pool, but you seem to
think my plan for the night was a violent drunken fight with
you. What's my crime? Looking. Yes that's right, looking at
you - a drunken ape grabbing his balls in the pub so you can
impress some poor girl who had the bad luck to cross your
path. Well, to be frank, the sight of you grabbing your balls is
not on my list of the top one hundred things to see before I die.
And if you don't like random members of the public looking
at you doing it, here's a suggestion from www.rocket scientist.
com - don't do it in a public place. Now why don't you go home,
get onto You Tube, and look up Alexei Sayle's song 'Who You
Looking At?' You'll learn a lot.'

At that point, a most bizarre sensation came over me. My
face froze and I could not move my tongue, or open and close
my mouth. It was like being anaesthetized at the dentist, yet
far worse, for my whole mouth was numb and immobile.
Thankfully, the rest of my body was working normally and I
could still move, an ability I put to immediate use by exiting
the premises.

It's easy enough to guess what happened, and realise I'd
fallen foul of the very power which was supposed to protect me.
I had begun as a victim, yet once the attacker was at my mercy,
I had turned into a thug myself, even if only verbally. I'd gotten
away with it in Canberra, but in Coogee, I'd certainly gone too
far. There was no call for me to slander and abuse my assailant,
even if he had been the aggressor.

It would not be the only time the powers of the Vortex
Winder turned out to be a double edged sword with unexpected

consequences, yet at this stage I did not know there were still many surprises in store for me.

3
Steer Me To The King

I suppose I should introduce myself. Does it really matter? I liked the way in the movie *Once* that we never learned the names of the two main characters. That's the one about the Irish busker and his girlfriend the piano player. Even in the credits, they were listed as 'Guy' and 'Girl.' That's easier to pull off in a film, though, rather than a book. OK then, the name's Jim. Jimmy Brandt. Mr James R. Brandt, if we're being formal.

I quite identified with 'Guy' actually. We had a bit in common. He was a songwriter, busking in the streets of Dublin, and the rest of the time working in his dad's Hoover repair shop. He was trying to get somewhere in the music world, without much hope, until 'Girl' gave him a kick-along by setting up a recording session so he could make his album.

Presumably, the rest was history, although the film ended at the point where he moved to London. He didn't even take 'Girl' with him, much to the disappointment of romantics like me in the audience. In real life, however, it ended very well for the two actors playing the lead roles. They had a hit record with the soundtrack, won awards, had an affair. It was a weird little blend of fact and fiction. Normally, it's the fiction that's the wild fantasy and the fact is the mundane reality, but this time it was the other way round.

I'm a songwriter too, although Guy's heart-rending acoustic ballads aren't my style. I'm more of a rocker. Retired now. Back in the last decade, I recorded a lot of songs when I was living in Adelaide, but I'd become disheartened by the frustrations of the biz, and given it all away. What a waste. I'd gone back to uni for a few years, and was now working part time in an office job. Still giving the odd guitar lesson and writing the occasional song, but had basically given up the ghost these last ten years. What I really needed was my very own 'Girl' to come along and inspire me to keep going, record my songs, and move to London. But instead of 'Girl' I had Sandra, whose main purpose was to inspire me to get a fulltime job, leave Coogee, and move out to the western suburbs to pay off a mortgage.

It wasn't her fault. It was I, not her, who'd given up on my youthful ambitions. Now in my late thirties, it didn't seem such a bad idea anymore to buy into the suburban dream and start living a 'normal life.' There's a lot to be said for it, especially when you start getting older. As someone once said, 'I don't want to be cool, I want to be warm.' Well, I may have been occasionally cool in my twenties, but those days were gone.

Here I was then: I wasn't young or old, rich or poor, handsome or ugly. I was just an average guy sliding into mediocrity like almost everyone else.

Yet the appearance of Iolango had thrown a large X factor into the mix. The idea of shape shifting beings with magical powers was rather bizarre, but I'd seen the effects of the Thug Repellent with my own eyes, so perhaps it was true. It was weird, but the world is *full* of weird things when you think about it. Most people simply aren't aware of them.

And there was the Vortex Winder sitting on the bedside table. With a tinge of excitement, I picked it up and got the news on special power of the week. It was something called the 'Waking Dream'- whatever that was. I peered into the screen

If you are confused, at a crossroads, or seeking direction, request a waking dream. Ask your inner oracle a question and, within seven days, the answer will be presented to you in symbolic form in the events of your daily life. It is up to you to form your own interpretation, and act on it.

Was that it? It didn't sound very exciting. Not as dramatic as the Thug Repellent. Just some symbolic message I had to find. Well, that was just great. I was already prone to over-thinking. Now I'd be over-analysing everything for the next seven days.

It all seemed rather vague. How obvious would this 'waking dream' be? Would it appear with neon lights flashing, or instead be a subtle sub-text hidden in the mundane events of the day? I tried searching the Vortex Winder for more information, but none was forthcoming.

As expected, I found myself hypersensitive to everything going on around me. The Indonesian guy who ran the local corner shop called me by the wrong name, and I spent half an hour trying to read a meaning into it. Channel surfing on TV, I chanced upon the classic 1970s series, *Catweazle*, and wondered if it contained a message. Other such trivial events followed, but after four days, I was still clueless. My question for the oracle had been right to the point: What should I do with my life? Which path should I take?

It was late in the week that the waking dream finally appeared. I'd dropped into a music shop in Coogee to buy some guitar strings. As I paid for them, the guy in the shop asked if I wanted to go to a concert by blues legend, BB King, that night at the Hordern Pavilion. He'd been given a free ticket by the promoter, but had a prior commitment and couldn't go. It was nice of him to offer, but I didn't exactly grab the ticket out of his hand.

'BB King?' I said. 'He still going then?'

'Sure.'

'God, he's been around for a while. Didn't he start out in the fifties? He must be ancient.'

'Doesn't matter. He's still playing two hundred shows a year.'

'That's more than every second night. What's he on, then - Viagra?'

'Whatever it is, I want some.'

I took the ticket. To be honest, I wasn't that keen. Blues was OK, but it wasn't something I listened to much at home. It was good live though and fun to play. Oh well, I supposed I'd better go and see BB King. It was like seeing Segovia play classical guitar if you had the chance. He was that kind of almost archetypal figure, so closely was he identified with one genre of guitar playing.

So it was that I found myself filing into the Hordern Pavilion that night with a few thousand other Sydney people. The crowd seemed a lot more civilised than the usual crowds I'd seen in that venue. It was certainly better dressed. Yet there was something a bit 'Melbourne Cup' about it. You know, the people who don't follow horse racing, but turn up for the big race once a year because it's *an event*. That's the sort of vibe there was at BB's Sydney gig. Apparently, the arbiters of public taste had made one of their random decrees and BB King was suddenly the coolest guy in the world, and everyone just *had* to be there.

As for the show itself, it was OK. I've never seen so many people on one stage. Two or three guitarists, bass, a horn section, female backing singers, two drummers for God's sake! A three piece like Cream would have hated to follow them. Then again, it's about quality not quantity, really. Don't get me wrong, BB and his band were pretty good, but frankly the old boy must have seen better days. There were so many slow songs, I nearly fell asleep. BB must've been hot once, but the guy was getting on. He wasn't really setting the place on fire. It was more of a slow smoulder, without actually reaching the point of flaring up. What the Melbourne Cup crowd made of it all, I don't know. They probably managed to brainwash themselves into loving it.

Like I said, BB's slow blues nearly made me nod off. Maybe that's what *did* happen, because that's when I had the dream. It was vivid, it was shocking, and it jolted me to my core, so that my whole identity came under stern interrogation, and the depths of my sad decline in life became clear. As I was nodding off, I casually looked over to my left and two rows in front of me, there he was.

Bill.

Bill Steer.

Bill Steer, the virtuoso guitarist from Carcass. He of the drastically detuned guitar, the lethal death metal riffs, and demonic guitar solos. And as I confronted this shocking apparition, this bewildering manifestation, one ineloquent thought cut through everything else: *what the fuck is Bill Steer doing at a BB King concert in Sydney?*

In sheer disbelief, I kept on goggling at Bill, and my eyes must have been burning a hole in his face because he turned round to see me staring at him. Quickly, I looked away. Just because the guy is famous (not that this crowd knew who he was) shouldn't mean he can't enjoy a night out on the town without being gawped at. He turned back around to look at BB onstage.

For the rest of the show my gaze kept returning to Bill, although I tried not to overdo it so that he turned round again. It was definitely him. Now that I came to think of it, the pieces started to fit together. There had been rumours that on the last Carcass tour of Australia, Bill had gotten together with a local girl and it had turned serious. At about that time, Carcass signed up with a major label record company but ran into big problems when the grunge fad took over. The hard rock scene had been turned on its head when the LA glam bands were killed off by grunge, guitar solos went out of style, and the people who signed Carcass to Columbia Records left the company. Carcass were coming off the back of *Heartwork* one of the best ever melodic death metal records, but there'd been rumours the new label bosses tried to make them go for a commercial sound, and even tried to force Jeff Walker to start singing properly. That was never going to happen. Eventually it had all fallen apart, Carcass had split up, and the world lost a great band.

So this is what happens to old death metal guitarists, I thought. They get married and start going to BB King concerts. That's when it hit me this must be the waking dream. Bill, BB, and me. Bill Steer was almost my contemporary. Of course, he'd made the big time, whereas I'd never even put out a proper record as such. Regardless of that, in the context of this dream, the former Carcass guitarist symbolised myself and the end of my own music career.

At this point, let me add a disclaimer. Bill Steer is a genius and what he does in his personal or professional life is no business of mine. His presence at a BB King concert was an event I interpreted in my own way, for my own reasons. The symbolism was purely my own, which I used it as a means of spurring myself to action.

I should also note that the events in this story happened several years in the past. That need not diminish their interest. Every historical era contains a million untold stories, of which mine is merely one. Telling such stories brings the past back to life, whether it was centuries ago, or just a few years. It also enables the power of hindsight. That's not some supernatural power conferred by the Vortex Winder, but one we all possess. It's the power to understand past events from the more knowledgeable standpoint of the present. And as they say, hindsight is always 20/20.

As it turned out, Bill Steer *did* reform the mighty Carcass some years down the track, but at the time of the BB King show, I wasn't to know that would happen. I went home that night and couldn't sleep. As a result, my girlfriend Sandra couldn't sleep either, and finally, about 4am, I told her about Bill. She didn't seem to be getting it, and maybe at that time of night, that was understandable.

'So you saw some old heavy metal guitarist at the BB King concert,' she said. 'So what?'

'It wasn't just anyone. It was Bill Steer from Carcass.'

'Never heard of him.'

'Typical. You probably don't even know who Tony Iommi is.'

'No, and you know what, Jimmy? I don't care. I'm not into heavy metal. Anyhow, why shouldn't he go to a BB King concert? Everyone's heard of *him*. He's a famous blues guitarist.'

'That's why I went too. If you play guitar, it's mandatory to see him at least once.'

'There you go then.'

'It's not just that, it's the whole package. The serious relationship, the blues concert, the death of Carcass.'

I looked at Sandra and saw she wasn't taking it seriously. Indeed she was smirking. She was just about to start winding me up. It was one of her hobbies - and like a fool, I rose to take the bait every time.

'Listen to yourself,' she said. 'The death of Carcass! Do you know how silly that sounds? Actually, your friend Bill sounds like a fine man. He's grown out of this adolescent phase of liking heavy metal, and started listening to some mature music like blues. If only a few others would do the same.'

Sure enough, I exploded.

'*Mature?* What's so mature about blues? They only use about three chords.'

'Eh?'

'Oh that's right, you wouldn't know. If you played guitar, you'd know blues is based on the I-IV-V progression - that's three chords.'

'Oh really?'

'They branch out occasionally, but it's mainly those three chords. That's the genre. At least, with metal you can go beyond that. So why is blues a superior art form? Something 'mature adults' listen to?'

'Must be the lyrics.'

'Why? It's all boy-girl stuff. Baby, you're hot, or you don't love me anymore, or you're a two timer. Or whining about how you've got no money or whatever your hard luck story is.'

'At least that means something. I suppose they should be singing about death, should they? Look at these silly bands you listen to. Carcass. Slayer. Suicidal Tendencies! Maybe you should see a psychologist.'

'Not all metal bands have death in their names.'

'Name one.'

'Sepultura.'

'Sepultura? What does that mean? I'm going to look it up.'

'Oh wait, bad example. It was just the first band that popped into my head. Sepultura means 'grave' in Portuguese. Scrub that. How about Metallica? There you go - nothing at all to do with death.'

'Yeah? Look at those covers,' Sandra said, going to my bookcase full of CDs. *Kill Em All*, *Death Magnetic* with a coffin on the front. And look at this one - *Ride the Lightning* with an ever so tasteful picture of an electric chair. Why don't you listen to some proper music for grown-ups?'

'Please. If growing up means listening to blues and other serious art forms, I'll stay as I am, thanks.'

I sank down onto the bed, putting my head in my hands.

'You don't understand, there's a history here. Back when I was in high school, I had a good mate, and we used to do this metal show on the local FM radio station just playing our own records. I had all the Sabbath, Priest, and AC/DC. He had Rainbow, Zeppelin, and Van Halen. We did good for the world by making sure that at least once a week, the poor downtrodden people finally had some decent music to listen to. But just a couple of years later, my friend fell into bad company. He started running with the wrong crowd, and after we left school, he starting to hang out with people who listened to blues. He totally changed. Every time you saw him it was Ry Cooder this, or JJ Cale that. Heartbreaking, it was.'

'It's not just him,' I continued. 'Even the big stars aren't immune to this mental decline. Look at Jake E. Lee. He was tearing it up with Ozzy back in the eighties. Then the next thing you know, he's formed some godforsaken Bad Company clone band. And what about Gary Moore? A total shredder in his day, until he turned into a boring blues guitarist. Remember that soppy ballad, 'Still Got the Blues'? His one big hit. Ironically, it wasn't even a blues song. It was ripped off from 'Autumn Leaves' that jazz tune.'

At this point, Sandra jumped up and starting singing 'Still Got the Blues' in an overwrought style, but changed the words so it was about Jake E. Lee. 'You used to play with Ozzy, back in the metal days. But I found out the hard way, you were just a music ho who strayed. On the wrong path, your soul you had to lose. You sold out to adulthood, and started playing the evil blues.'

I must admit, Sandra can be quite funny at times. I would have laughed if I wasn't so annoyed.

'Anyhow,' I said, 'Bill Steer is the last straw. Seeing him at the BB King concert just doesn't sit right with me. Bill should be out there touring the world with Carcass, not sitting there listening to blues. But now it's all come to me in a flash of inspiration. I've received guidance in symbolic form. Guess what I'm gonna do? I'm putting the band back together.'

'Like the Blues Brothers?'

'No, *not* like the goddamn Blues Brothers! Like Sabbath when they got Ozzy back in the band. You don't believe me? Just watch. I'm going to write some new songs and make an album, like the Irish guy in *Once*.'

'You don't *look* like a rock star. You haven't even got long hair.'

'I may very well grow it. Starting today.'

In the heat of the moment, I almost added *and you don't look like a rock star's wife*, but thought better of it. Although I'd had my fair share of girlfriends in the past, I wasn't born with classic rock star looks. This had annoyed me in the past, as Sandra's comment did now.

To be honest, I did find Sandra very attractive, with her pretty Italian-Australian face. She was also pleasingly voluptuous, as she neared forty, and I'd occasionally told her not to bother with the diets she tried from time to time. This morning, her sculpted eyebrows were raised in skepticism at my latest plan.

'After ten years, you're suddenly going to make a comeback?' she said. 'But you never even made it in the first place. How can you come back when you weren't even there? You didn't even release a record.'

'I had the songs, they just never made it to the airwaves. Still, better late than never. Maybe I'll make it big and set a positive example for Bill Steer to bring Carcass back to life. Carcass will live again!'

'Listen to you, Jimmy, you sound a bit mad. I'm worried about you. Last week you came home pissed and started talking about a magic cockroach or some rubbish, and now you're on about reborn carcasses and putting the band back together. Are you OK? Or is this just some bullshit midlife crisis?'

'No, the midlife crisis is when you get married and buy a house. That's my opinion. Midlife sanity is when you do something sensible like living your dreams.'

'You're nearly forty, you know. You think you're going to make it as a rock star at your age?'

'Even if I don't, so what? At least I'm doing what I really want.'

'I suppose you'll still be rocking out when you're seventy, like BB King?'

I stopped. That was the Eureka moment, and it was Sandra who led me to it.

'Exactly! Excellent point. BB King is a fine example to us all. A majestic and mighty blues guitarist who doesn't allow age or social norms to dictate his behaviour. We can all learn a lot from him.'

'Make up your mind. One minute you're talking like he's the antichrist, now suddenly he's a role model.'

'If you don't mind, Sandra, this is my waking dream, and I'll interpret these symbols as I see fit. It's all crystal clear! I asked for symbols to guide me on my life path, and here they are. Bill has been sent here tonight to *steer* me in the right direction. He has shown me I must *look to the King*. BB King, still rocking in his seventies, is the inspiration for me to follow - and it's taken Bill to show me that. Bill has sent me a message: *Look to the King*! My path is clear. I'm going to reform the band and rock for the next thirty years. Oh thank you, Bill and BB for showing me my true path!'

'I'll give you one year, and if you haven't made it by then, I'll buy a bloody house with someone else.'

At this none too subtle threat, I affected a benevolent smile and a lofty expression. I was now in a mood of euphoric megalomania.

'You fool, Sandy. Don't you see that, thanks to me, we won't have to buy a house out west? We can buy one right on Bondi Beach! One day you'll thank me.'

'Bugger off, Jimmy. You'll wind up in the gutter - and don't think I'm coming with you. Oh God, why can't I just have a nice, normal man? Everyone I've dated in the last ten years is a ridiculous dreamer. I'm just about over men, to be honest.'

'Thanks for your wise words and encouragement, Sandra. In this case, perhaps the optimum solution is as follows: go and find another of the many women who share your views, form a lesbian tryst, bask in the bliss made by the union of such perfect beings, and go buy a house in the western suburbs together. In the meantime, I'm putting the band back together. Thank you and goodnight.'

At that moment, Sandra's alarm went off. Swearing, she threw her pillow at me and got up to have a shower. I went to the kitchen to make us coffee, and began forming my plans for musical world domination.

4

An Interrogation

So, what am I doing preparing for a job interview?

Bloody Sandra! A few weeks earlier, she'd heard about a fulltime job at a company where one of her friends worked. She'd talked me into applying. Now, the day after my epiphany at the BB King gig, an email arrived telling me to show up for an interview.

How's that for timing? I'd just made a life changing decision to get back into music, and the last thing I needed was a fulltime job. My first thought was to pull out, but that didn't go down well with Sandra. What did go down was the temperature in our unit, at least 'til we argued it out. She said I should at least give it a go. Do, say, six months of fulltime work, while starting on my songwriting at night and weekends. Then, I could save up enough money to record my album, and if it did alright, I could quit the day job.

She did have a point. I had hardly any savings, and at this stage would have to finance my own album, at least until the major labels came knocking. On the other hand, I knew from experience just how draining fulltime work could be. You came home exhausted, and by the time you'd had dinner and relaxed, it was just about time for bed. Such conditions were far from ideal for writing great music.

My mind was divided between the desire to get on with my music and awareness of practical matters - the need for money, not to mention having to keep Sandra onside. Finally, I decided to go ahead with the interview and let fate take its course. If the job came through, I'd save all my wages for the album. If not, I'd get stuck into writing the songs.

In these circumstances, it would be interesting to find out what the Vortex Winder's magic power of the week would be. With any luck, something to do with making large amounts of money without having to work. Yet when I checked the screen, it turned out to be the *'Power of Right Speech - the ability to always come up with the right words for the occasion at hand.'*

Once again, it didn't seem a very exciting magic power. It may have been great for a politician or lawyer, but it was no use to me. Yet on reflection, the Power of Right Speech would be pretty handy for a job interview - which was exactly the problem. The timing was impeccable! Here I was going to a job interview for a position I didn't want, and suddenly I'd been blessed with the gift of always saying the right thing. Now I'd probably get the job against my will. My only hope was that the Vortex Winder would somehow know the job wasn't in my best interests and help sabotage the interview. Or if it *was* in my interests, so be it. I resolved to trust the magic and say whatever I felt, letting the Right Words flow out as they would.

On the big day I dressed well, even managing an uncharacteristic tie. That way, Sandra couldn't accuse me of not making an effort. I arrived at the Company office at 11.15AM, some fifteen minutes early. Job interviews are stressful, but not wanting the job relieved the pressure. That was also a concern. Sometimes when you really want something, you don't get it - but if you *don't* want something, it just falls in your lap. It's one of those perverse and infuriating facts of life. On that basis, perhaps it would be better to brainwash myself into wanting the job, so as to ensure it fell through.

It was in this divided state of mind that I entered the room to meet the interview panel. I saw three corporate types, two men and a woman. The men looked so similar – mid-forties, clean shaven, short black hair - I could barely tell them apart. Fortunately, the one introducing himself as Richard was sitting in the middle and wearing a black suit, while Graham on his right was wearing a grey one. Realising I'd be bound to mix up their names, I invented an instant rhyme for them: Richard in the middle and Graham Gray. Richard in the middle and Graham Gray. I was so busy repeating it to myself I forgot the name of the woman on Richard's left, and was embarrassed to have to ask for it again.

'Janine,' she said, with a frown. As she was wearing a red business suit, my rhyme for her was Janine, Janine, red jelly bean. Good, that should do it. No mix ups now. Richard in the middle and Graham Gray. Janine, Janine, red jelly bean. I was good to go.

The first few minutes were fairly routine, as I trod the fine line between confidence and humility, trying, for example, to show some knowledge of the company without coming off as a know-all. The panel discussed the job, along with my background and credentials. So far so good.

The job itself was a lowish middle management role. I won't go into the details as they aren't relevant to my story, but it's true I had the skills and experience to do it. That should have been enough, but at this point the interview took a left turn. The panel tried to put me through some kind of sneaky psych test, with a few off the wall questions. This sort of thing had come into vogue the last few years, although its ethics are questionable. I'm not sure a job interview is really the right place for psychoanalysis - but what can you do? Well, the normal strategy is to guess the type of answer the interviewers are looking for and give it to them. Richard, the guy in the middle, began by trying to lull me into complacency.

'James, you're well qualified for the position and you seem to have a good sense of what this company's about. What we're going to do now is step out of the square, think outside the box, and find out if we're all on the same page. We're going to throw a few random questions at you. Don't over-think your responses, just be yourself and say the first thing that pops into your mind.'

'I don't want to.'

'Why not?'

'I'm sorry. That was the first thing that popped into my mind.'

Richard laughed.

'A sense of humour. Just what we want! Right, here's an easy one. What's your favourite colour?'

My favourite colour? What on earth did that have to do with my capacity to do this job? Presumably this was some kind of colour association test. What was the right answer? I had a quick test run of colour associations in my mind. Blue: depression, BB King. Green: environment, hippies, marijuana. Red: blood, communism, Janine, Janine, red jelly bean. Gold: gold medal, champion, wealth. Silver: piracy, *Treasure Island*. Black: funerals, death, heavy metal. White: wedding, cricket, angels. Oh, bloody hell! What was the right answer?

'Don't think about it too long,' said Janine Jelly Bean. 'Remember, it's not a very serious test. Just say the first thing that comes into your head. We won't judge you on your answers.'

Then why ask me? Yet at that moment, I felt a sudden change of mood. A sense of abandon took hold and I no longer cared about guessing the right answers. I had the urge to speak freely, either with the candid truth of my actual opinions, or with the flippancy the questions deserved. The magical power of the Vortex Winder had taken effect. I looked my inquisitors in the eyes.

'You want to know my favourite colour, Janine? That is the answer you seek? Then by the Powers, you shall have it! My favourite colour is blue. The blue of the sky, the ocean, and

Peter Rabbit's little woollen jacket. By all the gods, my answer is blue.'

'Peter Rabbit? That leads on to the next question. If you were an animal, what kind of animal would you be?'

I furrowed my brow and adopted a Wittgenstein pose of deep thought.

'That's an interesting hypothetical. It's quite the conundrum. My head's telling me one thing and my heart another. But if you're going to put me on the spot, there can be only one answer: the Zambian water beetle.'

'I see.'

'Or the Pterodactyl, if I'm allowed to go prehistoric. It's not so much the creature itself, it's the name. Pterodactyl. I just love it.'

'Intriguing,' said Graham. 'Next question: who is your personal hero?'

'My personal hero?' I said. 'Hmm. Another tough one. I suppose I should say Nelson Mandela, Mother Teresa, or someone like that. But I'm going to think outside the box and say Tony Iommi.'

'Who?'

'Tony Iommi, the guitarist from Black Sabbath. When he was seventeen years old, he was working in a factory in Birmingham. On the very day he was going to quit and start fulltime with the band, he had a terrible accident and lost two of his fingertips so he couldn't play guitar. So cruel. It almost makes you believe there is no God.'

'Ouch!' said Graham, wincing.

'But that didn't stop him. He made some plastic fingertips, taught himself to play again, and went on to almost singlehandedly invent heavy rock. What a comeback from adversity. Even Mandela would have to hand it to Tony for that. And the funny thing is, losing those fingertips forced him to play in an unorthodox way. It's quite possible he wouldn't have invented heavy metal unless he had to do that. It almost makes you believe in God. Or Satan.'

The panel looked a little taken aback.

'I noticed on your CV you listed music as a hobby,' said Graham.

'You can call it a hobby if you like, but it was a hobby for Tony once too.'

'Any other heroes?' asked Janine.

'Plenty of heroes, but if I had to pick one off the top of my head... maybe Doug Walters, the great Australian cricketer of the 1970s. Without doubt, the finest embodiment of the ideal of work-life balance. He had the rare ability to mix heavy alcohol consumption with high work performance. His KPIs at the time involved scoring runs for Australia, as well as taking catches in the gully, and wickets with his canny medium pace. The thing about Doug is that no matter how many schooners he'd had the night before, he never for one moment wavered in the performance of his duties on the field for Australia. I would regard him as a real icon of Australian values.'

What was I saying? The words were just flowing out of me, like I was channelling someone. There was no way I was getting the job after an interview like this. Thank God. Yet bizarrely, the panel didn't seem to be taking it too badly. They were smiling at each other like they'd found their man. What on earth was wrong with them? With a pang of panic, I sensed they were sizing me up for the job. If I didn't do something very quickly, I'd find myself in gainful employment. I'd better up the ante fast.

Richard in the middle said, 'We're impressed so far, James, you really think outside the box. You wouldn't believe how many Nelson Mandelas we've had today. Gets very dull after a while. Now, next question: if you were prime minister for a day, what would you do?'

'Prime minister? The first thing I'd do is abolish the open plan office. Good fences make good neighbours, and those cubicles you've got out there are a poor excuse for privacy. I'd be down on this company like a ton of bricks. How can anyone concentrate on their work when they're surrounded by drivel on all sides? Noise pollution is the biggest enemy of productivity in the office, so the first thing we'd need is self contained, fully soundproofed cubicles so everyone can work in peace.'

'Might be a bit expensive, don't you think?' said Graham Gray.

'It would pay for itself through increased output. The second thing I'd do as PM is ban all school leavers from going straight to uni. Most of them are burned out from studying and won't work. They're more interested in partying and romance, so they're in no position to appreciate the wonderful gift of tertiary education. Also, they have very little life experience. They don't know themselves or their real ambitions, so they've no business making life changing decisions at that age. But what do they do? Sign up for some big old course. Then, they either drop out after a year or two, or reach the age of forty and wonder why they ever became a doctor, a lawyer or whatever. Sorry, guys, it's over. I'd pass a law that all school leavers have to work or travel, or go on the dole for a year, so they'd have time to get to know themselves and build some hunger for what they really wanted. Then you wouldn't have such a high dropout rate from first year uni students, and there'd be more places for people who really want to be there.'

Richard raised his eyebrows. With his dark hair, and wearing his black suit, for a moment I had the disconcerting impression he was some kind of insect.

'A mandatory gap year?' he said. 'That's a pretty bold plan, but it makes a lot of sense. Anything else?'

Oh no, I didn't want to be making sense. Better come up with something fast.

'Uh... you know how we have the minute's silence when someone dies? Why not put them all together and have a whole day of complete silence? Get them all out of the way at once.'

There was nearly a minute's silence then and there as the interview panel digested that one. Finally, Graham composed himself and continued with the next question.

'Getting back to the subject of work, where do you see yourself in five years?'

'That question implies a face value acceptance of the concept of time. In deeper terms, time is an illusion. If you think about it, the past doesn't exist, and neither does the future. We only have the Now. And as the Greek philosopher Heraclitus said, we can never step in the same river twice. What is the future anyway, but an imaginary, idealised projection of the Now? Realistically, we can only live in the Now, as nothing else really exists, and by the time we come to future Nows, the current Now won't exist either. But to answer your question in the way you mean it, in five years time I see myself as one of the biggest rock stars in the world, having the number one album on the charts, and headlining arena tours.'

'That's very ambitious.'

'You can call me a dreamer, Gray, but let's see you say that in five years. Music's not just a hobby for me. It's a vocation.'

'And in case it doesn't work out, do you have a Plan B in mind?'

'Yes, of course.'

'What would that be?'

'Well, I suppose this it.'

'What do you mean?'

'This place. Working with you guys.'

'I see.'

'Look, a man can dream. I'd love to be a famous rock star and have the world at my feet, but it might not happen. As Bon Scott said, it's a long way to the top if you want to rock n roll. So, in case it all comes crashing down and my dreams are crushed, I'll just have to face the hard, horrible, hangover of reality and keep on working with you guys.'

'How kind of you,' said Janine.

At last! I was finally starting to piss them off. Then Richard came in over the top. 'I love your honesty, James. I've had it up to here with yes-men and liars. Your attitude is refreshing. You really say what you think.'

I kept on following the standard body language advice about maintaining eye contact with the interviewers. As I stared into Richard's eyes, I felt a chill of recognition. There was an inhuman glint behind his gaze, and I remembered Iolango's warning. That guy in the Morbid Angel t-shirt at the hotel. Sonuvabitch! Was it Elijinx?

Well, maybe. I didn't know for sure, but it made sense. He was impersonating Richard, and trying to make me get a job. Somehow he must know about my musical dreams. Perhaps he read the blog post I'd published last week after the BB King gig. Now he was doing his best to sabotage those dreams by forcing me into gainful employment. A truly diabolical scheme.

I wondered how much hold he had over his fellow interviewers, and how he'd connived his way onto the panel in the first place. Then again, I suppose he'd simply changed his form and waylaid the real Richard in some nefarious manner. My only hope now was to annoy Graham and Janine so much they wouldn't let him hire me.

'What does your wife or partner think of all this, if you have one?' said Graham. 'Are you married?'

'That's quite a personal question, Graham, but ask a personal question and you'll get a personal answer. My Sandra's a lovely girl. She's smart, funny, and she hasn't been sucked in by this awful Brazilian fad girls are into nowadays. But to level with you, we don't share the same taste in music, and she thinks I'm wasting my time doing it at my age. She's given me a year to get it out of my system. In fact, she'd prefer I get a real job like this one. If it wasn't for her, I wouldn't be in this room now.'

'She wants you to fail?'

'No, not really. We simply have different concepts of what failure means.'

'Thanks, James,' said Richard smoothly, 'but we don't really need to know about your personal life. Let's get back to some more work related questions. Why did you leave your last job?'

'Well, Richard, I'd love to positive-spin it and say it was because my personal mission statement compelled me to seek greater challenges with a dynamic company like yours going forward. But the truth is, my co-workers had these awful ringtones on their phones. Seventies disco, techno, that sort of thing. I mean, come on.'

'Can you explain why you've had so many jobs?' said Janine.

'I just haven't found the right company yet. Someone I can commit to, someone worth more than a fling. Haven't found my Sandra, know what I mean?'

'And the employment gaps in your CV?'

I gave her a hard stare.

'There's something very wrong with that question, Janine. Why do we define someone by their job? The assumption is that if someone isn't working, they're not doing anything meaningful. Good Lord, there's more to life than going to work every day, that's for sure. What I was doing in those CV gaps was living life.'

At this point, Richard butted in and tried to close off the interview before I went too far. He - or rather Elijinx - wanted me to get that job. But he was too late. Graham and Janine were by now rather annoyed. My rudeness and high handed attitude had pissed them off. Who could blame them? Oh well, better finish it off. Graham frowned and cut to the chase.

'Mr Brandt, why should we hire you?'

'For only one reason - because you think I'm the best person for the job. Not because of my age, looks, racial background, political views, or anything else other than my capacity to do the work.'

'How can you value-add to our company?'

'What kind of a question is that? It doesn't make sense. But I assume you're rephrasing the previous question in silly management jargon. If that's right, then what you'll get is a guy who'll turn up and do a good job 9-5. As long as there's no attempt to blackmail me into unpaid overtime, I can promise I'll get it done. And you can put it in the contract that from my end, there'll be no office politics of any kind. Any progress up the ranks of this company will be through my own work related efforts. I might surf the net a bit from time to time, but there'll be no backstabbing or bootlicking. Just a guy who turns up and does the job, then goes home at five and forgets it 'til the next day.'

This answer didn't seem to impress Graham. He finished with a pretty mean question.

'What would you say are your biggest weaknesses?'

'My biggest weaknesses? Graham, we're going to have to get to know each other a little better before we start talking about that sort of thing. But let's make a deal. You, Richard and Janine can each tell me your own biggest weaknesses, then I'll tell you mine. How about that?'

That just about did it. The interview came to an end with everyone very pissed off: Richard because I wouldn't be able to get the job, Graham and Janine because they couldn't give me the job and then sack me, and me because I had no money and an album to record.

5
Adventures In The Black Art

Looking back, a number of factors took me to the Black Art. I lost the Vortex Winder, I found out how much the album was going to cost, and Sandra's work transferred her to Melbourne for three months.

After two years, Sandra and I had reached a crossroads and some time apart would help us decide if we should continue. Sandra's hard headed pragmatism and my stubborn idealism made for a shaky alliance.

Her loss hit me harder than expected. At first, I welcomed the peace and freedom, yet after a few days home alone, a sense of unreality crept in. It keeps you sane to have someone else around to share the banality of daily life. Without that, the prospect of madness takes a few steps closer. The sense of indifference is palpable. With no one around to praise, blame, help or hinder you, you begin to feel that your own actions are meaningless.

After a couple of weeks, I was in depression. Although I'd come up with some good guitar riffs for the album, there was still no clue how it was to be funded. It turned out that a decent recording studio would cost at least ten grand, if it was to be done properly. In hindsight, the job interview had been a missed opportunity. Perhaps Sandra wouldn't even have taken the transfer if I'd got the job. I certainly couldn't afford to follow her to Melbourne. Not for the first time, it seemed that a lot of my problems came down to being broke. Let's face it, without money there's not much you can do in this world. There are very few doors open to you.

In the midst of all this, losing the Vortex Winder was an act of very poor timing. Perhaps there would have been some magic trick to lift me out of this hole. Although I turned the house upside down, it was nowhere to be found. Once depression over Sandra's exit set in, it didn't seem to matter anyway.

Yet the Black Art was waiting in the wings. It all began one Friday in Randwick. I was having a late lunch in my usual Thai restaurant, reading the sports part of the newspaper when my eye was caught by the betting odds for tonight's football. North Queensland, playing away against St George, were paying three dollars for the win. That is, for every dollar you bet, you'd get three dollars back if they won the game. The odds seemed pretty high, so I checked if Jonathan Thurston, at that time the world's best player, was playing for North Queensland. Yes, he was - so why were they paying three dollars? Surely home ground advantage wasn't worth that much to St George. I walked across the road to the TAB - the local betting shop - and put on fifty bucks. It was my first ever bet on a sporting event, and the TAB lady had to show me how to fill in the card.

In hindsight, what stands out is the naive simplicity of this first gamble. A single leg, head to head bet! In time, I would come to view with disdain anything less than a complex multi-leg wager – that is, a bet hinging on the result of several games combined. Yet on that virginal evening, I watched avidly on TV as Thurston led his team to a gripping victory, and my fifty bucks turned into one hundred and fifty. Fists pumped in the privacy of my living room, and my turbulent affair with the Black Art was born.

I had never bothered with sports betting before, and barely knew it existed. Yet as I returned to the TAB the next day, a new world opened up before my eyes. It was astonishing the number of things you could bet on, even within my sport of choice, rugby league. Apart from the simple head to head bet of the night before, which is just one team against another, there was no end to the betting options. You could bet on whether a team would win by 1-12 points or by 13+, whether they would be ahead at halftime as well as fulltime, or with a handicap of 'points start' given or conceded. You could bet on first try scorer, the number of tries in a game, and dozens of other options. (For those who don't know, a 'try' is a scoring play. Like a touchdown in American football). The more specific your bet, the higher the odds, and the more money you could get back.

It soon became clear the real money was to be made by a multi-leg bet that ran over several games. This way, the odds multiplied to produce some big returns. Take the following, for example, with the odds in brackets. Say I bet on the Bulldogs to win by 1-12 (3.20), Melbourne Storm 1-12 (3.50), Newcastle to lead at half and fulltime (1.80), Broncos head to head (1.45), Penrith with 8 points start (1.90), and Wests 13+ (4.00). Surprisingly, if you multiply all those odds it ends up at about 220 to 1, so if I put on $10 it would win $2220. If I invested $25, it would turn into more than $5000!

Why hadn't I heard about this before? If I could master this strange new game, all my financial problems would be solved with one blow! Doors that were closed would open. All my dreams would come true: I could record the album, go overseas, buy a house, perhaps even marry Sandra - and all without having to sell out and get a nine to five job.

My mind is naturally prone to obsession, and this tendency came to the fore. I resolved to study this new enterprise, master it, and reap the profits. What would bring victory in this fight? First and foremost was vision - the ability to see opportunities most people can't. I saw that sports gambling, run with smarts and a system, was the doorway to my dreams. Second, you needed a certain amount of capital to invest. That was shaky, but I had just enough money to sign on as a starter. Third was an intelligent mind to understand the best strategy when placing bets. This was no exercise in blind luck. It required some canny knowledge of betting and the game of rugby league. Fourth was mastery of the science of mental energy, which is the idea that through willpower, faith, and concentration, you can draw wealth into your life. There's a lot more to the idea than that, but that's a tale for another day. Fifth and last was simply luck. A certain amount of luck would also be required.

Soon I was in business, and began my meteoric rise. Within weeks of my first fumbling amateur bet, I had learned enough to make a bold decision to turn pro. It may seem extreme, but that is my way. From now on this would be my job. I would be a professional sports gambler - although that was a boring job title to be avoided. I preferred to think of myself as an alchemist or sorcerer, and I dubbed this enterprise 'the Black Art.'

The alchemist's dream was to change base metal into gold. Seemingly by magic, but really by science. To modern eyes, it seems a childish quest. Yet the alchemist's dream has never really gone away. The wish to turn base metal into gold is as strong in the 21st century as it was in the 17th. We may use different words to describe it, but the quest is much the same. It's the attempt to create wealth out of poverty, to conjure a large amount of money from a small amount. That is the gambler's dream, and the gambler is the modern alchemist.

No doubt my view will produce some skeptical sniggers - and they sound a lot like the ones I heard at Sydney film festival one year during the film, *Shotgun Stories*. It was the story of a family of 'white trash' brothers in a small American town. They were all battlers, struggling day to day. The oldest brother was about thirty with a wife and child. Against the wishes of his wife, he was trying to make a living as a professional poker player. In a display of sadly justified stereotyping, the wife disapproved of his dream and wanted him to get a normal job.

At one point in the story, they were having the usual argument and she said that she didn't like his gambling. His response was to say, 'It's not gambling, it's a system.'

This was the cue for some condescending laughter from the audience - and what smugness there was in that collective laugh. The cultured, worldly film festival audience thought itself so much smarter than this specimen of white trash who thought he could make a living playing poker. *It's not gambling, it's a system.* Ha ha. This fool in search of fool's gold with his 'system.'

But why? There *are* professional poker players. Some people *do* make money playing poker. Some become millionaires, others make a good living while traveling the world. Those who make money from it don't do it through luck. They are the very people who *have* a system.

Why then the smug, condescending laughter? Perhaps you can blame the film for making the character fit the white trash stereotype - and sadly, in a victory for killjoys everywhere, by film's end he did toss it in and get a real job. That doesn't excuse the lazy laughter of the audience. The audience bought what the filmmakers were selling - the image of the hopeless, deluded gambler. They did not see past the surface to the character's view of himself as an aspiring master of the Black Art. Nor did they see the nobility of his ideal - his quest to be an alchemist and escape the mundane semi-slavery of the full time job.

That smug audience should remember two points: not every form of gambling is the same thing, and everything is a form of gambling.

If a newspaper report says Australians spend 100 million a year on gambling, it means everything from poker machines ('the pokies') to lotto tickets, horse racing, cards, or sports gambling. The reports imply that this is a fool's enterprise. Well, there are fools, and there are fools, and some of them are the ones writing the report. There's a vast difference between playing poker and playing the pokies. One involves intelligence, strategy, planning, and luck. The other needs only luck. And while there are poker millionaires, there are no pokie millionaires. Except, perhaps, the people making the machines. Nor are there those who travel the world pokies circuit making a living pressing the buttons on pokie machines. So, please, not all types of gambling are the same. Ninety-nine percent of those playing pokies or lotto are going to lose. That's just the way it is - but sports betting is a different story. There are ways of making money, and it's not all about luck. There may be 20% winners and 80% losers, but the trick is to be in that top 20%.

Apart from that, if you want to damn gambling, why stop at the most obvious forms of the enterprise? If you're trying to turn a small pile of money into a bigger pile by guessing the future, it doesn't matter if your game is real estate, business, or the stock market. You're a punter either way. Plenty of people have been burned in the real estate game, but go to one of those dinner parties with the people Sandra hangs out with and no one will laugh if you call yourself a real estate investor.

At the same dinner party, if you say you run a small business or you're starting one up, no one will call you a mug. You'll meet with polite responses. Yet statistics say at least half of new small businesses fail, so if that isn't a form of gambling, I don't know what is. Good luck with your risky wager.

As for the stock market, if you want to bet on which companies are on the way up or down, then again good luck, and no doubt what you're doing is not gambling, it's a system. For another example, take marriage. When you marry, you enter an arrangement which will have serious consequences financially (let alone emotionally). You will enter that union with as much optimism as the most hopeful gambler - but you'll have to live with the results, however it goes.

You're betting that you or your partner won't change, or if you do, you'd better change in the same direction. Good luck. Ask those who've been through a messy divorce if they knew the gamble they were taking. The old adage that one should bet with the head, not the heart, seems a little cold blooded here. Yet those men who ended up with a costly divorce settlement and child support realised too late the high stakes they had been playing with. In the same way, women who invested their resources for twenty years in a marriage, only to be left high and dry when the husband left for greener pastures, also found out love can be a crap game with many losers.

It's not gambling, it's a system. Every member of that smug film festival audience who ever invested in real estate, started a small business, played the stock market, or got married, should retract their condescending laughter. We're all gamblers, the only question is genre.

My form of gambling, at this time in my life, was betting on sporting events. I called it the Black Art for dramatic effect, and that pleasing scent of nefariousness. Like the alchemist, I wanted to turn base metal into gold. There is a system involved, but I ain't telling, because if everyone can make gold, the value of gold declines, ultimately becoming as worthless as the base metal from which it was formed.

There are sinister implications to the name as well. Believe me, the Black Art can burn you up. There's a dark side, which I'll come to soon, but first let's look at the appeal of the enterprise.

Before that, however, I must make a concession to whoever is reading this tale. I tend to fixate on things, but I realise that not everyone will share my obsessions - including the current chapter. Some readers won't be interested in my 'adventures in the Black Art' or will think that this chapter is too long.

Rather than have those readers give up on the book, I'm going to invite them to simply skip ahead to the next chapter.

I'll even make it official, like it's a magic gift from the Vortex Winder itself.

This is a free pass to move on to Chapter Six.

Go right ahead. It won't affect understanding of the rest of the book.

For those readers who remain, I'll explain why the Black Art was so appealing to me at the time.

Put it this way: there are magic doors of possibility which only certain keys will unlock. A person's life falls into limited patterns, but with just an ounce of luck, you can break through those limits. Take my biggest dreams of the moment. I wished to record my album, and maybe buy a house with Sandra. Taking an overseas trip had also been on my mind for some time. All those would cost a lot of money, and the only way to get that was to work long hours in a fulltime job. The tradeoff is that you have to sacrifice nearly all your time and energy, so the job becomes a vampire that sucks out your lifeblood.

If you do have that fulltime job, the idea is to save a certain amount of your income each week towards your goals. It becomes a slow, laborious journey in which you gradually inch towards your distant prize. With the Black Art, however, if you pull off a big win it's a magic carpet which flies you there fast - and if you're really lucky, you can get there instantly.

The Black Art is an X factor. Normally, your income is fixed. You know more or less how much money is coming in each week, which is pretty dull. The Black Art is a wild card because it opens up the chance you might get an extra five hundred or a thousand or more dollars that week. True, you can lose a lot - that's the risk - but at least the unpredictability keeps it interesting. It's a *Snakes and Ladders* board game come to life.

And there's always the chance a big win could open up those magic doors to your dreams.

As I saw it, the Black Art was the *only* real way those magic doors could instantly open. It was a striking realisation at the time. I suppose another option was to become a bank robber, or its modern equivalent, the cyber-criminal. Yet, leaving aside the moral questions, that would have been a gamble too far. There was too much to lose. Prison was totally out of the question. A brilliant aspect of the Black Art is that, as opposed to many other get-rich-quick schemes, sports gambling is 100% legal. It was a major plus and no mistake.

At this point, no doubt some people are thinking I'm a bone idle lay-about who wants everything to fall in his lap without doing any work for it. Well, they can ditch that moralistic misconception right away, and not just those who've ever bought a lotto ticket in the hope of becoming an instant millionaire.

The Black Art is a risky venture. It can make or break you. If you're smart and lucky, you can make a quid out of it. If you're dumb or unlucky, or even smart and unlucky, you might end up on the streets like that homeless guy who lives outside the TAB in Randwick. Seriously, there *is* a guy who's set up permanent camp right outside. It's like he's employed by the anti-gambling league as a warning to every punter who goes in there! So if I'm lucky enough to pull off a big win, don't begrudge it to me. Or at least have the decency to remember I was the one who took the risk in the first place.

Second, people have no idea how much work is involved in this business. The paperwork alone is frightening. All those little cards and forms you have to fill in. Before you do that though, you have to study the form of all the teams, the weather and other factors, and then come up with convoluted strategies for each weekend's betting. That is, unless you're one of those pin the tail on the donkey punters who takes 'mystery bets' and leaves it to blind chance. If you do it properly, you really have to study and use your brain. That's why it irks me when people lump sports gambling in with roulette, pokies, and lotto tickets. There's no actual thought involved in those games, no strategy, no intellectual aspect. What strategy is involved in pushing the buttons on a pokie machine or filling in lotto tickets? It's all magic and no art. Just wishes, optimism, and blind luck.

Remember, *it's not gambling, it's a system.* There is method, strategy, and thought. There's some kind of attempt to understand the game you're playing. You don't just push a button or tick a box.

The third factor to get the wowsers off my back is they have no idea what I've been through. I've spent years of my life trying to make it as a musician and a writer. I've put thousands of hours into it, basically working for nothing - less than nothing, considering what it's cost me - and I've never broken into either the music business, or into publishing.

It's not been for lack of talent. I've just never had the networking skills, the right looks, or the politics to make it. Meanwhile, plenty of far less talented people were given opportunities that never came to me. You see some of the books in shops, or even winning awards, and wonder why. It's maddening.

I gradually formed the view that neither the music or book industries were any kind of meritocracy, where entry was granted purely on the basis of artistic worth. Clearly, so much of it was down to front - looks, hype, celebrity - or having the right politics or contacts. It also seemed that opportunities were only given to those who had already attained power or fame, and those who were unknown got nothing. For example, the new books you see advertised at bus stops are the ones by already bestselling authors, and rarely by the unknown newcomer. So - surprise, surprise - the rich get richer and the poor stay poor.

Put it this way: is it any wonder the poor bastard who wrote *A Confederacy of Dunces* topped himself long before his novel became a posthumous hit? He just gave up, because no one would give him a chance to go from being a nobody to a somebody. It was only his grief stricken mother's attempt to salvage something from the tragedy that finally got him a start - but it was a bit late by then. If there's a happy ending to the story, it's that the royalties were able to fund a steady stream of fresh flowers for his grave.

Over time, I came to believe that the entertainment and culture industries were, more or less, deeply evil. In the context of that belief, the Black Art for me became an agent of justice. If the human world was corrupt and unjust, the Black Art was a means of bypassing that system. You won't release my album or publish my book? OK, I'll conjure up fifty grand out of nothing and put them out myself.

In a world ruled by the twin tyrants of stupidity and corruption, I hoped there might yet be a higher force of justice which could override it. I believed higher powers could deliver me from the evil of the human world. The Powers would save me (I will capitalise the word from now on as a sign of reverence). The Black Art would be the means by which such Powers would bestow upon me my rightful freedom. Every week, as I prepared my army of sporting bets, I called upon the Powers to deliver the infusion of energy so urgently needed. I held private rituals in which I lit an altar of symbolically arranged candles in my darkened room while visualizing planets aligning and sending bolts of immense energy into my world.

In one way and another, I became deeply obsessed with the Black Art. It became my profession and my religion. It was my means of restoring justice to this world, funding my music and writing, and escaping the slavery of the fulltime job.

Apart from working on the album, everything else became a distraction from my new obsession - football, betting, and making money. The financial crusade took up most of my resources. I was still working a couple of days in my part time job to provide basic fuel for 'the war.' (Let's not discuss that job - it's irrelevant). The rest of the time was spent analysing betting combinations and games for the coming weekend's 'battle,' as I came to call it, and using mind power exercises and 'spells' to attract money.

I made elaborate charts in my computer's Excel program, depicting my army of bets in the battle. Against a black background, the bets were drawn as coloured shapes. Using a chess terminology, any bet with a prize over $2000 was a king, between $1000-$2000 was a queen. Anything around $750 was a rook, $500 a bishop, $300 a knight, while my 'foot soldier' bets of about $100 were pawns. Those were the amounts I stood to win, of course, not what I invested.

I generally only spent two or three hundred dollars each battle for the whole squadron. One might think it was highly profitable. Yet to generate such high rewards, I had to run lengthy and complicated multi-leg bets, and the more results you needed to get right, the harder it was to win. Some battles were complete blowouts where my army was wiped out without gaining a single win. I tried to spread the risk, of course, by running various combinations. If I could get a couple of pawns or a knight through, at least it would cover costs, but the real prizes were the rooks, queens or kings. Higher still, up above even the kings, were the JMs, and we'll come to them soon.

Each Friday, I would complete my strategy for the coming 'battle.' After careful consideration of tactics, I'd head down to the TAB and fill in all the little cards, before handing over my cash. All that paperwork was a pain, especially as I had to stay in the TAB to fill it out and put up with some of the annoying people who hung out there. Apart from the homeless guy camped out the front, there was the goose who always yelled out in his stupid spruiker-like voice during horse races shown on the TV screen. I always tried to get out as fast as I could, then go for a sauna and a coffee, meditating on mind power and the riches coming my way. Back at home, I'd make up my coloured battle charts. They were beautiful to behold. Like a general standing over his mock battlefield, I watched the progress, or the death, of my kings, knights, and pawns as they progressed towards financial glory over the three days and eight games of football each weekend. I would hold back some troops until the second stage of the battle, Saturday, and send in the cavalry come Sunday.

It may have been beginner's luck, but in the early weeks of the war, I snared two big wins. Sure, there were a couple of wipeouts as well, but in Battle Four I captured a king worth $2750! In Battle Six, I followed up with a queen of $1685. From there, my obsession knew no bounds. I was sure the Black Art was the agent of my salvation.

Looking back now, I can see the dark side of it all, but at the time I believed I had found 'the way.' It was a man's dream job. You could make a living while watching football on TV and you hardly even had to leave the house. You could drink beer and listen to heavy metal music while working. How many other jobs can you say that for? My weekends were thrilling, dramatic adventures through gambling battlefields, secret wars waged in a noble cause and - win or lose - there was a beer to be had after (and during) the game.

I no longer missed Sandra. To be honest, I was glad she'd gone, for it would have been hard to live this lifestyle with her around. Indeed, it reached the point where I'd be walking through Randwick on a Saturday, see some guy with his wife or girlfriend, and actually feel sorry for him. 'That poor bastard won't be watching much football tonight!' That was my mentality. It sounds mad, in hindsight, but such is the compulsive nature of my mind. Once it fastens on some obsession, all else fades away.

It was only when I passed up the chance to see a Queensryche gig that I knew I was addicted. Normally, I would have lined up keenly to see this fine melodic metal band on their first Australian tour, but I skipped it in favour of watching an unremarkable game of footy between Manly and Penrith. As it happened, my whole army of bets was wiped out that night, and alarm bells began to ring that maybe this whole thing was going too far. I'd started to shun the outside world, turning down social events and invitations to see bands or movies, all so I could stay locked in my darkened living room obsessively betting on games of football.

There were other signs as well. I'd started to extend my betting beyond rugby league, and began taking an unprecedented interest in the other football codes like AFL, American football, and the English Premier League. I'd go to bed at midnight, then wake at 3am to check rugby union results from South Africa. Waking the next morning after a few hours sleep, strong coffee would fire my feverish mind into planning the next stage of the battle.

In a strange and ironic sense, I'd become a workaholic, focusing constantly on the business of my fulltime job as a sports gambler, or as I preferred to call it, a practitioner of the Black Art. At one point, Sandra, phoned and hinted at a possible return to Sydney. I made a weak attempt to muster enthusiasm for the idea, yet failed abysmally. Hurt and upset, she asked if there was another woman. In contrast to my previous utterances, my denial rang true, for the only mistress I had was the Black Art. Like a heroin addict, the only thought consuming me was the next fix, the next battle, the next victory, with the final prize being the opening of the magic door beyond which lay the recording of my album and the overseas trip.

At this point, I began to lose. The trouble with running complex bets over several games is that if only *one* of your selections loses, the whole bet is gone. You can get nine correct results out of ten, but that's as good as getting none. You get nothing for a near miss. For a while I didn't mind, and reminded myself that having been so close to a big win (often worth a few thousand dollars), if I kept the faith the next big win would be just around the corner.

I soon learned it was no good sulking when you have a disappointing loss, as the only person you hurt was yourself. There were many life lessons to be had. Sometimes after a big loss, I'd be proud of myself for retaining a sunny, optimistic mood. It showed great character and resilience. After a while, you became stoic about winning and losing. You learned to cultivate a Buddhist detachment about the results. Although you strongly desired the win, you tried not to be 'attached' to the outcome. But you desired it all the same. That's why you played the game. 'Born to lose, live to win,' as one of Lemmy's tattoos used to say.

There were other aspects of the enterprise I found strange. For example, suppose you backed the Bulldogs to win by 1-12 points. Obviously, a 13+ win was no good to you, so if they scored a 'try' (worth 4-6 points) you cheered… but not too hard, because if they scored again your bet would be in trouble. You wanted them to win, but not by too much. So sometimes you'd be flipping during a game, barracking first for one side then the other. It was also weird the way you treated teams like pawns, swapping allegiances week to week. One week, a team would be your staunch allies if you backed them, the next week your deadly foes if you backed their opposition.

However, the steady stream of agonising near misses did get to me after a while. There must have been six or seven weeks in a row where I was inches away from a lucrative win, only to have it snatched away at the last moment. It was real Tantalus material. (Tantalus was one of the damned in Hades, always hungry and thirsty, with food and drink visible but just out of reach - hence the word *tantalise*.) In the same way, the Black Art seemed to contain an element of real cruelty. I cursed the Powers and asked what I had done to deserve this. Was this torment to be the reward for my faith and hard work?

I was tormented by what I came to call the 'St George factor' though in truth Parramatta was nearly as bad. Both teams were almost entirely perverse, and could scarcely have done a better job sabotaging me if they'd been on the payroll of the TAB itself. The way it worked was that whenever St George were favourites they would lose, and whenever they were underdogs they would win. As someone who tended to bet on favourites, this would stuff me up royally.

Of course, this was in the era before Bennett took over as coach and made them one of the most reliable sides in the league. Before that, St George were so fickle you'd think they were led by Hansie Cronje, the bent South African cricket captain. They'd come into a game as hot favourites, only to lose to some lowly, no hoper opposition. Then, the next week, they might have key players out due to injury, be playing away from home against a strong team, and given no chance at all - before storming home with a bizarre upset win. This happened once against Brisbane, who were at odds of $1.10 for the win. Planning to skim a lazy $100 profit, I put $1000 on Brisbane, only to see the idiots from St George pull off a miracle upset.

Forget the Buddhist detachment, I came to hate St George with a passion and cursed them to the seventh pit of Hades.

Another time, I backed the same clowns to win by 1-12, and was on track with a minute to go when they led by seven. I should mention that scoring a try is worth four points, and if you convert the kick that follows, you get another two points. So there I was, up by seven. In the last minute, a certain winger, who shall remain nameless, scored a fluky try in the corner and converted, meaning St George got up by 13. Tortured again by the St George factor.

After a while, it was these agonising near misses I came to hate the most. It was so cruel to have a huge victory in my grasp, only to have it snatched away. Yet the closer I came to a win, the more addicted I became. In search of the ultimate victory, I became a man possessed. I might be losing battles, but swore an oath I'd win the war or perish in the attempt. I lost interest in music, forgot about Sandra, shunned social life, and focused only on form, tactics, and my mind power visualisation spells. Yet the season was drawing to a close, so if victory was to be had, it must be had soon. My pool of financial resources was draining rapidly. War is an expensive business, all generals know that. Yet a war, once begun, must be followed through to victory or defeat.

It was in the context of these desperate times that the JM appeared, and the final battle was at hand. The JM is the most lucrative prize of all. The official title is Pick the Margins. It's like the football pools in England, because you have to pick the correct result of all the games for that weekend's round. It's a tough one, because you also have to pick the margin of victory - either team by 1-10 points, 11-20 points, or 21+. Believe me, it's not easy, but if you can pull it off that's the alchemist's gold right there.

Because it's so difficult, Pick the Margins often isn't won on a given weekend, so the pool of money invested by punters jackpots to the next week's games. Hence it is a 'Jackpot Margins' or a 'JM' to use my own cultish jargon. This is the Holy Grail of the Black Art. If you can pull that one off, you've got it made. A couple of JMs had come up earlier in the season, but ethereal as the Grail itself, had eluded me. Now, in round 23 of the competition, the prize hadn't been won, so the jackpotted pool was up for grabs in round 24. 'JM24' as I called it, became my focus. The beauty of the JM is that the pool of prize money is so large. On a normal round, the pool is about $100,000, but for a JM all punters, large and small, have a crack, so the pool can swell to around $500,000. The more punters bet on it, the bigger the pool becomes, and vice versa. Now that's the kind of inflation I like.

With a pool like this, the trick is not just to win it, but to win with a few upset results. The prize pool is divided between all the people who correctly guess the winning sequence. So let's say the pool is $500,000. If ten people win, they get $50,000 each. But if a hundred people win, they only get $5,000 each. So the thing is to pick a sequence with some surprise results. That way, if you get it right, not many punters will have guessed it and you get the lion's share of the pool.

It was easier said than done, but I vowed to have a crack. I could see a magic doorway standing right in front of me, and if the key could be found, what lay behind that door was full funding for my album, an overseas trip, and maybe even some superannuation money! Once again, I realised there was only one possible key to open that door and that was the Black Art and JM24.

That week was the full moon of my obsession. There were daily invocations of energy from the Powers, and rigorous study of form, weather, and betting tactics. Indeed my preparation was as thorough as that of any actual team preparing for a game that week. On Friday, I filled in the large amount of paperwork required and sat back earnestly to watch the first game.

My demise was rapid. Parramatta were playing away to Canterbury Bulldogs, and the Dogs were certain victors - or so everyone thought. Of the $400 worth of combinations I'd backed, I'd taken the Dogs by 21+, 11-20, 1-10, and also covered the upset Parra 1-10 and even 11-20. So what happens? Parramatta play like supermen and get up by 22 points.

Game over after one match. I felt like a formula one driver who'd spent months preparing for the big race, only to blow a tyre on the first lap. To push the analogy, it was utterly deflating. All that energy, all those wishes, floated off into the ether like so much mist. The one saving grace was that most of the other punters would have been caught out the same way, so hopefully the JM would not be won, and would grow to an even larger pool the next week. After a couple more odd results, that's exactly what happened, and JM25 loomed large for the following weekend.

Determined to see this war through, I launched another army with $400 worth of combinations at JM25, yet this time we were all bamboozled by a couple of draws. That is, when two teams are locked on the same points at fulltime. While this is a common result in soccer, it's unusual in a high scoring game like rugby league. It's impossible to guess draws, and as there were two of them in round 25, the prize pool was again not won. It would all come down to JM26, which was the final round of the season.

At this point, my money tank was running on empty, and prospects looked dire. I had not a single dollar saved for the album and my only hope to finance it was JM26. If it had been a magic door for JM24, it was now an immense window of opportunity by the time the prize pool had swelled for JM26.

It was sure to be at least two or three million by now, perhaps more.

This was it - the final battle. The last stand. I beseeched the Powers, implored the gods, focused on positive energy and the worth of my dreams, along with my wish to avenge the wrongs of this evil world. I studied all the form and weather, ran combinations and permutations, looked for weak spots in my predictions, then finally by the Friday, filled out all the little cards and sat back waiting for battle to commence.

I had decided to run a final $500 worth of combinations on it. Ironically, I had St George to thank. Having foolishly backed them again last week, they'd been down 34-10 with twenty minutes to go and I stood to miss out on a prize of $350. Yet with typical perversity, they'd staged a miracle comeback and I'd got the cash. So, I resolved to include these 'miracle troops' in my assault on JM26.

It was a hard round to pick. As it happened, the top eight positions for the finals were mostly decided and couldn't be affected by this weekend's results. Thus, it was hard to know how motivated some of these teams would be. The one exception was game three, Newcastle vs Wests. The result would affect teams' attitude for games four and five, because if Newcastle won, there would still be a chance for the other teams to make the finals. If Wests won, the following games wouldn't matter, so the teams wouldn't care. Thus, it was not known ahead of time whether games four and five would be motivated, hard fought encounters or nihilistic free-for-alls.

After all that, I again blundered on game one. How dumb could I be? Penrith had been in great form, but I'd mainly taken them by 1-10 and 11-20 at home, largely ignoring the 21+ option. With mounting dismay, I watched them hand Brisbane a flogging, and three quarters of my army was wiped out. It was a military disaster as my brave boys went to their deaths, and an economic winter threatened to engulf the land. From a squadron of 500, I only had about 50 units left for the other seven games.

Yet surprisingly, I got through the Saturday games with nearly half of those intact, and a wild and desperate hope glimmered in my heart. There were only three games to go on Sunday, and there was still a chance my troops could get through for the prize.

The trickiest one was Melbourne Storm playing away to an out of form Manly. As the Storm couldn't improve their position on the ladder, they'd rested key players, so it was very hard to tip. I'd split my forces half and half between Melbourne 1-10 and Manly 1-10, and was praying for a close game. In a state of dread, I watched a tight, close match where the lead changed hands several times. Each time either team threatened to get to a lead of more than 11 points, I faced oblivion. Yet as the final minutes passed with Melbourne hanging on to an 8 point lead, I collapsed on the floor in exhausted relief.

Now I just needed the Dogs by 11-20 or 21+ over New Zealand Warriors, then the Roosters to flog Parramatta in the last game. The stress was not over, and the Dogs' game was further torture as they failed to produce the commanding performance I required. With ten minutes to go, they led by only six points. If they could not score another converted try to get past a ten point lead, financial ruin was staring me in the face. As they launched another strong raid on the Warriors' line, I implored them to please, please not kick a field goal. The one point would have assured them of the win, but been utterly useless to my own campaign. Miserably, I stared at the screen, and didn't know whether to laugh or cry when Luke Patten scored for us in the corner. Great, we had the try and were ten points up, but now we'd have to kick the goal from right on the sideline for my hopes to stay alive.

Thank the gods we had Hazem El Masri - El Magic, as the fans called him - to kick for us. He's widely regarded as the best goal kicker of all time, yet there was no guarantee he'd get this one kick today. Of course, everyone remembers El Magic's goal from the sideline to win that game against Newcastle a few years back, but no one remembers this last minute goal from the sideline against the Warriors to take us to from a lead of ten points to twelve. The only one who remembers is me - because it was worth a goddamn fortune. I almost couldn't watch, but peeked through my fingers as the great man's kick swerved like a banana and sailed ever so sweetly between the posts. Then I was turning handstands and running round the flat like a lunatic.

From there, JM26 only needed the Eastern Suburbs Roosters to flog Parramatta by 21+ and the prize was mine. Yes, it was Parramatta, which was a major concern, but the Roosters had the form and motivation to do the job today...

...and by all the gods and Powers, there was no disappointment! The final victory was by thirty-eight points. I cheered in relief at every try scored.

I had finally done it. The magic door had opened at last! I ran around the apartment in ecstasy, leaping over the sofa, jumping up to touch the ceiling, then rolling around on the floor like Angus Young doing a guitar solo.

I headed straight to the pub to check the TAB computer and discover the size of the winning dividend. What a breathless moment. My heart was beating triple as I flicked through to 'Pick the Margins' results, eager to find out how much I'd won. It hit me right in the face - $89,635! The number exploded in my brain. I'd never had that much money before. The magic doorway was opening in front of me. I could step through and fund the recording of my album, make that overseas trip, and learn the true meaning of freedom.

I bought a bottle of Jack Daniels and went home to celebrate my rebirth. The next morning, with remarkably little hangover, I planned the near future. I'd take a short break overseas with Sandra. Already, I was imagining the moment when, with casual largesse, I'd show her the airline tickets. Then I'd come back and record my music, before using a portion of my winnings to promote it.

Sandra did indeed come back to Sydney later that week. I had the airline tickets ready to surprise her, but it didn't quite go to plan. It was clear there was something wrong as soon as she walked in the door. Turned out she wanted to end it. She felt that she and I had different dreams and weren't pulling in the same direction. Maybe it was time we went our separate ways. And, as she finally admitted, she'd met some guy in Melbourne.

I said very little. It's not wise to speak too much in the heat of passion - better to think first and speak afterwards. So I said nothing about the Black Art, the money, or the overseas tickets. A spiteful impulse tempted me towards flaunting the airline ticket and ripping it up in front of her, but I got the better of it and held my tongue. Let her go if that's what she wanted. Couldn't really blame her, as I'd done nothing to try to win her back these last few months.

Sandra took some time to collect her things and return some of mine. She emptied a box with a few odds and ends, and there it was - the Vortex Winder. That old thing. Turns out it had been mixed up with some stuff she'd put in storage before going to Melbourne. Now she was moving out, she was clearing house. I grabbed it at once before she could throw it out with the trash. It might well come in handy overseas.

We parted with no tantrums or harsh words, and no tears, although on the latter score it was purely a matter of dignity on both sides. We took a respectful leave of each other and exited into separate futures.

Looking back with clarity, I saw this was one of the fruits of my infatuation with the Black Art. To some extent, it had cost me a relationship. Yet what had really cost me the relationship was my previous state of poverty, a state which the Black Art had now rectified. That's the Black Art for you. I never could work out whether it was good or evil, savior or destroyer. There's a fine line between a passion and an obsession. In hindsight, it had brought me within a whisker of financial ruin, yet I'd escaped rich as a king. This type of sorcery was too dangerous and too exhausting. It was probably best to go out on top and quit this enterprise now. Having stared oblivion in the face and escaped, I would use the bounty to fuel the adventures that loomed so large and imminent before me.

Part Two

6
Trade Winds

Centuries ago, before the world was fully mapped, adventurers used the trade winds to cross the seas. They reached new lands, and separate worlds came into contact. People who were aliens to one another met, then traded with, fought, or married each other. Goods, cultures, and concepts were exchanged. For better or worse, new societies were formed as a result of those meetings.

The old style explorer is now obsolete, for there are no more uncharted waters, missing continents, or lost tribes. Everything has been found and catalogued. In a way, the world has shrunk. It is no longer the land of the endless horizon, for almost any part of it is within reach of a twenty-four hour flight. The modern human is a superman who crosses continents almost as easily as going downtown.

The trade winds no longer act as midwife to cultural exchange. As a physical force, they've been made redundant by the aeroplane. In a metaphorical sense, the trade winds blow ever onward, bringing people from all parts of the Earth together. The commerce is continual. Yet these winds may not be benevolent forces. They are neutral powers that carry the traveller towards beauties and hazards alike. They enable the human urge to travel, but care nothing for the consequences of that urge. Some will flourish, others perish, and there are no guarantees.

It takes courage to ride these metaphorical trade winds, just as it took courage for the old style explorers to cross the wild seas. Travellers take their chances and ride those winds as well as they can. It had been quite some time since I'd done so myself. Now, after a few years exile in my homeland, and thanks to the

Black Art, the door was open once again. There was the album to record, of course, but that could wait. A quick voyage would rejuvenate the spirit before that serious endeavour was begun.

So it was that I found myself alighting from the plane in the curious city of Amsterdam. After a week in this strange place, there followed a rambling excursion through France and Italy, down into Greece, and back through Eastern Europe. Let the tale of that voyage be told another time. For now, I'll focus on the return to my old home away from home, Germany itself.

It had been a few years. The trip was no random move. It was confirmed as soon as the Black Art came through for me. Although the return was planned, my original visit had been the result of a stray throw on the roulette wheel of romance. Some years before, I'd fallen in love with a German woman who lived in Australia. It had been quite a surprise.

I'd met Freya, a tall and attractive artist, in Sydney a few years before. She'd spent a decade dividing her time between Germany and Australia, but had now made the decision to return to Germany for good. Even so, she wanted to qualify for dual citizenship, and the rules said she had to spend one more year in Australia. If not for this rule, we would never have met, so you could say bureaucracy worked in my favour for once.

It was about halfway through this twelve month period that I met her. She was more or less at a loose end, and we began a casual affair. She told me she was leaving at the end of the year, and it didn't bother me at all. On the contrary, it was a relief, as there would be no need either to keep the affair going or take any steps to end it.

After a while, my feelings changed. A couple of months into the affair, it dawned on me that I would miss her when she left. Wanting to preserve something of our time together, I began to jot down some memories of Freya in a diary. Little by little, these musings wove a spell over me so that I became bewitched into a state of strong emotion.

There's that well known Hemmingway quote, through a character who'd been rich and then lost his fortune. When asked how he'd gone broke, he said it happened gradually and then suddenly. That's the way I fell in love with Freya. The emotion crept up little by little, then suddenly and without warning assaulted me. One moment I was in control of myself, sipping a cocktail of mild melancholy as I mused on the transience of human relationships, the next I was violently drunk with the urgent wish not to lose her.

How had this happened? Apart from the power of Freya's unique charms, something in me had awakened. Realising the mortality of our relationship had sharpened my emotions. By coincidence, I'd been listening to that song 'Falling Slowly' from the *Once* soundtrack, a bewitching tune to which I fell prey. Also, Freya had told me many tales of growing up in Germany, and I, a man who had not travelled much, was haunted by a yearning for distant lands foreign to my own.

Finally, there was a day when we walked in the waterside parklands near Rozelle. It was one of those crisp Autumn days when the air automatically arouses the spirit. As opposed to the tropics, which induce in me only languor, the sharp tang of Autumn always awakens my sensitivities. As we walked round the gardens I saw three roses clustered together like the prongs of a trident. The first was a bud yet to open, the second a flower in full bloom, and the third a rose past its peak and on the path to death and dissolution. It was a poignant image, to be sure, but the fact I'd even noticed was a sign my mind was flirting dangerously with that state of temporary madness known as being in love.

There ended my resistance. I no longer wanted to be separated from this woman, and thought urgently of a plan by which we might stay together. This new state of affairs was inconvenient, to say the least. Freya was returning to Germany, and I was in no financial position to follow her. Yet I was compelled by this newfound insanity to somehow find a way.

The heightened emotional state made me look back in wonder and regret at the type of life I'd been leading in recent years, which was now lost to me. I remembered the time when I was not in love, the lost innocence of just a few days before. That type of life seemed cold, plain, even rather trivial, compared to the state of being in love. Yet it was easier for all that, and far more comfortable. It had been a simpler life. Perhaps a little naive, somewhat callous - but vastly easier. Now, I'd been jolted from my peaceful slumber by this temporary madness that compelled me to thoughts of following Freya to Germany.

To complicate matters further, Freya was ten years older than me, and this was in the days before this so called 'cougar' trend became socially acceptable. Yet love is single-minded and bows to no obstacle, whether age, distance, or money. Not at first, anyhow.

In some ways, it makes sense to marry an older woman. Women tend to live longer, for one thing, so the life spans balance out. All too often, when a man takes a younger wife, he dies at the usual sort of age, and she's left high and dry as a widow for twenty years. In my own case, I've not always lived, shall we say, the *healthiest* life. I've had my share of partying. Perhaps there'll be a price to pay. I don't really expect to reach eighty. Sixty looks a better guess, and given this prospect, it might not be right to take a wife ten years younger. If I take one ten years older, well, to put it bluntly, we're more likely to die at about the same time. It seems only fair.

This was my mentality at the time I confessed to Freya that I'd fallen for her and wished we could stay together. She was taken aback and baulked at the practical difficulties, yet she was not unwilling. My love wasn't in vain. With great relief and optimism, we conceived a plan whereby I would live and work part of each year in Germany until such time as Freya was in a position to return fulltime to Australia. We walked once again in the park at Rozelle. This time there was an otherworldly feel, as if I had broken through dimensions. I felt the autumn woods through which we walked were European forests, as if from a Bavarian fairytale.

Sadly, it was not to last. Although we kept it going for a couple of years, which in its own way was a victory, it was too hard to sustain love at such a distance. After many years of dual country living, Freya was tired of going from one place to another. In my case, the nemesis had once again been money. Dual country living is a rich man's game, not one for the likes of me. Slowly, the money ran out. I still remember the last day in Germany when we knew I'd probably never return. On that mournful day we faced the mortality of our love. Much as when a family member is in the last stage of terminal illness, a point comes when nothing more can be done but endure it until it passes. When the moment arrives, the death is almost a relief, for there's no longer anything left to lose.

Even so, those two years together contain many fond memories. The city of Augsburg is one of the oldest in Germany. Dating back to the Romans, it's ten times older than my own hometown. I loved the old medieval streets in the heart of the city, the vein-like miniature waterways flowing through them, and the nearby mountains.

I also enjoyed the sheer foreignness of living in a non English-speaking country. It's like a second childhood as you try to learn a new language from scratch. In a sense, I was indeed born again, yet it struck me that learning German was a consequence of the romantic roulette wheel. It seemed rather random. The roulette ball had fallen on Freya but if it had landed elsewhere, I could just as well find myself in love with someone else and learning French, or Icelandic, or Portuguese. Or, as actually happened a few years ago, Mandarin.

That I was now speaking German was almost entirely arbitrary. In a larger sense, perhaps it was just as arbitrary that I was speaking English in the first place. Why should I have been born in a small Australian city when I could just as well have been born in Russia, Thailand, or Tunisia? That it was Australia and I'd grown up speaking English seemed a matter of chance. The sense of isolation made me yearn for the exotic otherness of the foreign. It was as if the English speaking Jim was one small petal in a flower whose other petals were scattered to the four corners of possible worlds, each in their own existences. Now, I rejoined with another of my random, imaginary counterparts, and felt less lonely for the experience.

It's said German is one of the easier languages to learn. If that's true, then thank the roulette wheel I didn't fall in love with a Russian or Greek girl, because German wasn't easy for me. There's the thing about nouns having a gender, for example. As with French or Italian, every object is classified as masculine (der), feminine (die), or neuter (das). Now, what is the point of assigning gender to a noun? Why should a rock, a spoon, a tree, or a potato salad be classified male, female, or neuter? If that's not bad enough, the gender ripples out to affect the ending of other words in a sentence. Then there are the four cases - nominative, accusative, dative, and whatever the other one is - which affects the order of the words. It's all very confusing.

Complaints aside, it's wonderful to become immersed in a new language. You learn everything from scratch, as a child does, and it's humbling to realise what a low mental age you now possess. Even six year old kids can out-speak you, reeling off fluent German without thinking. In the meantime, you mumble a few halting inanities like a dumb *auslander*. You feel like the local village idiot, especially when plan B is to fix an affable grin on your face and trust in the kindness of strangers.

But so what? It's refreshing to get this foreign flavour into your mind, to become a stranger to yourself. I loved living in Augsburg, grappling with the new language - and I was nothing if not ambitious. I may have been the village idiot at that point, but each year when I returned, I planned to move up a step. You've got to rise up the ranks bit by bit, that's how it's done. This year I was the village idiot, but next year I might rise to become the village moron. The year after that I could graduate to the level of village simpleton and possibly, with further effort, I'd ascend to the level of village dickhead. From there, the sky was the limit. With further study, I'd be able to pass for being thought slow witted, and then it's only a short step to reach the level of dinner party bore. Finally, before I died of old age, I might just about be able to pass for a native.

Sadly, those lofty ambitions were scuttled by my poverty and the demise of my relationship with Freya. On that final bleak Autumn day, I'd thought I would never return to *Deutschland*. Yet now the Black Art had magically opened doors which had been bolted shut, and as Sandra had conveniently dumped me, it was a perfect opportunity to revisit Augsburg and my old love Freya.

How pleasing it was to arrive by train at the *Hauptbahnhof* that morning and walk once more down the cobbled road of *Maximillian strasse*. It was cold and grey - nothing unusual for Augsburg with Summer just passed - but I didn't mind a bit.

I checked into a hotel near the *Fuggerei*, had a shower, and got ready to call on Freya. I'd decided to try the old surprise visit routine. A risky venture to be sure, as there was the chance she'd be out, at work, or perhaps even with a new boyfriend. If that turned out to be the case, it wouldn't matter, we could spend time together as friends. I was only planning to stay a couple of weeks anyway, so it was best not to revive the old emotions. As the taxi drove up *Morelle strasse* and pulled into the *Prinz Wilhelm* quarter, they were reviving anyway.

It was therefore an anticlimax to find out Freya no longer lived there. Her aunt was still around and although surprised to see me, she invited me in for tea and we resumed our old habits of bad communication featuring my appalling grasp of the German language and her even more tenuous acquaintance with English. I went straight into village idiot mode, fixing the usual simpleton's grin on my face. My German had become even worse, so I'd now regressed to the level of apprentice village buffoon. Suddenly none of the words were coming back to me, as if I'd been away ten years instead of three. After a long and arduous struggle, Freya's aunt managed to convey to me the complex message that Freya wasn't around, but might be visiting later.

That left some time to kill, so I dropped in at the music shop in *Werder strasse*. An old friend, Stefan, worked there. He played in a metal band and I'd given him some guitar lessons when I was trying to make a few Euros on the last trip. He was a good guitarist, but I found it odd that he didn't use the little finger on his left hand. It was absurd. The great Django Reinhardt only had two fretting fingers, due to injury, and Tony Iommi from Sabbath had his own disability - but why would any able bodied guitarist voluntarily take on a handicap by not using the little finger? By using only three out of four fretting fingers, he was running at 75% capacity.

Anyhow, Stefan lived in the same block of flats as Freya's aunt, and it was through him that I'd first heard the German band Rammstein. He'd played their live *Volkerball* DVD on his home theatre. Watching that mighty performance, and the charisma of the singer Til Lindeman, was to understand why some say they're the best live band in the world. As we chatted, Stefan casually delivered the news that Rammstein were playing Munich in a couple of weeks time. *Unglaublich!* What timing. I would get a ticket, whatever it cost.

I went back to Freya's aunt's place, having first, through much miming, sworn her to secrecy about my return. So when I knocked on the door and entered, Freya's face went white, as if it were she and not I who was the ghost. She touched me to make sure I wasn't a hallucination, then put her arms around me. We adjourned to the local cafe one block away. It turned out she was single, so it was possible our love might be resurrected for a time if that's what naturally transpired.

Unfortunately, two of Freya's friends dropped into the cafe and came over to our table. I remembered Annie and Ulrike from years before, and they seemed very friendly. They spoke to Freya in German, and ventured a few remarks in my direction in halting English, as clearly my German wasn't up to much. Finally, after inviting us to their house for drinks in a couple of days' time, they left Freya and me alone, and the two of us went back to Freya's flat.

I woke the next morning in my hotel, having returned there after leaving Freya's place. I turned on the TV in case there were some children's shows on, as that was about my level. I flicked around the channels, then settled on a news program, my eye having been caught by some highlights from the football *Bundesliga*. I watched with only casual interest and it was a good minute or two before I became aware of something very odd. The news readers were speaking fluent German, and I could understand every word they were saying.

What on earth was going on? Normally, I could only get a few words here and there, and suddenly they were all making sense. Confused, I changed channels, and got lost in the intricate banalities of a local soap opera, once again understanding every word. And so it continued, each new channel bringing fresh confirmation of this miracle. It was not that the German words were magically translated into English, or there were subtitles on the screen. It was a case of being suddenly able to understand the German language itself as if I'd been speaking it all my life. It was as if a new software program had been installed in my brain, but there was more to it than that. There was a real feel for the language, a sense of familiarity, though it was hard to see how that could be possible. The word order and grammar felt 'natural.' No effort was needed to form and articulate thoughts. I wondered if this new ability manifested verbally too, so I began an impromptu speech, giving voice to whatever thoughts entered my head. With immense delight, I heard fluent, complicated German sentences echoing within my hotel room.

A suspicion formed about the likely source of this miracle. I felt through my luggage, searching for another old friend I'd recently been reacquainted with. There it was - the Vortex Winder. It had been a long absence all through the time of the Black Art when Sandra had unwittingly taken it with her. I'd been afraid it wouldn't work anymore, but in previous weeks it had come through with a couple of special powers on my travels through Europe. (Again, that is a tale for another day.)

It was by now about the time when there might be a new one, and when I fired up the Vortex Winder, my suspicions were confirmed. Special power of the week was *the ability to master a foreign language*. According to the screen, I'd be able to blend into a foreign environment, to speak and understand like a native!

Not for the first time, I speculated that the Vortex Winder had the ability to anticipate its owner's needs and come up with the gift most suited to the current situation. At the moment, there couldn't have been a magic power that pleased me more.

There was no time to lose using this gift to the full. I dressed and walked to *Thalia*, the three storey bookshop near the markets. I picked up a book, and instead of the usual laborious progress and ten percent comprehension, my eye flew down the page and meaning flooded into my mind. Like a child prodigy with ADHD, I moved from book to book, reading a page or so of one before putting it down and moving on to another. At the shop counter, I engaged a staff member in a long conversation about the novel of the week by a trendy German author. With delight, I found that I could understand her perfectly and form a reply with no effort.

Determined to duplicate this feat, I left *Thalia* and began walking the streets of Augsburg, visiting shops and museums, initiating as many conversations as possible. I was never this garrulous in English, but this new ability was a gift to be used to the max for its brief lifespan. At the local evening college, I prevailed upon the receptionist for a long discussion of course options for the coming term, although by then I'd have toppled back to the level of village idiot. When the receptionist finally tired of me, I wandered into an arthouse cinema complex and watched part of an international action film which had been dubbed into German. Finding that there was not enough dialogue, I walked out and switched to an English period drama in the one next door. Amusingly, the same voices from the action flick had performed the dubbing in this historical piece, and I tut-tutted in a knowing and disapproving manner.

Growing bolder by the hour, I hailed a cab and demanded to be taken to Augsburg university, where I bailed up some poor fellow from the philosophy department. I introduced myself as a visiting professor from Sydney and subjected him to a tirade on Kant's verbosity being even worse in the original *Deutsch* than its English translation.

After a further gratuitous rant about the Vienna circle of the 1930s, I took my leave and decided to have a laugh with Freya. We were meeting for lunch, along with her aging but still physically robust mother. Previous such meetings had seen Freya caught in the middle, conversing with me in English and her mother in German, and translating every line for the benefit of the other. Today, I walked up to Freya's mother and, employing formal high German for comic effect, greeted her gallantly and at length. I proceeded to annoy the waiter with a long discussion of the menu before, in a presumptuous and high handed manner, ordering for all three of us.

Freya and her mother were staring at me open mouthed all the while, amazed at my transformation from dunce to genius. '*Übung macht den Meister,*' I pronounced with a jaunty wink at Freya's mother, before proceeding to dominate conversation for the rest of the meal. It was rather rude, yet it was such a novelty for Freya and her mother to hear my articulation that they didn't seem to mind. After the meal, I told Freya the truth, relating in German the astonishing tale of Iolango, the Vortex Winder, and all that had transpired since then. The story seemed a wild fantasy, to be sure, yet no more miraculous than my sudden mastery of the German tongue, so she seemed to believe it.

I barely slept for the next day or two, not wanting to waste the chance to take in as much German culture as possible while the magic power lasted. I was slightly annoyed when Freya reminded me of our dinner appointment with her friends Annie and Ulrike that evening, but Freya suggested we have some fun with them. The idea was for me to spend the first hour in my usual state of tongue tied idiocy, and then suddenly let loose with an outburst of fluent intellectual discourse after the main meal was served. It would be a good laugh.

We turned up at Ulrike's place, and at first everything went as expected. Annie and Ulrike were about the same age as Freya, and they patronised me in the familiar way as if I were a child, which in fairness was the truth as far as they were concerned. Apart from my limited powers of verbal ability, I was ten years younger than the three women. To set up the gag, I stayed fairly quiet while we had a glass of wine and some cheese, listening to the three of them chatting among themselves. Every so often, they would offer me a sentence or two in English, to which I'd reply either in English or in deliberately slow and clumsy German. Freya asked me to play classical guitar while they talked, and I did so as my way of contributing to the evening's ambience.

It was hard not to laugh at the thought of what would be coming up next, yet the joke didn't quite go as planned. As we were finishing our wine, Freya had a phone call from her aunt, who wasn't feeling at all well and was thinking of going to hospital. This wasn't that big a deal, because her aunt is prone to hypochondria and often had these little episodes. However, Freya excused herself, and as her aunt lived only ten minutes drive away, she said she'd quickly call on her to make sure she was alright, then return at once.

After Freya left, I resumed playing classical guitar. Annie and Ulrike smiled at me, then kept on talking. They seemed a little tipsy, laughing and chatting between themselves, not bothering to include me at this point. Still eager to drink in as much German language as possible, I kept listening to their chatter, and was surprised to take in the following exchange, which of course was all in German. I translate it for the benefit of English speakers.

'Keep playing, boy, that's one thing you can do well.' said Annie.

'Mail order brides have to be good for something,' Ulrike replied. 'Freya said he can cook too.'

'Yeah? Maybe I should get one, do you think?'

'Sure. A nice young one like him. Freya's a real cradle robber. Typical. She never did date her own age group. Remember after school, she only went with a guy if he was ten years older. Now she's almost fifty and look at him - nearly young enough to be her son. Disgraceful!'

'A scandal - but who really cares anyhow? I'll take one of them too. Did you check him out when he was getting the wine glasses off the top shelf? Nice! I'm finished with German men. Ever since Andreas went off with that Austrian whore. Twenty years of my life I gave him.'

'Forget him, Annie, he doesn't deserve you. He'll be back in a while begging forgiveness.'

'He can tell it to my lawyer. If he wants to pick up some girl half his age, he's dead to me. Two can play that game. Freya's got the right idea. I'm going to get one of these Australian mail order brides too. He can't talk, but who cares? He can cook, he can clean, and he can play guitar.'

'That's not all he can do.'

'Yeah, look at him, the little tart. I'll bet he knows how to do it.'

'Sure. That tongue's not talking much, he can find something else to do with it.'

'Let's order one! I wonder how long before it arrives. Maybe a week or two.'

'I can't wait that long. Maybe we should take him upstairs now before Freya gets back.'

The two tipsy women collapsed in bawdy laughter. I was shocked. To think that these two mature, respectable German women would carry on such a sexist, scandalous conversation right in front of my face as soon as Freya was out of the room. Treating me like some kind of third world sex object. Mail order bride indeed. Of course, they assumed I couldn't understand a word they were saying.

Flushing red, I excused myself and went to the bathroom so they wouldn't guess from my complexion that I had understood the conversation. This would have caused them unnecessary embarrassment. As I walked away, I felt them staring at my body again. Yet by the time I returned, they seemed to have forgotten me. Such is the lot of a 'mail order bride.' Once the 'owner' has had their fun, you become invisible again. The topic of conversation had changed in my absence.

'Where does she get off with the idea she's this big artist anyhow? She's never exhibited in Munich or Berlin.'

'She showed me her CV. Strange that all her big shows were in Sydney, and hardly anything at home.'

'It's not hard to make a CV like that. It's not like anyone's going over there to check, are they?'

'She thinks she's pretty good, eh? I'll believe it when she does something in Munich. So now she's an artist? There was no sign of it in her twenties. Not until she started hanging out with that crowd at *Kulturhaus Kresslesmühle.*'

'Oh, let her have her fantasies. They're harmless, I suppose.'

This was all quite unfair to poor old Freya, and I was tempted to jump in with an outburst of fluent German to defend her. Freya did have art shows in Sydney, and had created a lot of quality work. It's a pity her friends weren't aware of it. It is a sad aspect of human nature that often the people least appreciative of your work are your own family and friends. Because they know you, for some reason they assume you're no good. It's not unless you get public recognition through awards or sales they finally see you're actually pretty damn good at what you do.

At this point, the doorbell sounded and Freya returned to the party. I explained to her in English that our planned joke was off, and would tell her the reasons later on. We passed the rest of the evening happily enough, although I was slightly embarrassed by the earlier conversation.

A few days later, I made it to Munich for the Rammstein concert, and by all the gods and powers, they did not disappoint.

It was an amazing show, and Till Lindeman is surely one of the best front men ever. Rammstein could probably have taken on Slayer in their prime and held their own, and in my eyes there is no bigger compliment.

Before and after the show, I took the chance to talk music with some of the German fans. But as the night wore down, I was aware of an imminent sadness. The power of foreign language mastery must end soon, and I would return to my dunce like ways. Yet I hoped some memory of my experiences would remain and provide the impetus for a renewed study of the language.

Another sadness was that I would again have to part from Freya. The brief revival of our love also brought a reprise of its death. I was determined to return to Australia to record the album, and Freya was still stuck in Germany, so we were set for another painful parting. There is no beginning without an end, that is the way of these love affairs. Yet we must hope each ending contains the seeds of a new beginning.

In spite of that sad end, we can draw solace from the beauty of what has been. The trade winds brought us together. In the great and mysterious commerce of human interaction, they joined two people from opposite ends of the planet. With our meeting, a new world was born. From my side, I found a rich relationship, and also a fond acquaintance with a culture that was foreign to me. I became part of that country and discovered a hidden 'German' side of my personality, one which felt oddly familiar but had been latent until then. There are more things in Heaven, Earth, and human nature than are dreamt of in your philosophy. Let the trade winds blow ever onwards and lead us where they will. They may take us to heavenly places of which we never dreamt, or to hells we never suspected to exist - and unfortunately, that brings me to the next chapter.

7

Amsterdam to Bangkok

I'm going to keep this chapter short, because it contains some memories that should never have existed. It goes in only because it must as part of the story, yet it's a pity I was ever caught up in such vile events.

I was back in Amsterdam, my final port of call before the long trip back to Sydney. The flight from Munich was a short one, and here was a chance to savour the Amsterdam nightlife one more time before I left the next day.

Once again, I walked the winding, Escher-like streets of this strange city. Even the harsh winter weather was no deterrent. As I took refuge beneath my many layers of shirts, jumpers, great coat, and warm winter cap, it felt as if my body was safely ensconced inside a luxury hotel of garments, with only my face peeking through the window at the extraordinary view. The icy night air was a tonic to the spirit as my eyes took in an endless parade of odd little shops, canals, fellow travellers, and also the prostitutes so openly advertising themselves in the 'shop windows' of the red light district.

I was only a browser in that department, but like many a traveller before me, it was a blast to find such a liberal attitude to life's so called vices. Prostitutes in the windows, marijuana sold in the cafes. In truth, this was no more Sin City than any other in the world, the difference was the honesty. What would elsewhere be hidden away, here was openly on display. The sense of freedom was invigorating. I entered one of the famous cafes. It still felt odd to buy marijuana over the counter and light up a joint at the table. As the change of consciousness seeped through me, I reflected in wonder on recent adventures

- the comeback to music, the Black Art, the overseas travel, the reborn *amour* with Freya in Germany, and of course the Vortex Winder itself. At that point, it seemed the way was ever forward and the trade winds would blow forever.

In this euphoric mood, I got talking to a stranger, a young guy who looked to be in his late twenties. He'd come to my cafe table and asked for a light, then bought me a beer. He introduced himself as Jonathon and said he'd just travelled over from Norway. Maybe it was the weed, but it struck me that Jonathon had a most remarkable face. During our conversation, I kept staring at it, trying to place him. After he told me he was a pro guitarist himself, I figured that I may have seen his photo in one of the rock mags.

There was something enigmatic about the guy. His face was naturally angelic, yet with a hint of moral corruption. If anything, this added to his charismatic aura. Longish blond hair set off a pair of ice blue yet bloodshot eyes. He looked simultaneously young and old. This, I speculated generously, was because he was an old soul, and less generously, was also due to the 'road' lifestyle he admitted to have been living in recent years. With a flash of stoned insight, I decided he was the embodiment of how Dorian Gray's portrait would have looked after a couple of years in the attic. Halfway to hell, still handsome, but starting to fray round the edges and crumble from within. I couldn't place his accent, but he spoke English well enough.

When I told Jonathon I was a guitarist myself, his reaction was lukewarm. As he revealed, he was jaded with music, burned out after touring nonstop for the last three years, and retiring from the biz altogether. Noting the coincidence, I ventured a remark.

'That's funny, I did the same thing when I was your age. What are you, nearly thirty? That's when *I* quit. Ten years later and I'm back. Maybe that'll be you too.'

'Nah,' Jonathon almost snarled. 'I'm done. Been at it since school and what've I got? No money, no fame, nothing. I'm over it. The travelling, the setting up, the sound checks. Even the partying.'

'So why are you here tonight?'

'Old habits never die.' Jonathon muttered with a laugh that turned into a long racking cough.

'Only their owners,' I said, before realising the comment was uncalled for and a touch hypocritical. To change the subject, I said, 'What kind of guitar do you play?'

'Les Paul.'

'Ah, you're a Gibson man too. I've an Explorer, myself.'

'Nothing but the best - but it's all got to go. I'm broke and I've got to get home. You want to buy a couple of Marshalls?'

'I've already got an amp, and my plane leaves tomorrow. The airline fees would kill me.' I paused for a moment. 'What about the Les Paul? You selling that?'

'I wasn't planning to. Then again, it's not much use to me now. Make me an offer. Cash only. I ain't waiting for no bank transfer.'

I couldn't believe my luck. My last night in town, and a Gibson Les Paul was falling into my lap.

'Ah, OK. I don't really know. I don't have much cash,' I lied. 'Five hundred Euros?'

'Be serious. You insult me.'

'Well, *you* say a price.'

'Two thousand.'

'Whoa, that's out of my league, mate. I'm only a backpacker, you know. Forget it.'

'It's not just any old Les Paul,' said Jonathon. 'There's a history. You wouldn't believe some of the owners.'

'Who's that then?'

'I'll give you a hint. The initials are JB and JS.'

'JB and JS... JS, JB, JB... is he English?'

'Correct.'

'Surely you don't mean... Beck?'

'The very same.'

'Jeff Beck? You can't be serious!'

'He used it on *Blow By Blow*. It's the one on the cover.'

'Awesome! So how the hell did you get hold of it?'

'It's a long story.'

'Who's the other one? JS... JS? You've got me there. No idea.'

'Think of the eighties. Pretty boy, big blond hair in the still of the night.'

'You mean...?'

'John Sykes. He played it in Lizzy, Whitesnake, and on the first Blue Murder album.'

'John Sykes! One of my heroes. Sykes was a genius back then. That first Blue Murder record should've been huge.'

'Right you are, mate. Sykes killed on that record.'

'This is blowing my mind! You're telling me this guitar was owned by Beck and Sykes? No offence, but why should I believe you?'

'I've got papers for it. Sales receipts and a certificate of authenticity.'

'Can I see them?'

'I can call home and get them sent to you, no problem. If you want to see the guitar, it's back at the hotel locked up in my room. You can see it tonight if you like - but first make me an offer.'

'OK... a thousand Euros.'

'Out of the question. Eighteen hundred or nothing.'

'I can't get hold of that much cash this time of night. There's a limit on the ATM.'

Jonathon paused, and seemed to be considering. 'Fifteen hundred cash, and that's my last word. Take it or leave it.'

'OK, Jonathon, how about this? Give it to me for thirteen hundred Euros, and if you make a comeback in ten years, like I am, I promise to sell it back to you. I'll put it in writing, sign it, whatever you want.'

'I told you, I'm done with all that. There'll be no comeback.'

'If it's in your blood, you'll be back. So, what do you say?'

'Alright mate, done. Thirteen hundred, and you sell it back to me in ten years if I make a comeback. Maybe you're right and I'll change my mind.'

We shook hands on the deal, then walked through the icy streets to Jonathon's hotel, stopping on the way so I could withdraw cash from the ATM. Sure enough, it looked like the real McCoy - a black Les Paul, and it had a definite aura. It *had* to be genuine. We shook hands again, and I walked back to my hotel with the guitar. I decided not to worry about the papers of authenticity just yet. Jonathon could email them to me later. There'd be no time to worry about it tomorrow, that was for sure.

II

I woke the next morning and there it was, the Black Beauty Les Paul. I gazed in wonder upon Beck and Sykes' old weapon. Truly, the gods were with me, to bestow such an ally for recording the album! I was unstoppable now. If only there'd been an amp in the room. Yet even unplugged, the class of the instrument was clear. The sooner I could get back to Sydney, the better.

I checked out of the hotel and walked a few blocks to Amsterdam's central railway for the short train trip to the airport. With a couple of hours to kill before the flight, I browsed the airport shops, all the while keeping the guitar case at close hand, looking round every minute or two in case some Dutch thief was eying it off for a grab and run.

At the same time, I'd check that my passport was secured in the money belt at my waist. As an infrequent traveller, my paranoid nightmare was the thought of losing the passport and being at the mercy of airport officials. Without it, identity was erased in the eyes of the bureaucracy, and you were at the mercy of the arbitrarily good or bad souls that lurked within it. I still felt a bit stoned from the strong weed of the night before - hardly the ideal state for negotiating the stressful transition points of international travel. Someone observing me would have seen a man with a nervous tic that went: Guitar, wallet, passport: check. Guitar, wallet, passport: check. In an endless loop.

The best thing was to check in my luggage as soon as possible. The guitar went through as excess baggage. After politely harassing the counter staff about safety and insurance for the instrument, there was still time to get a coffee and wait for boarding.

Those long flights don't bother me much, at least if there are a couple of good books to read on the way. There's no cause to complain because really, you're looked after very well. The flight attendants care for you. They check that you're safe and comfortable, they come round with little biscuits, cheese, and wine. They offer pillows or eye masks if you wish to sleep. These small kindnesses are often taken for granted by fools. For me, their value was soon to be underlined by visiting a place where they were entirely absent.

I would never complain about a flight. Sure, it's not the best way to spend ten or more hours, and there are some hellish aspects. You're in cramped conditions, packed in with more than a hundred other people. You've got to share a tiny bathroom, there's not much freedom. But it's a small price to pay for being able to cross from one side of the world to the other in a day. Of course you want the trip to end as soon as possible, but they try to look after you. You have films to watch, music to listen to, and they think about your needs and take care of you.

I was reading one of the Irvine Welsh books – *Trainspotting* - feeling a mix of repulsion and admiration. It was a vile world brilliantly drawn. To think that such squalor existed in the 21st century. So much for progress. The drugs were only part of the problem, as much symptom as cause - but they didn't help. Here was the dark side of the drug experiment, laid bare. Yet there were many forms of stupidity in the world. Take the front cover of the book, for example. It was a copy of the poster for the movie version, showing photos of the four guys who were the main characters, and also one of a minor character named Diane. Yet all five photos were the same size. The thing is, while the four guys were in the story from beginning to end, Diane was in it for about three pages somewhere in the middle. So why did the movie poster have her equal size as if she were a major character? Apparently the film promoters wanted to appeal to the vital 15-35 year old female demographic, so they pretended that *Trainspotting* is not a tale of the drug fuelled adventures of Renton, Sick boy, Spike, and Begbie, but the drug fuelled adventures of Renton, Sick boy, Spike, Begbie, and Diane.

Why bother? The novel was a smash hit anyway. The masses already knew what it was about and who was in it. The film didn't need marketing, let alone false marketing. The fact is *Trainspotting* is a book about those four Scottish heroin addicts, and if they're all male, that's just the way it is. There's no point pretending Diane's a major character when she only appears in one scene. You'd hate to see them remake *Treasure Island* these days. The one female character is Jim Hawkins' mother, and she only appears in the book's first two chapters. If *Treasure Island* were made into a film today, the poster would show Long John Silver, Jim Hawkins, and Jim Hawkins' mother. Most likely, with her recast as an intellectual with a black belt in karate who went on the voyage, outwitted Silver, and found the treasure. For God's sake, if you want to create positive role models or reach a wider demographic, come up with your own stuff. Don't butcher the classics.

The first leg of the flight passed quickly enough, yet I was aware of a jarring note, a vague sense of threat and unease. Maybe it was just the Irvine Welsh book. As I dozed, however, I dreamt I was landing back in Sydney to learn that the Les Paul had been lost in transition. The feeling of devastation seemed awfully real, and I was relieved to wake and find it was just a dream. It was disconcerting, however, that the sense of unease had not gone away.

We had to change planes at Bangkok. After making a circuit of the airport to stretch my legs, I decided to check in for the last part of the trip. The first sign of trouble came when I handed my passport to the girl at the gate. Instead of handing it back and waving me through, she scrutinised it, looked at me, then checked her computer screen.

'There is a problem with your luggage, sir. Could you step this way?'

Immediately, the air travel paranoia kicked in, though there was no real reason to be afraid. Yet as soon as she spoke, I saw a couple of airport security guards standing by. They asked me to come with them. There was no choice but to comply and get it over with so I could board the flight. I was taken into an office a couple of minutes' walk away. The first thing I saw was a bunch of Thai airport cops standing around in the office, and the second was the Les Paul guitar case lying on the desk.

'Is this yours?' the head cop asked.

Of course it was. There was no reason to deny it. He took the guitar out of the case (how dare he touch it!) unscrewed a panel at the back and removed a lump of black hash about the size of a squash ball. With the sudden clarity of shock, the ramifications were obvious: Thailand, drugs, prison, death. But this was impossible. I was landing in Australia in a few hours time. My whole life was there, the album was to be recorded, everything was about to begin. Whatever lay in my personal future, Thailand played no part in it. It was just a stopover on the flight home. Trying to stay calm, I said, 'That isn't mine. The guitar is, but I've never seen that before in my life.'

'You know what it is then?'

I was already falling into a maze of mental traps. Having betrayed an instant recognition of the composition of the black ball, I had clearly shown myself to be no drug virgin. Yet it stood to reason that the black stuff was something dodgy - why else would the cops be holding it up for my inspection? It looked like a big ball of hashish. Of course I would have denied ownership. Whatever I said now would no doubt incriminate me - for something I had never done. In such circumstances, the simplest path was to tell the truth.

'I only bought the guitar yesterday in Amsterdam. I had no idea that stuff was in there.'

'Amsterdam,' the cop said with a knowing expression. It was another black mark against my credibility. Just another drugged up Westerner from the Sin City of Northern Europe. Not that Bangkok had much of a reputation as a moral exemplar, when you thought about it.

'I'm a professional musician. I bought that guitar yesterday for only 1300 Euros. It was a bargain price, that's why I bought it.'

'Maybe worth a lot more... when you got home.' The guy smirked at his colleagues.

'I'm a musician, that's why I bought the guitar yesterday. I don't know anything about that black stuff. I swear I had no idea it was in there. Please, my flight is boarding in about twenty minutes, I've got to go.'

'You talk to police first. Drug smuggling is a very serious offence.'

'Drug smuggling? What are you talking about? I'm not into drugs. This is all a mistake.'

'Mistake?' A malevolent laugh. 'Big mistake!'

I knew then I was doomed. Despite further protests and explanations, the airport cops would not be swayed, and I may as well have been arguing with a machine. In hindsight, that's exactly what I was doing.

There was no chance of catching the flight now. My best hope was to explain to the police and the Australian Embassy what had happened, then pick up a flight tonight when it was all sorted out. After all, I was completely innocent. Surely an innocent man had nothing to fear. Yet when I was transferred to a cell in a Bangkok police station soon after, I began to suspect that guilt and innocence were quaint concepts from childhood with no relevance to the present situation. Once away from the air conditioned airport, any facade of a sympathetic world melted away in the face of an oppressive, relentless wave of heat. This was South East Asia in summer, and in the current circumstances, any allusions to Hell would have been quite redundant.

There were fifteen or twenty other captives in the police cell. We were left in there like a herd of sheep in a truck, with all the dignity that entails. We could either pace around the cell or slump, sweat soaked, on the floor. In the absence of any other options, there was nothing to do except think. My mind was a stew of happy recent memories, devastated by a new awareness that they would have no successors. I recalled the memory, vivid yet now utterly dreamlike, of walking the icy streets of Amsterdam in my greatcoat less than two days before, the brilliance of the Rammstein concert from last week, and the sight of Jonathon's face when he'd sold me the guitar. Through the heat haze of the prison, my memories of his face shimmered and distorted. I could no longer recall his features in any detail.

After several hours - a miserable droplet of time in the looming eternity - I got to speak to Liz McDonough, a rep from the Australian embassy. She was a middle aged woman, kindly enough, but her sympathetic face was jaded by the déjà vu of her profession. I explained what had happened, but it was clear from her expression there was little hope of an early release. Did I have a receipt for the guitar? No, of course not, why would I? It had been a last minute purchase from some guy in a cafe. Was there anything to back up my story? No, and my fingerprints were all over the guitar from playing it unplugged the night before in my hotel room. There was nothing the Australian embassy could do then, apart from arrange some legal representation and notify any family back home in Australia. In the meantime, I'd be held in prison 'til the case went to trial.

The horror of the situation was worsening by the moment, with the realisation there'd be no escape from this country any time soon, that Australia was so far away it may as well be on the moon, and that even my family was going to be dragged into this mess. But there was some good news, the embassy rep said. There was no death penalty for hash. That was for heroin and the harder drugs, so I'd only be looking at a few years in prison.

If that was the good news, she could keep the bad. There was no way on Earth I'd be rotting five or ten years in a Thai prison. I'd kill myself first. My predicament was hideous beyond belief. I did the old *pinch me it's a bad dream* routine, but there was no mercy there. Dreams had never been *this* vivid. Well, if there was no escape route via a pinch, more drastic measures would have to be considered.

My fellow inmates and I were left in the cells overnight with nothing but a thin mat each to sleep on. Blankets weren't necessary, and would only have served as a forlorn shield against reality. Not that there was much sleep available. Sleep is for those with freedom, or those who've given up all hope of it. I was lost in a damned netherworld, doing the Limbo shuffle as I twitched miserably on my mat. Uncomfortable, friendless, afraid, and tortured by the thought that right about now I should be flying into Sydney and catching a taxi home. There I would be able to lie in a comfortable bed, have a shower, go out and buy a newspaper to catch up on news of home, and read it while drinking a coffee or going to my favourite Thai restaurant. Thai? Fuck Thailand, I'd never eat that food again, even if I made it home. Tears formed, and dripped into oblivion like my dying qi. At least they were silent tears, I'd try to hold on to dignity as long as I could. Why was I here? I'd done nothing to deserve this. This. Was. Not. Right.

The next morning, most of us were taken from our cells and herded into a prison van. In our current conditions, any kind of change aroused a glimmer of hope. Yet this journey was about as cheery as a wartime train trip to Auschwitz. We were simply transferred from a temporary hell into a permanent hell, namely the Bang Kwang prison, nicknamed 'Big Tiger' as I later found out. From the windows of the police van, I caught glimpses of this fiend which was to swallow us whole: the grim walls and towers, and the ironically pretty gardens near the entrance. Never was there so lying a facade as those gardens.

One might think I'd be spared prison until my case had gone to trial, but that wasn't how they did things around here. As far as the Thai authorities were concerned, I'd been caught trying to smuggle drugs through Thailand. I was clearly guilty, in their eyes. The trial was a mere formality and my sentence had already begun. I was now an inmate like any other.

Inside the prison's reception area, the new prisoners were registered. Then placed in irons. Leg irons, like some eighteenth century convict. This served the dual purpose of subduing the body and crushing the spirit. If ever a reminder was needed we were no longer considered human and had lost all rights, this was it. We were then taken into the main body of the prison, the belly of the beast, where presumably we were to be slowly digested, then finally absorbed or excreted.

Once inside the prison, it quickly became our whole world. Everything was shocking at first, because it was so far removed from normality. Many prisoners were crowded together in a small space. The heat and stench were oppressive. The food was terrible, and the guards had a palpable air of menace. Some of the new prisoners were given an introductory beating so all of us would have no doubt who was in charge. I got off lightly in this to begin with, but that was only a matter of luck, and my luck didn't last for long.

Most of the prisoners were Asian, but there were also some Westerners like myself. All of us, regardless of race, belonged to the same social underclass. The prisoners' faces bore expressions ranging from stoic endurance to sullen toughness, to ill concealed fear on the faces of the newer ones. Those who'd been there a long time simply looked blank, as if they could no longer muster the effort to pretend to be human.

The prison also housed an informal population of rats and cockroaches who, for reasons best known to themselves, had decided to make the place their home. They loitered in and around the drains, coming and going as they pleased, although I noticed they did not venture too close to the human inmates. The presence of these despised creatures added to the overall hellish atmosphere.

A more immediate menace was the prison guards. They all wore the same uniform, as well as favouring a particular type of mirrored sunglasses with large lenses. If you dared look into those sunglasses, you'd see your own wretched face looking back at you before feeling the sting of a cane on your body.

The guards were at liberty to dish out violence to the prisoners at any time. I witnessed some beatings which shocked me at first, but after a while they began to seem just part of the normal routine. Some of the guards were obvious sadists who had clearly found the ideal profession. Others did their job of controlling us without the need to labour the point with overt viciousness. After a while, it became clear which guards were the main ones to avoid.

Once you became acclimatised to the horrible atmosphere of the prison, boredom also set in as an extra demon to fight against. As long, pointless days stretched into blank, interminable weeks, the mind began to shut down. The daily routine was dull, empty, and futile. As the time wore endlessly on, I began to wonder which of the demons would finish me first - boredom and futility, hunger, heat, or a fatal bashing from the prison guards. In sheer boredom, I even framed a bookies' market on the likely victor. But unlike in the time of my gambling with the Black Art - an era which seemed years ago - this time there would be no winners at all.

III

To this day, I'm not sure which was worse - the physical discomfort or the mental suffering. The backdrop to the physical hardship was the oppressive heat. On top of that, you were always hungry, endured barren surroundings with few home comforts, and were often ill one way or another. Bed was no more than the simple mat on the hard floor. The leg iron became absorbed into one's consciousness as if it were an extra leg, or a cancerous growth. Added to that, the threat of violence was ever present. Some of the other prisoners were dangerous enough, but at least you could fight back if attacked. The guards, however, could lash out with no fear of reprisal.

Nearly all the normal physical comforts were absent, the things one takes for granted - a comfortable bed, enough to eat and drink, the freedom to shower and be clean.

The mental suffering was also wretched. Some of it was related to those harsh physical conditions. For example, I'm a guy who needs his own space. My parents recognised this and had the kindness to grant me my own room, apart from my siblings, at the age of eight. So to now be forcefully herded together with scores of other human beings was my idea of hell. When Sartre said 'hell is other people' he didn't realise how far that concept could go.

The human body has both its beautiful and disgusting aspects. In the Thai prison, you could say all the beautiful aspects were minimised to the point of invisibility, and the disgusting ones were magnified and took centre stage. The authorities saw prisoners as sub-human, so the basic rights to dignity were not thought to apply to us. As we found out, everything taken for granted in the civilised world was no longer granted to us.

Another key strand of the mental suffering was the sheer boredom of prison life. There were very few daily activities open to us. There was little to do, other than to think and dream of better days. The boredom of our routine was soul destroying. In a strange way, prison life was a bit like being on a long flight on an aeroplane, but one hundred times worse and with all the good parts taken out. You're crowded together in cramped conditions with a bunch of people you don't know, the food's not that good, you're bored, and you just want to get it over with as soon as possible so you can get on with your life. The difference - and all of this is totally relative to conditions in prison - is that on the plane you have comfortable chairs and cushions. The food is gourmet. The toilets are immaculate. You can listen to music, read a book, play games or watch movies, all of which help ease the boredom and discomfort of the flight.

The plane trip isn't much fun. It's not an experience you would seek for its own sake, and you want it to end sooner rather than later. But the movies, games, and books help make the time pass and you don't mind putting up with it all because you know it's only for twelve or twenty-four hours, so it'll soon be over when you reach your destination.

If you want to know what prison is like, think of an aeroplane trip that never ends - not in twenty-four weeks or twenty-four days, let alone twenty-four hours. A flight that grinds on and on aimlessly into the future, with no destination even in mind, let alone in sight. It's a flight in which all the little comforts have been stripped away. The food is next to inedible. The toilets are vile. The seats are uncomfortable. You don't have movies, books or music to ease the boredom of the trip. There are no smiling air hostesses who comes around to look after your needs with small kindnesses like food, drinks, or eye shades and pillows. Instead, there are prison guards who, if you're lucky, will ignore you. If you're unlucky, you'll get one of the sadistic ones who dispenses random acts of violence instead of after dinner mints.

Prison life is the plane flight that never ends. The flight without comfort or consolation, in which there's no destination other than physical and spiritual ruin. If you ever eventually find your way to the end of the voyage, there won't be much left of you.

After a few weeks, I had already begun to be ground down by the harshness and futility of the conditions. Under duress, the mind begins to shut down, as a defence mechanism. The initial shock of my incarceration gave way to a numbing state of acceptance. It was less and less of a shock each morning to wake to the grinding heat of another day in Hades. It was still a vile awakening, make no mistake, but one to which I was becoming accustomed.

I found that pessimism, oddly enough, was a far more useful state of mind than optimism. I'd made a few abortive attempts at positive thinking but found it impossible to sustain, especially without the physical health to reinforce it. It was actually less painful to adopt a mentality almost of defeat. In the early days, thoughts of my former life, and my musical dreams, had been a cruel torture. Those dreams may have been unlikely to come true, but there had been a chance. Not now though. They were all but extinguished. If I ever managed to get out of this place alive, I'd be an old man. Too old to play rock music, that was clear. But after my hopes were ground down with a few weeks' incarceration, my musical dreams seemed so remote and incredible that they were forgotten. I wanted only to get back to a normal life and the day to day freedoms most people take for granted.

Despite the pessimism, I retained a flicker of hope justice would be done at the coming court case. Liz McDonough, the woman from the Australian Embassy, came to inform me when the trial would be going ahead, and ask if there was anyone I wanted to contact back home. I took the chance to repeat my innocence and implored her to help free me.

'Thanks for coming to see me again, Liz.'

'You're welcome to any help we can give you. Are you OK?'

'I'm as far from OK as you could get without being dead. Please, you've got to get me out of here.'

She looked at me, expressionless, no doubt having heard it all before. I continued my plea.

'I was talking to a couple of guys who are in here just for possession, and they're doing five or ten years. So that's what I'm looking at, right? Except it might be worse for me if they decide it's trafficking. Right?'

She nodded.

'In that case,' I said, 'I'd like you to make a special request of the court and ask for the death penalty. If they're going to give me ten years, I'd sooner take the firing squad. Death is better. Why deny it? One thing's for sure, after ten years in this place, there's no such thing as being set free. Whatever walks out in this body after ten years would no longer be human, or alive. So if the Thai judicial system wants to make an example of me, they might as well get it over with.'

Liz McDonough gave me a kindly look.

'I know it's not what you want to hear right now, Jim, but you can get through this. It seems impossible now, but you'll find ways to adapt. You're not the first guy to be in this position, and you won't be the last. It doesn't seem real at the moment, but one day this will all come to an end and you can go home. Then you'll look back on this moment and realise what I'm saying was true. When it gets tough, think of your family and what's waiting for you at home.'

'That's the last thing I want to think of because it only reminds me where I *should* be, instead of this place. You talk about my family? My parents will be dead by the time I get out of here, and I'll be an old man myself. What's the point? Can't the Australian government do anything to help me?'

'They'll do everything they can, but they've got no jurisdiction here. You're not under Australian law, so there's not much the government can do.'

'It's not fair. I'm Australian, and I wasn't even visiting Thailand, only passing through on my way home. I should be tried under Australian laws.'

'That's not how it works. You were arrested in Thailand, so you're under Thai law.'

'Thai law is ridiculous. I'm not even guilty, but if I *was* guilty, it's only a bit of hash. You can smoke that in the cafes in Amsterdam. It's not even illegal. In Australia, you'd only get a fine for that much hash. At a guess, maybe $500 or $1000. But here you get ten years in a prison where the conditions are so bad you wouldn't house a dog here if you went away for the weekend. This is insane. What's so special and moral about Thailand anyway? They have, like, fifty cent prostitutes in the main street, don't they?'

'I'm sorry, but there's nothing we can do about the law, and I strongly advise you not to say anything critical of Thailand. It will only make it worse for you. It's in your best interests to show respect for the Thai authorities at all times. Then at least we've still got the chance to apply for a royal pardon after a couple of years.'

'A royal pardon? For a crime I never committed? I don't want a pardon for that. I'm innocent.'

'Tell me what happened again.'

'OK, Liz. As you'll see, my story is exactly the same as I told you before. I was in Amsterdam for my last night before catching the flight back to Australia. I met a guy in a cafe who said he needed money fast and had to sell his guitar. It was a Gibson Les Paul worth several thousand dollars, but he let me have it for 1300 Euros. It was perfect for me. I went back to the hotel, then straight to the airport the next day putting the guitar through as luggage. Next thing you know, I'm here, but I swear I had no idea that hash was in the guitar. I'll swear on any holy book in the world.'

'But you've no receipt for the guitar. There's nothing to back up your story.'

'Go on my website - there's pictures of me playing a few different guitars, but not the Les Paul. That proves I've only just bought it.'

'That won't convince anyone.'

'Please, Liz, I'm innocent. Surely the court will be logical. Why would I risk my life to smuggle a small amount of dope? I could get that much in Australia for a few hundred bucks. If it was heroin, maybe I could have made a profit, but to risk my whole life for a ball of hash - why would I do that?'

'I'm sorry, but I see examples of bad judgment all the time in this job. People do crazy, illogical things for no good reason. And why? Because they didn't realise the risk they were taking, they didn't imagine the consequences, or they just didn't think it would happen to them.'

'I'm not a fool, Liz. Why would I do something as stupid as taking dope on the plane? It's just not logical. It must have been Jonathon's stash. *I* certainly didn't know it was there.'

'Maybe you were just having too much fun and you didn't think ahead. If you're going to talk about logic though, there's something the court might wonder about. If the hash belonged to this Jonathon, why would he leave it inside the guitar when he sold it to you? Why wouldn't he take it out first?'

She was right. I had to admit it, and after Liz had taken her leave, it was this question which puzzled me most. As I pondered the riddle, fragments of memory from that dope-hazed final evening in Amsterdam came back, leading to a growing realisation of what had occurred. *Look for a certain malevolence that can't be hidden by change of form.* Could it be?

Surely he would not have bothered to track me to the other side of the globe. And for what: just because I'd accidently helped his mortal enemy? Perhaps these beings crossed continents as easily as they changed their form.

It began to make sense. I remembered his face now. The darkness in his eyes, the smile that oscillated to a sneer. In my *joie de vivre*, I'd been a soft touch. He'd played me for a fool, and no mistake. All that talk about Sykes and Jeff Beck, how the first Blue Murder album had been criminally ignored, and the rest of it. He'd flattered me by quoting my own opinions back to me. And where had he found them? That stupid music blog I'd written on my website. I'd even been fool enough to reveal my current location - boasting about having seen the Rammstein concert in Munich - so he knew where to find me. Just as he'd heard me brag about how I was going back to Sydney to record my album. From there, it must have been easy for him. Hacking the airline computers to find out which flight I was booked on. Tracking my movements in Amsterdam. The Les Paul laced with hash, the impersonation of a proud but failed muso down on his luck and forced to sell the instrument. Then an anonymous tip off to airport authorities in Bangkok. It was a simple but wily plan, perfectly executed. I'd fallen for it completely, a victim to my own ego and carelessness as much as his malice. Elijinx had beaten me.

The hopelessness of my position was brought home with renewed certainty. As Liz had pointed out, even if the court accepted my story about having bought the guitar one day before the flight, why would its previous owner have left all that hash inside? I was doomed, and as I returned once again to the horrible conditions of the lockup - crowded together in hellish humidity and vile proximity to other lost souls - I once again considered a more desperate means of escape.

I was already dead. This was no kind of life worthy of the name. The conditions of this existence were putrid and callously cruel. It would be kinder to take us all outside and put bullets in the back of our heads. That would be a mercy. But not this living death. To kill the person is to end his misery. To keep him alive, as a kind of living corpse, with awareness of what is outside the prison walls and what has been lost - that is a kind of cruelty no creature deserves.

As I simmered feebly within the prison cauldron, my will to go on existing came to an end. In the oppressive heat, I longed for something far away: the icy blast of the Dutch Winter night, or the cool breeze of easygoing Australian liberalism. Yet those worlds were no longer within reach, and if they were denied me, I would seek out the only possible escape. There was no more hope in this world, for I had been swallowed by this vile monolithic entity, the Thai prison. There was only one way out of here now. Yet, perhaps because of my proximity to death, I suddenly had an almost out of body experience in which an idea struck my mind with tremendous clarity. The idea was as follows:

In physical terms, this vast tiger of the prison was an illusion. It was not walls or chains which kept me here, it was the human concepts behind them which were the real source of the illusion. In purely physical terms, there was nothing stopping one of the prison guards unshackling me, leading me to the prison gates, unlocking them, and saying, 'Goodbye, Mr Brandt, you're free to leave. Please go, with our best wishes, and have a great life.' Nothing physical stopped this happening. Yet behind the walls, within the bars and the chains and the guns was something far more powerful and depraved. A black spirit. The same dark heart behind every vile regime in history, every systematic abuse, every act of cruelty.

I saw, in that moment, that even the perpetrators of the system were just part of the body of the tiger. There were those whose innate sadism found easy license to fulfil itself. They made up the claws and teeth. Then there were the grey administrative classes - everyone from the airport receptionist to the lawyers and judges - who enabled the running of the system with the mindless compliance of the cells within a vast smashing fist. The physical prison was simply the embodiment of an immense retributive urge.

There was no hope against such a fiend. My desires were of no consequence to the beast which had swallowed me. The Thai prison system cared nothing for the microscopic dreams of Jim Brandt. Those dreams were so much chaff to be ground beneath the twin wheels of indifference and malevolence.

Yet for all that, in greater terms, the prison was an illusion. I suddenly knew it beyond all doubt. The prison guards were phantasms. This was all an elaborate dream, a dream from which I could awaken. If a pinch would not do it, the blow from a cane, or even a bullet, would finish the job.

I walked straight up to one of the most violent of the guards – believe me, I had witnessed his handiwork upon my fellow unfortunates - looked directly into those inhuman sunglasses and spoke the truth.

'This prison does not exist. This place is fiction. I am a free man, and by the authority of my freedom I command that this dream ends now.'

The guard looked so surprised that his usual first impulse to violence was short-circuited. In disbelief, he asked me to repeat what I had said.

'You are a phantom,' I stated. 'You have no power over me, and I command you vanish.'

The cane landed with the sting of a pistol shot across my cheek, and within moments I was curled into a ball on the prison floor as several guards beat and kicked me. I vomited and, barely conscious, was dragged across the ground to be thrown into a cell.

IV

There I lay in ruin. This must have been one of the feared isolation cells. Solitary confinement, it was said, could sometimes last for weeks in one of these holes in the ground. Another metaphor for the grave, it seemed. Yet enough of this symbolic interpretation - if this was a dream, it had just become even worse than before, which barely seemed possible. The only good thing was I'd escaped the crowd of my fellow incarcerates, although I had not gained much in the way of personal space. The cell was about the size of a small kitchen. There was barely enough room to lie down, although by rights I should have been in a hospital bed. Now, in this tiny cell I simply existed bloodied and bruised, closer to death than to life, but not as close as I would like to have been.

I recoiled in this state for what must have been hours, although time had by now lost any meaning. I drifted in and out of consciousness, unsure if I was dreaming or hallucinating. Sleep was a mercy and wakefulness a burden. There were moments I feared that any remnants of my sanity were about to depart altogether. In an effort to distract my mind, I set myself simple tasks - turning words into anagrams, recalling in order the song titles from Black Sabbath albums, or trying to remember the events of my life year by year.

There wasn't much light in the cell, just enough from a small window to stop it being totally dark - not that there was much to look at. One thing that scared me was the thought that one of the prison rats might come into the cell through the window or the drain. I decided that if one came too close, I'd lash out with the last of my strength to keep it away. Yet no rat came. There were only a few of the prison cockroaches, and they weren't so bad, as long as there weren't too many at once.

My mind drifted back into the long pointless arc between dreaming, sleeping, and hallucinating, so when one of the cockroaches began ever so faintly to glow, I thought it was a further hallucination. Then it began to grow as well as glow, and the outline of luminous blue around the creature wakened a tiny spark of hope in my violated body and spirit.

The cockroach continued to expand, and within its shimmering aura, it began to lose the outlines of its insect form. Six limbs transformed into four, the body elongated, and the head became human, the face recognisable from a brief encounter one night long, long ago. I was looking at the form of a man - albeit a bonsai version! Barely daring to believe that here was the prayed for miracle, I uttered through parched lips.

'Iolango, is that really you?'

'Who else would it be?'

'I didn't recognise you at first.'

'I prefer to travel incognito. It's always wise to blend in with the locals.'

Iolango glanced at the four or five other cockroaches loitering near the drain. God knows what they thought of him.

'How did you know I was here?'

'Elijinx has always been a braggart.'

'So it's true. It was Elijinx who put me here.'

'Didn't I warn you about him?'

'I let down my guard. Please Iolango, get me away from here. If you get me out of Thailand, I'll serve you for the rest of my life.'

'Don't worry, my friend, the debt is mine. You won't spend another night in this place.'

'How will we escape?'

'We'll go out the same way I came in. Through the drains.'

'Those little pipes there? That's alright for you - you're a shape shifter.'

'And so will you be. This is something that only happens in very rare circumstances. I'm going to allow you to share our technology and change your form.'

'What? You mean, I can become a cockroach too?'

'It's not really my preferred species, but it'll have to do. No offence,' he said, looking down at the insects on the cell floor, not that they would have understood him anyway.

'I'll do anything to get out of this place,' I said. 'But I have to confess I'm scared to go down that drain. I'm not really an insect kind of guy, and who knows what else is in there? What about the rats?'

'Do you have a better plan?'

'Is there any chance we could go out the front door? You could change me into a prison guard and we could just walk out.'

'Too risky. They all know each other. We'd never make it out the gate.'

'You're right. Now you mention it, the humans in here are far worse than the rats. Alright - whatever it takes. Let's go! What do we do at the other end of the drainpipe when we get outside?'

'We'll worry about that at the time. Now, I've got to warn you this shape shifting is very strange at first. We'd normally train with small changes of form, rather than something as major as this - but there's no choice, so you'll just have to cope. Whatever you do, stick close by me at all times and don't panic. Right, close your eyes. As soon as we're changed, we're going straight into those pipes.'

I closed my eyes and told myself that there are more things in Heaven and Earth than are dreamt of in Bang Kwang, then felt the change begin. It was a sensation like nothing I'd ever felt. I would have simultaneously laughed and cried out in terror, had not my mouth and vocal cords both vanished. The closest comparison from my experience was the feeling you get when an elevator makes a rapid drop from the fiftieth floor, but it was far stronger than that. The feeling was brief but intense, then came to a sudden stop.

Even before I opened my eyes, I was aware my body had changed entirely. I sensed that I no longer had a vertical orientation, rather my torso and head now ran parallel to the ground. My hind legs jutted out at odd angles on either side of my body, while my front legs, although shorter, did the same at the front. The middle set of legs felt odd at first, yet turned out to be a steadying influence. The antennae at my front felt acutely sensitive, and I guessed they might provide some kind of sensing capacity to be used for navigating dark spaces.

I opened my new eyes and discovered that my tiny cell had become a gigantic cavern. I looked towards our escape route. The small drain hole near the floor had turned into a railway tunnel. The greatest shock, however, was finding myself surrounded by gigantic cockroaches! My impulse was to panic, but I reminded myself I was now one of them and had nothing to fear. Iolango too had reverted to his cockroach form, and I could recognise him by the faint luminescence around his body.

At once, there was an almighty crash and the door of my cell was thrown open. A terrifying colossus appeared in the doorway, a brown skinned ogre in the familiar prison guard uniform. With a surprised grunt, the ogre saw that his prisoner had vanished. He looked round the cell in puzzlement and when his eyes took in the group of insects by the drain, he brought down his cane among us with a vicious cry of rage, yet never dreaming he was staring at his former captive. From my new insect eyes, I saw this ogre's sceptre descending like the wrath of God, and joined my brothers in bolting on all six legs for the safety of the drain.

There was no time to learn how to manoeuvre this new body, so it was lucky the extra limbs served as a set of training wheels, making it hard to overbalance. The sensation of walking with my body parallel to the floor was not entirely alien, given that the same posture is used for swimming. The most disorienting sense was that of vision, not only due to the differences between insect and human sight mechanisms, but because I'd shrunk to a hundredth of my normal size. Thus, the human world was now a land of giants, and the insect world was at a suitable scale for me to navigate. Yet it was with some trepidation that I entered the dark tunnel of the drain pipe.

At the mouth of the tunnel, I took a final peek into my former prison cell and its overlord, the prison guard. I'd feared the guards even at normal size. Now that they were giants, it struck me what ogres human beings must appear to most of the animal species in our world. The ogre slammed the cell door with an impact that reverberated through my sensitive new sense receptors, and I turned back up the tunnel of the drain pipes.

It was almost pitch dark, very warm and humid, and I had not the faintest idea what to expect in there. It goes without saying that this environment was quite alien to my human consciousness. The saving grace was that my consciousness was no longer fully human. My memories were intact, yet the possession of an insect form changed my perceptions so that I could adapt to the foreign conditions with less trauma than may have otherwise been possible. My shock threshold was considerably higher in any case, after enduring the horrible conditions in the prison for months on end, so the fact I was travelling down a dark tunnel among a steady traffic of 'giant' insects was not quite as terrifying as it may have been. All things are relative.

However, this was no walk in the park! If my consciousness had still been human, I would have been frightened out of my wits. Certainly, there were moments of panic, and I could only hold my nerve by reminding myself I was now a cockroach, and pretending this was my natural environment, one quite normal and familiar.

Although it was dark inside the pipes, I was conscious of some kind of 'extrasensory' ability, the nature of which was unfamiliar, which enabled me to navigate my way around. Also, Iolango's faint phosphorescent glow allowed me to tail him, something I was desperate to do given my dread of being separated and having to navigate this terrain alone. In this way, we made our way steadily through the network of pipes, among the traffic of a number of fellow cockroaches.

From time to time, a glimmer of light appeared, indicating some kind of outlet into one of the prison rooms. When passing such a point, Iolango would move to the juncture and take a peek into what lay beyond. Presumably, he was trying to find an exit from the prison, and searching for an outlet near the external prison walls. From this, I deduced that he didn't really know his way around, which was a little alarming. Somewhat unreasonably, I saw him as an omnipotent saviour, so to realise that he didn't fully know what he was doing made me nervous.

At each juncture, I'd follow him to the outlet and peek out at the harsh world of the prison, and those poor souls who had been my fellow incarcerates. From time to time, I'd recognise people I'd known, feeling an odd mix of pity for them and a sense of excitement at my own lucky escape. Yet I was highly reluctant to pass through any of the outlets. Having escaped once, I had no wish to re-enter the prison in any form, not as man or beast.

There was a more grisly concern, and being presently unable to speak to Iolango, I felt afraid whenever he passed too close to one of the prison outlets where we could see people on the other side. It was rumoured that some of the prisoners were driven by starvation and madness to some barbarous habits, one of which was to eat any form of living being they could get hold of. This might include the cockroaches or even the prison rats. I'd not yet myself fallen to such a desperate level, but I was still a relative newcomer.

I wanted to warn Iolango of the danger. In one instance, our party of roaches came up beneath a grille in one of the overcrowded cells, and I spied a vile looking desperado eying us with murderous intent. Gesturing wildly with my front legs, I tried to stop Iolango going any further. The dim light from the grille reminded me I was in the midst of a number of insects, yet I felt safer with them than I would have with the miserable giants in the cell, enslaved by their fellows. At least we cockroaches were free.

The journey went on and on through the network of tunnels, and I became aware of a growing sense of hunger. I'd become so used to being hungry the only reason I noticed it now must have been due to my unfamiliar cockroach body. What on earth did cockroaches eat, anyway? It wasn't really a question I wanted to answer, so I hoped Iolango could find a way out of the prison before much longer and we could revert to human form.

On the subject of food, what, apart from starved human prisoners, ate cockroaches? This was a question to which I had even less desire for an answer. Yet before long, the inevitable happened, and near an intersection in the highway of the pipes, we came upon a couple of rats. As a human, rats and mice had never worried me, although it had been disconcerting to see them in the prison. As a cockroach, however, the rat was now something of a brontosaurus. Yet far from being a slow moving, dim witted herbivore, this 'brontosaurus' was a lightning fast carnivore.

It goes without saying that these monsters caused me great anxiety, the only mitigating factor being that there were dozens of other cockroaches around Iolango and me. If the beasts attacked, we were at least a statistical chance of survival. To my great relief, the rats ignored us. After all, the sight of cockroaches was no novelty to them.

Finally, after what seemed like hours of travel through the hot moist pipes, Iolango and I reached an outlet which came out in the prison garden near the entrance. If we could cross the gardens, surely we could find room to squeeze underneath the gates or the wall somewhere.

We left the safety of the pipes and entered the gardens. The sunlight was blinding, and in an odd way foreign. Cockroaches are nocturnal creatures after all. Yet we weren't going to wait for nightfall, preferring to leave the prison as soon as possible. As a result, the next stage of our journey saw us navigating the unfamiliar terrain of giant flowers and plants, a forest of tree-sized blades of grass, and huge mounds of dirt which I would have crossed with seven league boots in my former life. I wondered why Iolango did not simply change us both into birds that we might fly over the prison walls, but he later told me that there was a limit to the number of transformations he could pull off with a novice like myself. It was easier to stay as we were.

We crossed the forest of grass with maximum haste, casting fearful glances left, right, and skyward. I recalled the memory from a day long ago, when I'd actually seen a magpie swoop down upon a lone cockroach which had been foolish enough to venture outdoors in daylight. Now I feared a similar fate, and prayed that the gods and powers were with us for just a little longer.

Finally, the prison gates loomed ahead of us. We found a gap through which we could crawl, and at last I was beyond the vile confines of the prison. It would have been premature to make any assumption of safety, of course, and the wave of traffic noise signalled fresh challenges ahead. For one thing, we were now fully resident in the land of the giants, with all the dangers that entailed. A constant stream of vehicles and individuals roared past us as we cowered in a gutter, making our vulnerability clear.

There was nothing for it but to follow the gutter and get far away from the prison without further delay, and Iolango conceived a daring plan on the run. At a street corner near us, a young giantess on a bicycle had pulled up at the traffic lights. Boldly, and with an urgent shake of his front leg, Iolango scooted forwards and ran up the tyre, with myself in hot pursuit. We ran along the bike frame, crawled onto the woman's cloth bag, and ducked inside it. No sooner had we done so, than the giantess rode off down the street, on a ride we hoped would take us as far from the prison as possible.

This was the safest we had felt since exiting the prison pipes, and we had a few minutes to gain some much needed rest. Finally, the bike came to a stop and we peeked over the top of the bag at our new surroundings. It looked like some kind of Bangkok backstreet, quiet and free of traffic or passersby. Iolango and I jumped to the ground and scuttled off before the giantess noticed our presence.

Of course, the danger was not yet over. We were still stuck as insects in a giant world, subject to any number of hazards. Seeking privacy, Iolango led us around a corner into an alley way which seemed to be deserted - at least by humans. Yet there was no warning for what happened next. I sensed a presence behind me, and turned to find myself staring into the cruelly cold eyes of a Bangkok street cat. I nearly fainted in terror, yet within seconds was gripped by a newly familiar sensation and found myself growing rapidly larger and my assailant smaller. Iolango had decided enough was enough, and returned us to human form. The shocked cat beat a hasty retreat, and I found myself once again a man, beaten up and exhausted, but at least a man.

Iolango joined me in human form, and we walked out of the alley. Now the streets were human scale again, it didn't take long before we reached a populous area, full of people and shops. I was still in a paranoid state of mind. What if the prison guards were out looking for me? As if anticipating my fears, Iolango nudged me to observe my reflection in a shop window. Both Iolango and myself had rejoined the human race with the camouflage of Thai features. I was now close enough to being a local to travel incognito through the streets.

With the immediate danger removed, I was conscious once again of a great hunger. We entered a local restaurant and ordered several dishes, and for the first time since leaving Amsterdam long ago, I ate a decent meal. Iolango warned me not to overdo it, but I was too famished to resist. Sure enough, I was sick soon after the meal - but it was worth it.

We adjourned to a local hostel to rest after our ordeal. The very next day, we returned to Bangkok airport, the scene of my arrest a couple of months before. Through methods I didn't question, Iolango had arranged passports and a flight back to Australia for us both. Some ten or twelve hours later, we landed at Sydney airport. Iolango took his leave, saying he would soon be in touch. I caught a taxi to my flat in Coogee, and opened the door to a home I had thought never to see again.

Part Three

8

Battle of the Voices

After a European winter and an Asian summer, it sure felt good to be back in the world's best climate in Sydney. The little flat in Coogee was exactly as I'd left it at the time of the Black Art. Luckily the rent was on auto payments, or I'd have come back homeless. It had been nearly six months. Two in Europe, the rest in the prison. It was profoundly touching to be back among familiar things which had seemed lost forever. Books, photos, even mundane household objects like a bed and a washing machine. Such simple items and some personal space give you a sense of basic dignity.

There was a lot to do, yet it took a while to even begin. No wonder. You don't walk out of a prison like that with any sense of *joie de vivre*. Many don't walk out at all. That kind of systematic brutalisation of the body and spirit takes its toll. After the months inside, my body was lighter than when I was eighteen. Mentally, the wounds were still fresh and would not heal for some time.

I wish I could say my time in prison turned me into some fine humanitarian, driven to make great reforms and a better world. Instead, it only confirmed my long standing view that the task was futile. The brutality of the prison system was simply a more extreme version of the many other unjust systems in place.

The very fact it's a system makes it impossible for one person to effect change. As I tend to be a lone wolf rather than a team player, I see little chance of bringing about general reforms. It might be *easier* if I were a team player, but relying on other people means dealing with their limitations and the gulf in communication. To avoid this frustration, my solution is simply to act morally in my own life, and try to deal fairly with those few beings in my immediate orbit. You can be a humanitarian on a small scale. It seems futile to try to take it any further, as you are constantly running into obstacles of one sort or another.

It would take *at least* a few weeks to get back to normal. The healing process was to be found in simple acts - walking from Coogee Beach to Clovelly looking out to sea, strolling freely among shops and markets, visiting old friends and my family. I told no one about my time in the prison. What would be the point, and how could I possibly explain it to them? To say nothing of the means of my escape. It was simpler to pretend to have been in Europe the whole time.

I shuddered at the thought that, if not for Iolango, I'd still be rotting inside the prison. Yet one day it struck me there was no point holding on to anger or self pity. Save the pity for those poor souls still incarcerated. Having been given a second chance to live, the gift must be honoured. I was free and would use this opportunity to the full. I decided, as best as possible, to banish the events of the last few months from my mind. It wouldn't be easy but I would try.

My greatest wish was to unleash my creativity. Having escaped one prison, I now found all prisons anathema and sought to escape from as many as possible. Apart from the music, I felt a sudden urge towards writing. A few years earlier, I'd written a book of short stories which was accepted by a small publishing house. At the last minute, the deal had fallen through. Well, now was as good a time as any to resurrect this lost book. I still had most of my Black Art winnings in the bank - why not go for broke and get the book published as well as the album released? Now I'd been given a savage reminder of the value of freedom, it was vital to use it.

I went back to *Harness and Heath*, my collection of stories. It had been a few years and I was able to read them with fresh eyes. To my surprise, the stories seemed both inventive and funny. They deserved to be read. Nothing would stop me this time. I decided to print up a few demo copies and take them round to every publishing house in Australia until someone gave me a deal.

Of course, there was also the album to record. The dream which had seemed dead and buried a few weeks ago was back within reach. I dusted off my electric guitar and got to work.

When it comes to hard rock songwriting, it's all about the riff. Other styles of music are vocal driven, but here it's about the guitar riff that kicks off the song. Like in 'Smoke on the Water,' 'Iron Man,' or Highway to Hell,' to take some examples from classic rock. I had a few riffs kicking around from the time before going overseas, enough to make six full songs. As for the lyrics, why not write about my own recent adventures? Maybe it could end up as a concept album. I wrote lyrics for the songs 'Black Art,' 'Trade Winds,' and 'Vortex Winder.' Before long, there were six songs written and ready to go.

The next step was to find a drummer and a studio in which to record. With the help of Google, I found a few likely candidates. From there, it was just a case of trying them out to see who could do the job. I eventually settled on a drummer named Dave, and a producer called Steve who had a studio and the technical skills to lay down the songs.

That was the easy part. More problematic were the vocals. In past recordings from a few years ago, I'd come to the microphone by default, for reasons which will soon be clear. I hoped for better this time. It's hard enough playing guitar on stage, let alone singing as well. I placed an ad for a singer, with the optimistic promise of a guaranteed album release if they got the job.

I went into the studio to put down all the instrumental parts, as well as my own vocal guide tracks which the real singer could then record over. My vocals sounded alright - and it was a buzz to hear the rough mixes of the songs once they were done - but with luck a 'real' singer could make them even better.

For the singers who answered the ad, the process was to give them the rough mixes, get them over to sing, then have a chat to them to check for any personality problems. But after a few interviews, I began to realise why there are so many solo artists in the world.

The first guy, Derek, looked as good as he sounded bad. A typical show pony, he had the visuals down pat and the look-at-me vibe of a vintage David Lee Roth. I would have put up with it too if he could sing, but when he opened his mouth, all that came out was some out of tune warbling and a few wild squawks. It would never work. Looks will take you a long way, but no one can see you through the headphones.

The second singer was Lucy. Another show pony, but one who could actually sing. The problem was she looked a bit *too* good. Natural beauty and no attempt to hide it. On the contrary. Indeed, the six inches of cleavage was just overkill. I mean, you try to be polite and maintain eye contact, but...

Look, the thing is, you don't *want* someone like that in the band, otherwise it turns into Blondie or No Doubt - one beautiful camera-hogging girl, and a few faceless sidemen up the back. Can't stand that. Everyone in the audience loses 50 IQ points as soon as you get someone like that in the band. On the other hand, maybe her vocals would be so good we could put up with it, as long as she agreed to play down the visual side. A few days later, we spoke on the phone.

'Hi Lucy, sounded alright the other day. Maybe you can come to the studio and put down some vocals.'

'I'd love to.'

'One question, though - if you joined the band, would you be happy doing videos and live shows to promote the record?'

'Of course.'

'I'm a bit worried about your appearance.'

'What's wrong with it?'

'Nothing. That's the problem. What I mean is, would you be prepared to tone it down a bit? Your... attractiveness.'

'What for? I don't understand.'

'In this business, the record companies always push the sex thing. Going for the lowest common denominator as usual. So all the photo shoots, the music videos, and the press would be all about you. They'd be exploiting you and your body.'

'Not really. I'd be the one exploiting them.'

'I see.'

'Hey - what's the problem?'

It may be empowering for you, Lucy. It's just that, well, your breasts have got nothing to do with my music.'

'Excuse me?'

'My music's not about being sexy. Why should it be? We don't want guys coming to the shows drooling over you instead of listening to the songs. We want them to hear your great vocals, not look at your outfit. Can you wear a hijab or something? Well, maybe not a hijab, that's going too far. Can you just wear normal clothes like they do in AC/DC and bands like that?'

'Bon Scott dressed sexy.'

'I'm thinking more jeans and a t-shirt like Malcolm Young.'

'I'm not wearing that.'

'Bon was singing about sex half the time, but my lyrics aren't about that. Don't get me started on today's lot, especially the girls. I'm sick of seeing it on every music video, like it's compulsory. The music channel is a soft porn channel now. It's all pole dancers and posing.'

'What's wrong with being sexy?'

'If it doesn't fit the lyrics, it's just annoying. Even in hard rock. Remember that old Whitesnake song 'Here I Go Again'? One of David Coverdale's best songs. It was all about him being on his own, walking down a lonely road towards his destiny. But in the video, he had his girlfriend of the time rolling round half naked on the bonnet of a car. How was that even remotely related to the song?'

Lucy didn't sound very convinced. The idea of not trying to promote my music by dancing round like a nymphomaniac exhibitionist was too radical a concept these days. I hung up, relieved we wouldn't have to work together.

The next one due to try out was Lewis, a well known singer on the local live scene. He'd been in a couple of bands, recorded, and even toured the US, so it might be a real coup if I could get him. As he lived locally, we'd arranged for him to drop by my flat at 11am. When he hadn't turned up by one, I gave him a buzz just in case I'd got the time wrong.

'Hey Lewis, is that you?'

'Yeah. Who's this?'

'Jimmy.'

'Jimmy Who?'

I paused for a moment.

'From the band.'

'Jimmy...? Oh yeah.'

'What happened?'

'What do you mean?'

'You were coming here at eleven, weren't you?'

'I just got up. The Zep Heads had a gig last night.'

'Oh right - your Led Zeppelin tribute act. I didn't know you guys had a gig. On the other hand, you *did* know. Oh well, see you round.'

'Why don't you come over here? Bring your guitar and amp.'

I paused again. Should I give the guy a second chance? Or would this sort of scene just be re-enacted with endless variations in the future?

'I had time at eleven,' I said, 'but I'm busy now. Got some urgent vacuuming to do. Might even wash my hair. Let's give it a miss.'

'Don't you know who I am?' said Lewis.

'I do now.'

'What's your problem, man? You sound a bit uptight.'

'I've got plenty of problems, but you won't be one of them. If you're not going to turn up, you could have texted me.'

'Hey, it's only a jam. Take a chill pill, dude.'

'Sure, I will. By the way, Zeppelin retired thirty years ago. I heard Jimmy Page wants to reform but Planty won't be in it. Why don't you give him a call?'

I hung up on the call. Maybe it was a bit harsh, but screw these guys who aren't even professional enough to show up. They play in some Led Zep tribute act, then carry on like they're the real thing. It's bad enough when real rock stars act like divas, let alone the wannabe impersonators. Imagine what he'd be like on tour. Forget it.

The next one was Ritchie. Inevitably, there was another problem with him. No matter how much is right with someone, there's always something wrong. He could sing, he wasn't a show pony, and there was no attitude problem. The issue this time was that he was a songwriter himself. He'd heard my songs and already had a few changes in mind.

'Jimmy,' he said, 'your songs are cool, but I don't get your lyrics. What's this black art, anyhow? And the vortex winder? Don't take it the wrong way, but I want to write my own words.'

'Oh yeah?' I said, hackles rising, picturing airborne swine and melted snowballs in eternal damnation. But wait, I told myself. I should at least keep an open mind. Maybe Ritchie was a great lyricist as well as a good singer.

'How about you sing these songs as they are, then you write some on the next album?'

'Yeah, maybe. It's just that the 'Vortex Winder' song, I've got some lyrics that would be perfect for it.'

Ritchie pulled out a notepad and showed me a page of handwritten lyrics about him riding his motorbike down the highway. I said nothing for a minute, poker face, silently scanning the page.

'Not bad,' I said, at last, 'but didn't Priest already do the motorbike thing about ten times? 'Freewheel Burning,' 'Heading out to the Highway,' Hell Bent for Leather'?

'Who?'

'Judas Priest. What - you don't know the Priest? How old are you - twenty five? A bit before your time, maybe. Anyway - why don't you leave your lyric book here and I'll have a look?'

As soon as he left, I cast an overcritical eye over his rhymes. Not that I'm the best lyricist, but as it turned out, Ritchie wasn't either. He had the hip hop self obsession thing, the me-and-my-girlfriend thing, the clichéd political statement thing, and the what-the-hell-are-you-on-about 'Stairway to Heaven thing.' No offence, but it just wasn't my thing.

Ritchie's lyrics weren't that bad really, but I didn't want them sung over my guitar riffs. Put it this way. Imagine you're a visual artist - let's say a painter - who did eighty percent of a painting and got Ritchie to come and finish it off. Do you really want to paint eighty percent of your still life, or your abstract impressionist or whatever, then have Ritchie on his motorbike painted right in the middle of the canvas?

Nothing against the guy, you can't blame him for wanting to sing his own words. And by now, after four interviews, the problem's pretty clear. It's obvious who the bad guy is in all this

- me. A control freak? When it comes to my songs, sadly it's true. Goddamn it, I might just have to sing them myself. That would be my punishment. What a drag. By all the Powers, if only I had Derek's body, Lucy's voice, Lewis's connections, and Ritchie's... No, actually I didn't need Ritchie.

It was while pondering this whole dilemma that there was a knock on the front door. Registered post. I signed off on it, then opened a small cardboard box. There was a note inside.

'Jim. I hope you're feeling better. Here's your replacement Vortex Winder, the new model. It comes with three complimentary wishes. Be careful what you wish for, and remember each wish will only last a week. Iolango.'

How very timely. I'd lost the old Vortex Winder back in Thailand at the time of my arrest. Well, the first wish was a no brainer. I sat down in front of my CD collection, placed my hand on the new VW, and said, 'I wish I could sing like the best singers in metal.'

Looking back, my wording was a little ambiguous. Surely I should have remembered all those fairytales where the wishes turned out wrong because the wording was unclear, or the consequences not imagined. What happened was, for reasons best known to itself, the new Vortex Winder interpreted my wish in a completely literal sense. Not only could I now sing like the best singers in metal, I could sing *exactly* like them. All it took was a moment's concentration on a particular singer, and suddenly I could open my mouth and pull off a perfect impression of that singer's voice!

I spent the next couple of hours playing with this amazing new gift. One minute I'm doing Rob Halford from Priest, the next, Bruce Dickinson from Iron Maiden. Even better, it seemed I was getting the voice from when each singer was at his peak, before it started to go downhill. So I'm getting Ozzy circa 1973 and Brian Johnson from the *Back in Black* album.

Next thing you know, I'm channelling Slayer's Tom Araya, and, let's see... yes, even Til Lindeman from Rammstein (although my German was still terrible). *Unglaublich!* Hmm, wonder if I can do a woman? Angela Gossow from Arch Enemy, yes, and even the operatic vocals of Tarja from Nightwish.

The only disappointment was I couldn't get Bon Scott, and when the attempt to copy Dio also failed, the likely theory was that deceased singers couldn't be copied. Apart from that, it was all go. I got straight on the phone to Steve, the producer, to make an urgent studio booking for the next day.

In hindsight, the whole thing wasn't at all thought-out. For one thing, what was Steve going to say about my little reverse-karaoke act? But never mind that. The priority was to get into that studio and get it done. On the day, I did warn Steve, and tried to spin him a farfetched yarn that I was a professional mimic. He wasn't buying it.

'You been down to the crossroads, Jimmy?' he asked, after a few songs.

'What do you mean?'

'How are you doing it?'

'Doing what?'

'The voices. It's freakish.'

'Oh that. Look, I told you, I'm a mimic. It's part of my stand up comedy act.'

'Come on. No one can sing like this. It's impossible.'

'A foolish word - but thanks for the compliment. People say that all the time after my act. I'm glad you like it.'

'I can't say that I do. This is weird and unnatural.'

'Come on, Steve, it's just showbiz. Anyhow, you're getting well paid, so just do your bit.'

The rest of the session, Steve wouldn't look at me. He couldn't believe what he was hearing, and was clearly spooked. But that was his problem. It was really none of his business.

I drove home and spent the night drinking beer and listening to the playbacks of my album starring the best voices in metal. In that state of intoxication, I conceived some wild ideas about how to put it out. One plan was to release it as an anonymous record, get it out there, and let the consequences fall as they may. Another was to write to each singer requesting a guest appearance on the record, and send them the track with their own voice. When they heard that the song was already done, they'd realise they could get paid without even having to show up. Who knows, maybe they'd go for it.

A more sober mood the next day brought the realisation it was impossible. Even if I could get in touch with these big rock stars, how could I possibly explain that their voices were on my songs? There'd be lawsuits, contractual issues, you name it. You don't want to make enemies of your own heroes.

By the end of the day, I came to the sad conclusion there was no way these tracks could ever see the light of day. A private treasure they would remain. Oh, the pain! So where did this leave me? Right back where I'd been a couple of days ago, without a singer I could stand, and stuck with doing the vocals myself in my own natural voice.

I did toy with the thought of using a second wish to sing like myself, only six times better, but this would have also ended in tears. The ability would only have lasted a week. It might have been alright for the studio recording, but what about when I sang live and sounded six times worse than the record? It wouldn't do, and there's no way I was going to go out and lip synch like a fake teen pop star.

So there it was. I was just going to have to sing the songs myself and hope for the best.

Damn.

9

The Matthew Effect

There's an old Chinese proverb that says *when choosing a restaurant, pick one where people are already eating.* Can anyone spot the flaw in the logic here? By the end of this chapter, it will be perfectly clear.

By now, both the book and the album were nearly done, and it was only a matter of finding a publisher and a record company to put them out. To pitch my work to these people, it had to be well packaged. Most of the Black Art money was still in my bank account, so I could afford decent covers. I had fifty books and fifty CDs printed up. These copies weren't for sale, they were purely to negotiate a deal with the publishers and record companies.

The mention of CDs is going to date my story. Then let it be clear - this story didn't happen yesterday. It was around the year 2010. However, even in 2010, CDs were going out of style. We were moving well and truly into the digital age. My persistence with CDs, even then, indicates my status as an aging dinosaur becoming out of step with the times.

Nevertheless, the very next day after getting the books and CDs, I sent them to all the leading publishers and record companies in Australia. That was only the opening salvo. You've got to follow up fast, or nothing happens. Publishers, in general, are pretty useless. It takes months before they'll get back to you with a rejection letter. There was no point sitting round at home waiting for that, and past experience had shown the humble approach gets you nowhere. So, just a few days after mailing the book, I rang a couple of the publishers who would by now have received it.

Of course, I never made it past reception. Yes, they'd received the book, but no, they weren't able to look at it. Company policy was that submissions were only accepted through an agency. To be an author these days, you had to have a literary agent. The second and third publishers I rang had the same policy. No agent, no book. OK, if that's how it works, so be it. I went back a step and mailed copies of the book to all the main literary agents in Australia.

A few days later, I was back on the phone. The first agent gave me short shrift, stating curtly that he wasn't taking on any new clients. The second agent was far more loquacious.

'I received your book,' she said. 'Self published, is it?'

'It's not published at all yet. That's why I sent it to you. It's printed up like that so you can see what the end product will look like.'

'You don't have a publisher?'

'Not yet.'

'I only take on clients who have a publisher.'

'But the publishers said they only take on clients who have an agent.'

'That's probably right.'

'Where does that leave me then?'

'I wish you all the best with it. Keep trying, and never give up.'

'What should I do then?'

'Keep trying and never give up.'

Then she hung up on me. Just like that. I rang a couple more agents, to no avail. The impression given was that they were only interested in taking on clients who were already successful authors. The best I got was the promise they'd have a look at my book when they had time.

Suddenly it was all coming back to me. I remembered why I'd quit writing in the first place, a few years back. It was this sort of thing, where the people in power were about as fair and helpful as the contrary characters in a Lewis Carroll book. The publishers won't take you on unless you've got an agent, and the agents won't take you on unless you've got a publisher. After stewing on the paradox for a couple of days, I reached the conclusion that sitting back and waiting would get me nowhere. It was time for action. Bugger the middle man, I would go in and front these publishers directly.

I caught a taxi to one of the largest publishing houses in Australia. Dressed in my smartest clothes, I hoped to bluff my way past reception and front the managing director. Let's call her Barbara, although that's not her real name. My storming of the citadel all went to plan. I warmly greeted the girl at reception, saying I was here for a meeting with Barbara, and before the young gatekeeper had time to check my credentials, I breezed past her and strolled down the corridor.

I didn't have to look very hard. Her name was on the door. Knocking boldly, I entered the room and found myself smiling at a surprised looking woman sitting behind a desk. Barbara was an attractive woman in her mid-forties, short haired, bespectacled, and dressed for success.

'Forgive me barging in on you, Barbara, but I'm on a very tight schedule and didn't have time to make an appointment.'

'And you are...?'

'Jimmy Brandt, at your service. I'm just up from Melbourne for a couple of days,' I lied. 'It seemed like a great chance to have a chat with you. Did you get my book, *Harness and Heath*? Doesn't matter, I've a copy right here.'

I handed Barbara the book. She accepted it with a distinct lack of enthusiasm.

'You can't come in here without an appointment.'

'Can I make an appointment then?'

'Not really. I only meet with contracted authors.'

'Looks like I did the right thing skipping the appointment then.'

'If you've a book you want to submit, leave it at reception and we'll get someone to take a look at it.'

'Please, Barbara, I feel like I'm being fobbed off again. I hate being fobbed. Please don't fob me. I'm sorry to barge in on you, but I've come all the way from Melbourne. Can I just have five minutes of your time?'

There was a pause while Barbara decided whether or not to call the police. In the end, she seemed to conclude that the easiest way to get rid of me was to hear me out.

'Your time starts now.'

I began a short, fast talking spiel about how *Harness and Heath* was a fine book full of wit, pathos, topical relevance, and potential mass appeal. I assured her that given a chance and just a little promotion, it was almost a guaranteed hit. Furthermore, the short story genre was coming back into vogue thanks to everyone's attention span being shortened by YouTube, Twitter, texting, and so on.

I finished my spiel and looked at Barbara hopefully, almost daring to believe I'd won her over. So, it was most annoying when there was a knock at the door and a man walked in. He looked vaguely familiar, and after a few moments I recognised him as one of Australia's better known authors. Let's call him Larry. He must have been one of Barbara's clients. What the hell did he mean by barging in like this during our meeting? Didn't the prick get enough attention already?

Barbara, however, greeted Larry like a husband come home from the war. The effusive warmth on display could not have contrasted more with the cold and muted reception I had received. Barbara didn't introduce us. Indeed, she seemed to have forgotten I was there. It was only when her client gave me a quizzical look that Barbara remembered me, before apologising deeply for the inconvenience. No, not to me - she apologised to him.

'So sorry, Larry, just give me a minute to deal with this and I'll be right with you.'

Larry left the room, and Barbara sat back down behind her desk. She looked again at the copy of my book, *Harness and Heath*.

'Well, Mr Brandt. I've heard you out. As soon as you've gone, I'll give your book to one of our junior readers.'

'I'd really rather you read it yourself.'

'It's got to go through the others first. If they like it, they'll let me know.'

'Look, no offence, Barbara, and you're obviously very busy. Why don't we cut all the crap and agree that you can publish the book? It's a great book, and if you read it you would know that. As you don't have time, let's skip that step and just sign the contract now.'

Barbara stared at me, taken aback by my audacity.

'Just who do you think you are?'

'I'm Jimmy Brandt. Guitarist, songwriter, and author - if you'll allow me to be.'

'Jimmy who? Tell me something - how many literary awards have you won?'

'None, but if you publish my book, that may change.'

'How many bestsellers have you had?'

'None, but if you give me a chance, I'll have some.'

'Have you had any books published at all?'

'Not yet.'

'Then what on earth are you doing wasting my time if you haven't even had any books published yet?'

'Well for God's sake, that's why I'm here!'

I was starting to lose my cool. Better watch it.

'Do you have an agent?'

'I can't get an agent unless I've got a publisher.'

'Do you have any media profile?'

'No, but how about this? Publish the book, set up some interviews, and give me a bus stop ad like you did for Larry's new book.'

'A bus stop ad! Why on earth would we give you a bus stop ad? No one's ever heard of you.'

'Exactly. That's why I want the ad.'

'Why would we even publish your book?'

'Because it's a good book, and it deserves to be read. It's certainly better than some of the others you've published lately.'

'But you're a nobody. No one's ever heard of you. Why should they buy your book?'

'Sure, I'm a nobody - but the only way I can go from being a nobody to a somebody is if you help me out and give me a start.'

'It doesn't work like that.'

'Well how the fuck *does* it work?'

'I beg your pardon. You can't speak to me like that. Get out of my office or I'll call the police!'

I paused. This wasn't how the meeting was supposed to go.

'I'm sorry, Barbara, my emotions got the better of me. Allow me to apologise. It's just that I know the book will succeed if you give me a chance. Of course, Larry's a successful author, but how about sharing it around a bit? Instead of putting out Larry's twenty-seventh book - which, as we both know, really isn't as good as his old ones - how about putting out my first?'

'This is not a charity, Mr Brandt, it's a business. Come back when you're a somebody. Then we can talk.'

'I see. So you won't lift a finger to help me turn from a nobody into a somebody, but if I somehow achieve this miracle on my own, you'll talk to me then - and you expect me to welcome you with open arms. Well guess what? If I ever do make the big time on my own, your company is the very last one I'll consider, because I won't forget the way you treated me when I was a nobody.'

'A word of warning for you, Mr Brandt. This is a pretty small town and a small industry. It's not wise to make enemies. No one's going to help you then.'

'They're certainly not helping me now, so what's the difference? Might as well blow up the bridges and be done with it. So, you're advising me not to make enemies and not to offend anyone? That's the same advice Liz gave me in the Thai prison. Ha, I see the arts world is just another crappy little prison. Just another hierarchy with masters and slaves.'

'You arrogant fool! You come barging in here demanding to be published. What do you expect us to say? You're clearly very naive. Do you have any idea how many manuscripts we receive each week? Do you know anything about how the publishing industry works? You're not the only unpublished author in Australia, you know. You're just a queue jumper. Go to the back of the queue where you belong.'

'Do you think I want to have to barge in here? Of course I don't, but you guys won't look at my book otherwise. The normal processes are useless, so this is what authors are driven to.'

'Much as we'd love to publish more unknown authors, it simply isn't possible. There are certain economic realities to consider. I'm sorry you find it frustrating, but it's not my problem.'

'No, you're doing OK. You're at the top of the tree. Can you at least advise me on how much arse I have to kiss to break into this biz? Whose arse should I start with? Is there a manual or something?'

'You could start by learning some basic manners. Then, why not take some courses on how to get published at your local writers' centre? You might learn something about the industry. Now I'm afraid you'll have to leave. You've wasted enough of my time. If you like, you may leave your book at reception.'

'How magnanimous of you, Barbara. Shall I save you a stamp and pick up my rejection letter on the way out? Let's see, how does it go again? *Thanks for your submission. We regret that it is not suitable for our current lists, but we wish you all the best for future publication.*'

'I see you've had a few already.'

'It's about time you came up with a new one, don't you think? How about, *Dear author, thanks for your submission. Unfortunately the Writers' Club is full. There are no vacancies for the next ten years, so you may as well shove your manuscript up your arse and set fire to it.*'

'I think you'd better leave. If you're not out of here in one minute, I really will call the police.'

'Don't worry, I'm going. Fuck publishing, I'm going back to the music business.'

Oh no. I never intended the meeting to turn out like that. All those memories from a few years ago came flooding back and I totally lost my cool. Maybe I'd blown my chance of getting published now. I went home, got on the booze, and tried to forget it.

The next day, I changed my focus to music. If I couldn't find a book publisher, at least there was still the album. Maybe the music biz would suck less than the writing biz. Then again, from what I recalled, the music biz sucked pretty hard as well. Who knew which one was worse? It's a real clash of the titans between those two. Anyhow, you've got to try.

I rang up a few of the rock managers who'd been sent the CD. There were some remarkable parallels to what had happened with the literary agents. The rock guys only seemed to want to take on clients who were already successful. Did

I have a record deal? No. Was our band playing gigs at the larger Sydney venues? No. Were we getting any airplay, and did we have an industry profile? No and no. In that case, go away. Come back when you're successful.

After a few calls, I again tried a more direct approach by visiting one of them in person. I set up a meeting with a well known manager. Let's call him Baz. To his credit, he did agree to see me. This time I promised myself not to blow up, no matter what.

Baz was sitting at his desk. He looked like he might have once been a rocker himself, but had moved into management when his youth faded. He had thinning, slicked back hair, and a slight paunch, but still looked good for someone just on the wrong side of fifty.

'Hi Jimmy,' he said. 'So you're the guy on the CD.'

'Did you hear it yet?'

'Yeah, three or four songs. Not bad. There's something different about your music.'

'So, you think you can help us?'

'I don't know.' Baz looked me up and down. 'You're not what I expected.'

I shrugged.

'I don't look like your typical hard rock guy, if that's what you mean. No tatts or long hair. But that's good, isn't it? Bit of a cliché buster.'

'People are pretty shallow. It's easier to reach a demographic if we can pigeon hole you as a type. And let's be upfront - how old are you?'

'Well, ah... I'm about mid-thirties. So what?'

'Leaving it kind of late, aren't you?'

'Who cares about age and looks?'

'The market cares, and the market is always right.'

'BB King played last year and he's over seventy.'

'That's blues. Different genre, different expectations - and he's been doing it for decades. Have you ever thought about getting a young guy in to sing? Or maybe a hot young girl singer? Like that band - what's their name? Oh yeah, Garbage. Three older dudes and a bombshell. That might work.'

I frowned and felt my blood pressure rising. I'd better not lose my temper this time. I took a slow breath.

'Is that really what you have to do to get on music TV these days?' I said.

'Sex sells,' Baz replied.

'How about if I just hire a few strippers to go on stage with the band? Will that work?'

'Now you mention the stage, what sort of venues have you been playing lately?'

'To be honest, we haven't done any live shows yet. We're more of a songwriting and recording band.'

'So what do you want from me?'

'A record deal. Help us get signed to a label who'll put out our album. I'm not so much into playing live. Singing and playing guitar are fine in the studio, but live is a tough ask. I'm more into just putting out records at the moment.'

Baz looked at me in disbelief.

'What do you think this is - the twentieth century? How are you going to sell any albums if you're not playing live?'

'There's radio airplay, TV, press interviews for a start.'

'Australian radio doesn't play hard rock. As for TV, nothing personal, but no one wants to see some forty year old nobody. So, if you're not on the radio, TV, or playing live, there won't be any press interviews either, you can bet on that.'

'Thanks for your encouragement, Baz. What an inspirational manager you must be.'

'That's just the way it is, mate.'

'But you said the CD was good.'

'So what? News flash: people don't buy CDs anymore. The whole downloading thing has taken over. In a few years, it will be digital streaming. These days, your album is just a free ad for your live show.'

'Bullshit it is! The album is what matters.'

'Even if that's true, why should someone buy your album when they can download it for free off the net?'

'Uh... basic ethics and regard for the artist.'

'No one gives a fuck about that, mate. They expect your music for free, and if you want to make a quid out of it, it's up to you to get out on the road and play it for them live.'

'Why should I go out and play for a bunch of thieves?'

'That's how it is now. Take it or leave it.'

'I don't want to go out on the road six months a year. Why should I? Living in cheap hotels, slogging my guts out, setting up gear, and playing the same songs every night. What about my personal life? What if I've got a wife and kids - how can my marriage survive this lifestyle? I wonder how all the downloaders would like it if they had to go on the road to do their jobs. Oh yeah, it's so glamorous... maybe for a couple of weeks, not for six months.'

'I'm sorry, mate. This ain't the twentieth century anymore, and if you don't like it, you're in the wrong business.'

'Looks like I am. Well, fuck the music biz, I'm going back to publishing! Oh wait...'

'Have you got a day job, Jimmy?'

'This is it.'

'Has anyone out there even heard of you?'

'Not really.'

'Look, if you're not famous by the time you're forty, forget it. No one's going to give you a start now. You may as well get a real job.'

'Thanks Baz. You've made my day.'

What a waste of time. After a couple of days rest, I decided to take a more grassroots approach. Stuff the big record labels and publishers, I'd put out the damn CDs and books myself. So, I got another thousand copies of each printed up, and started trying to promote and sell them.

OK, I was a little naive. I didn't realise how hard it is to get into book or record shops on your own. I went to a well known chain music store and they didn't want a bar of my CDs, because the band wasn't on a record label. Likewise, I took the book round Sydney bookstores, and because it wasn't with a big publisher and going through a distributor, they wouldn't touch it. If you weren't part of the system, you were locked out.

I even rang a bookshop in my old home town in the country. Told them there was a feelgood story going in the town newspaper about a local boy made good, and all I needed was the bookshop to allow me a book signing event for a couple of hours on a Saturday morning. The owner of the shop didn't want to know. 'Who is Jim Brandt?' she said imperiously. Jesus Christ, it was Barbara all over again. Even the lower-downs in the food chain were afflicted by the same rankist bullshit. Who is Jim Brandt? A nobody who could be a somebody if you give him a chance. For Christ's sake, I might as well quit if some scummy little bookshop in my hometown wouldn't even give me a break.

Finally, I resorted to trying to sell the book and CD to people I knew. Some bought copies and some declined. Some were too tight to buy one and expected freebies, or they assumed that if your stuff wasn't in the shops it was no good.

After one particularly fruitless day, I went home and had a few beers. All that effort writing my music and books, and for what? I put on an old Prong album and found relief in Tommy Victor's angry musical outbursts. 'Shouldn't Have Bothered,' he vented in one song. There was no point reaching out to fools. Why waste your time?

Flicking through the TV channels, I came across another Tom. Tom Baker, the guy who played the most popular *Doctor Who*, back in the seventies. It was an interview show, *Parkinson* or something like that. Tom Baker was reminiscing about his days as a struggling actor. 'You know what I found odd? When I was a young unknown actor, I'd go to the pub and sit on one drink for a couple of hours. I couldn't afford a second drink, and nobody would buy me one. But as soon as I became well known as *Doctor Who*, I couldn't go out without everybody wanting to buy me drinks, and by then I didn't need them to. I could afford to pay for my own drinks.'

Flicking to another channel, a different Tom appeared. It was a documentary about the notorious cult leader, Thomas Swan. The toms were certainly beating tonight. My ears pricked up. Maybe this was another waking dream, like on the night of the BB King concert. I flicked again. Sure enough, another documentary, another Tom. This time on the 19th century English engineer, Thomas Matthews, who'd designed over a dozen lighthouses during his lifetime. Lighthouses were cool. There was something special about them.

Tom. Tom Matthews. Matthews... the Matthew Effect. Yes, now I remembered. It was coming back to me from my uni days studying philosophy of science. It was something Robert Merton had said about the strong getting stronger and the weak getting weaker. He'd taken it from the biblical quote.

For to all those who have, more will be given, and they will have an abundance; but from those who have nothing, even what they have will be taken away.

Matthew 25:29

Merton had been talking about the scientific world, in which the more famous and prestigious scientists were given more funding and opportunity, which in turn lead to more fame and prestige... which lead to more funding and opportunity. Meanwhile, an unknown scientist was rarely given the same support. Yes, of course - it was an obvious feedback loop. It was the same in the business and investment world. Those with money could afford to invest, thus creating profit, while those with none couldn't compete and remained poor.

It was even true in the social world. I remembered back to my teenage years. At first, I'd had no girlfriend, and none of the girls wanted anything to do with me. But as soon as I'd had one or two girlfriends, my perceived social status rose, and numerous girls suddenly wanted to know me.

So much for the old Chinese proverb that says, when choosing a restaurant, pick one where people are already eating. Has anyone spotted the flaw in the logic? It's a circular argument if ever there was one. It's assumed the restaurant is popular because it's better, but really it's popular because it's popular.

If diners act on the principle suggested, it's a self fulfilling prophecy. People choose a restaurant only because it's already successful, and reject another one because it isn't. Thus, the established restaurant is full of customers. The new one has less customers only because it's on the wrong side of the feedback loop. In line with the Matthew Effect, people assume the empty restaurant is no good, and choose the crowded one. The empty restaurant won't be able to pay its rent and goes broke, while the crowded one goes from strength to ill deserved strength.

What an insidious principle. The rich get richer and the poor poorer. Clearly, the arts world was also riddled with this cancer. Established authors or bands enjoy the full weight of their industries' promotional efforts, while unknowns get not even the chance at publication, let alone any promo. To the public, famous artists are assumed to have succeeded on merit, and the unknowns are assumed to have *failed* on merit. That is, if they are thought of at all.

How to break this vile feedback loop? That was the question. To answer this, I had to ponder whether the Matthew Effect was a natural phenomenon, like gravity, or purely man-made. After some deliberation, I chose the latter. The Matthew Effect was a manifestation of the shallowest side of human psychology. Whatever one thought of the natural world, the cultural world was a human construct. An immeasurably foolish one, perhaps, but one I had to come to terms with.

Oh well, when in Rome. Shouldn't have wasted my time reaching out to fools? No. It's not that I shouldn't have bothered. I just went about it the wrong way. In naively reaching out purely on the basis of reason and artistic worth, my cause was doomed. If you want to rule a fools' paradise, you must become a fool yourself, and operate according to the rules and principles upon which such a paradise is based.

Now wait a minute. Hadn't Iolango said the new Vortex Winder allowed me three wishes? If so, there were two wishes left. I took hold of it, and uttered the tragic words.

'I wish I was famous.'

10
Fifteen Minutes of Fake

I woke up the next day and felt no different. Maybe I wasn't famous yet. I walked to the corner shop and there were no paparazzi waiting. I passed the house of the barking black dog, and he ran away when he saw me coming. He wasn't to know the thug repellent power only lasted a week, and that was ages ago. As for this latest magic, apparently fame only lasts fifteen minutes, so if I could get a week out of it that was a bargain. It might be just long enough to break the feedback loop of the Matthew Effect, and allow me to go to the haves from the have-nots and sign a publishing deal.

Back home, I googled myself, and nothing came up. Maybe it would take a day or two for the power to take effect. Whatever. I went back to bed.

About mid-afternoon, I got up to work on my songs. By nightfall, I decided to hit the town and caught the bus into Darlinghurst, an inner city suburb. I had a drink at a local hotel but as everyone ignored me, it was clear fame had not yet arrived. Soon after that, I was denied entry to a nightclub. Must've been still on the Z-list, and a long way to go before the cool people would give me the time of day.

Stuff it then, I'd go up the Cross. King's Cross, the red light district. No prostitutes in the windows like in Amsterdam, but a few in the streets. I was more interested in having a couple of drinks. There were plenty of other Z-listers around the place, so there was no problem getting served this time.

In one pub, I got talking to a guy who tried to sell me cocaine. He didn't look like a cop, so I asked if he had any weed. He produced a small amount, which was a rip off for the fifty bucks, but what can you do? It's not legal here. The guy rolled a joint, and I stepped out into a back alley to smoke it. I put the rest of the stash into a hiding place to collect later. There's no sense carrying drugs if you don't have to.

My head was spinning, and I decided to hit one of the nightclubs. The doorman let me in this time, and I walked into a pit of darkness illuminated by chaotic strobe lighting and filled with the booming bass of a techno beat. At least, I think it was techno. Or house. Whatever the hell they call it. Normally it's not really my thing. You had to be on drugs to appreciate this sort of music. Luckily, tonight I was, even if it was just a puff of weed rather than the Es most of this crowd was probably on.

I crossed to the bar and yelled out over the music a request for a vodka and V. V is one of those energy drinks with caffeine, guarana, and so on. They're legal, but in my view a bit dodgy. They get you going, but you wouldn't want to OD on them. Tonight, though, it was a V kind of mood, and by the time I'd knocked back a couple of those and another beer, the techno music sounded a whole lot better.

I got onto the dance floor and began dancing with a young South American girl, a Brazilian she said. There was a big screen above the dance floor, showing video clips of the songs being played. It was the usual soft porn, wall to wall show ponies. God, these young people are such posers. In my current mood, bring it on. My eyes were transfixed alternatively by my dancing partner and the posers on the big screen.

A song called 'Chica Boom,' or something like that, came on to the screen. There wasn't much subtlety to it. It was just some guy plus a few half-naked Latina girls simulating sex with him while he sang the words 'Chica Boom' over and over. The whole club was into the song and the dance floor was full. It was a catchy techno beat, and I wasn't the only one singing along - 'Chic, Chica Boom!' I was pointing at my young Latina dance partner, and laughing, every time the chorus came on. At the end of the song, she kissed me.

She sat down and I went to the bar to buy us a couple more drinks. It took about ten minutes to get served, and on the way back to our table, I walked past the DJ and offered him $100 if he'd play the 'Chica Boom' song again. $50 now, and the other $50 when he played it. He pocketed the cash, and I walked back to my new friend. Maybe it was the booze, but there was no doubt in my mind she was the most beautiful girl I'd seen for a very long time.

After the DJ eventually played 'Chica Boom' again, I gave him the other $50, but by the time I'd returned to the dance floor, my partner had vanished. I looked all over the club, but she'd disappeared. Oh well, there were plenty of other girls. It was time to move on from this club and try another one. I was still in a great mood, buoyed by the weed, V, and alcohol. I stumbled down the stairs of the nightclub and spilled into the main street outside.

There were people all over the place, everyone rowdy and intoxicated, having a laugh. For some reason, there was a film crew on the street corner just a few metres away. Whatever they were there for, they weren't being given much respect. Drunken guys and girls were walking up to the camera yelling and yahooing and carrying on like fools. I got in on the act myself. I can be as big a fool as the next guy if the time is right. I walked in front of the camera and did a sarcastic, silly little dance before blessing them with a hearty 'Chica Boom!' and flashing the heavy metal 'horns' symbol with both hands. That's the one with the middle and ring fingers folded, and the index and little fingers extended.

I went along to another nightclub, trying to look sober as I lined up outside. The doorman wasn't fooled and he didn't let me in, the bastard, so I had to try somewhere else. However, the night soon began to peter out, and about 2am, I finally caught a cab back to Coogee.

I got up early the next day and got busy, as that's usually the best way to get rid of a hangover. Even went for a swim at Wylie's baths, the ocean pool near Coogee beach. After a good swim and a coffee, everything was AOK, or near enough. Maybe BOK. There was still time for a productive afternoon of guitar practice.

I switched on the evening news on TV to catch up on the latest from our crazy world. But it was quite a slow news day - so slow, in fact, the station had to screen a filler story on the rise of drunkenness and mischief in Sydney's trouble spots. It was nothing to do with current events and probably could have been used whenever they were short of real news. Some guy from the ambulance service came on, complaining that they were sick of seeing the consequences of drunken mishaps. Then a police officer talked about introducing alcohol curfews after midnight. The whole thing was a bit hard to swallow. Was drunkenness really any worse than twenty years ago when I was a teenager?

The story was accompanied by footage of drunken yahoos walking round the streets. Those streets looked quite familiar. Oh yeah, looked like the Cross. Well, speak of the devil, I was there only last night.

The next thing I know, hitting me in the face without warning, there I am on TV doing a silly little dance, yelling out 'Chica Boom,' and flashing a double horns symbol right at the camera! Wait - what?! I was so shocked, it was impossible to focus on the next news story, and I didn't even make it through to the sports.

Oh well, that was pretty funny, I thought, shrugging it off. I wondered if any of my family or friends had seen it. I turned the TV back on during dinner, and the next show began. It was the current affairs show, which usually targeted middle Australia with some kind of whinging story about rip offs, dole bludgers, or rising crime rates. It should have been called *A Current Complaint*. Tonight, they were also running with the public drunkenness story, and I felt a small stab of anxiety. Sure enough, they ran the same footage of me doing my silly little dance and the hand signal. Then the smug presenter interviewed a policeman and asked him what they were doing about getting idiots like that off the streets. Idiots? Me? Oh my, fame at last. Fame... fame? Oh no! Surely not. Goddamn it, the Vortex Winder! I'd forgotten about my wish. No, surely this wasn't it. But what else could it be?

The next day, I got straight up and googled myself again. Still nothing. It was almost a relief this time. Then, out of mild curiosity, I went on YouTube and looked up the Chica Boom song. Turns out it was actually 'Chica Bomb' by some guy called Dan Balan. It wasn't quite as exciting at low volume and without the drugs. I went back to the YouTube search results to find a nasty surprise waiting. One of the other video results was titled 'Chica Boom guy.' And you know who that was? Yep, there I was looking like a total goose doing my sarcastic little dance, flipping the heavy metal horns sign, and yelling out 'Chica Boom!' like it was one of those martial arts war cries.

Whoever put it on there had clearly taken it from the news show. I checked out how many views the video had, and it was already up past the 100, 000 mark. Huh? Didn't people have lives? Had they nothing better to do than watch some silly guy dancing around yelling Chica Boom?'

This was unbelievable and more than a little weird. I went to the shopping centre and it may have been my paranoid imagination, but some of the people were looking at me funny. It wasn't funny to me. As I lined up to get lunch, there was a bunch of teenagers standing nearby. Next thing you know, they're nudging each other, staring at me, and one of them goes, 'Eh, Chica Boom!' The guy's mates immediately joined in and it was Chica Booms all round.

I went straight home and back on YouTube to see the clip. It was already up to 200,000 views. I was a viral sensation! The mortifying thought was that by now I was popping up on social media all over the world, being sent from phone to phone, and turning into some kind of mass joke.

That night on the current affairs show, I was back for an encore screening, but this time they were far kinder to me. After all, they'd gotten some great publicity out of it, considering the footage had come from their network. The presenter smirked as she read from her autocue.

'Drunken hoon one day, internet sensation the next! Meet Australia's newest social media star. In just twenty-four hours, he's had over half a million hits on his YouTube video. Last year, there was the Chk Chk Boom girl, but this guy seems to have trumped her. The only question is, who is the mystery man? If you're out there, or if anyone knows who he is, let us know.'

Oh no, I groaned, the Chk Chk Boom girl. The same thing had happened to her last year. She'd given a news crew some kind of bogus 'eye witness account' of a shooting at King's Cross, appeared on TV, and become an internet sensation for about a week, just like I was. So this was the calibre of celebrity I was mixing with now. I was really on the rise.

After the ad break, the presenter came back on and said, 'The search is over. We've had a tip off that our Chica Boom mystery man is one Jimmy Brandt. Jimmy, come on down. You're a star!'

By the way, if I ever find out which of my so called friends rang in with the tip off, thanks a lot. I'll get you for that. Oh, and speaking of gratitude, thanks very much Vortex Winder. I wanted to be famous for my art, not some Chica Boom bullshit.

That was just the start of the craziness. The next morning, there was a knock on my door. I opened it to see a bunch of cameras outside. I went back inside and the phone started ringing off the hook. Some of the callers were friends - but would you believe it? - there were also a couple of entertainment agents wanting to get me on their books. What do you know? I put years of my life into making quality books and music, and couldn't get an agent for love nor money, and now they were calling me unsolicited because of some silly YouTube video. Well, I supposed it would behoove me to seize the day, so I set up a couple of appointments for later. Better sign some contracts quick before the fame wore off.

I checked the YouTube video. It was well over half a million views, and there were already a number of spin off videos. One of them featured me saying Chica Boom repeatedly, at different speeds, over the backing of a hip hop track. My silly little dance had been slowed down and run backwards. This spin off video already had 200, 000 views itself.

Just after lunch, I caught a cab to the office of one of the entertainment agents. Introducing himself as Harry, he stood up from behind his desk and shook my hand.

'Great to meet you, Harry,' I said.

'Jimmy Brandt, the pleasure is all mine. You're a star.'

'It's nice to be famous, I suppose. But I want it to last so it's not just some flash in the pan, right? That's why I'm here.'

'Absolutely, Jimmy, couldn't agree more. A word of advice, though - milk it for all you can. You're red hot right now. Don't waste it.'

'Don't worry, Harry, I'm not one of your fifteen minute wonders. Today's your lucky day, because I've got some actual talent.'

'Of course you have. You're the Chica Boom guy. That's awesome!'

'No, not that. That's just a stunt. What I really do is I'm a writer and a songwriter. And guess what? I've already got product for you to sell - a book and an album.'

'A book? What, you mean with words and stuff? That's a bit highbrow.'

'It's not highbrow, mate. Anyone can read it. It's a good book.'

'And you've got an... album as well.'

'Here's a CD if you want to check it out.'

'A CD? That's pretty retro.'

'Oh no, not you too.'

'I don't even have a CD player anymore, Jimmy. What sort of music is it?'

'It's hard rock with a twist. Sort of Motorhead meets Radiohead, if that gives you some idea.'

'Why don't you do a techno track, like the Chica Boom song? That's more your *forte*, wouldn't you say?'

'Techno! My *forte*! You've got to be kidding me, Harry.'

'I'll level with you, mate. I don't think books and CDs are really the thing nowadays. But wait until you hear the fantastic offers I have on the table for you. You're going to be a big, big star.'

'Really? What have you got?'

'Wait for this, you're not going to believe it. I've got offers from *Big Brother* and *Master Dancer* already.'

'Eh? You mean that reality TV stuff? I'm not into that.'

'*Big Brother* is coming back with a bang this year, and you'll be right in the thick of it.'

'You mean that *Lord of the Flies* type show? I'm no good at social politics. I'd be the first one voted off.'

'I've also got *Master Dancer* and *Singing Idol*.'

'You mean, those shows where you've got three authority figures, and the contestants have to win their approval? Like lost puppies looking for a pat on the head.'

'Come on, it's great. Who are you to knock it? People love it.'

'OK, I'll think about it. That *Master Chef* was pretty good. I've got a bit of a chip on my shoulder about that sort of thing. It's the rankism.'

'Rankism?'

'You know, all that hierarchy, master-apprentice stuff. It pisses me off.'

'And how about this? I've got some big companies lining up to sponsor you travelling round the world with your Chica Boom act.'

'What do I have to do?'

'Just go to exotic spots around the world, shout *Chica Boom*, and put it on YouTube.'

'Seriously? Someone's going to pay me to travel the four corners of the Earth just to say Chica Boom? Is that it?'

'Why not? You're a star, kid, and you're going global.'

'Oh my god, Harry, this is unbelievable. Can I have some time to think it over?'

'Sure, but don't wait too long. Fame's a fickle flame. You gotta grab it while it's hot.'

I caught a bus to Maroubra Beach, one of the less crowded beaches, and thought it over. Things weren't working out as I'd hoped. Eventually, the compromise solution occurred to me. I'd meet Harry halfway, if he'd help me out in return. I called him up and said I'd do *Master Dancer* and *Big Brother*, as long as he agreed to get me a deal for my book and CD. He agreed, and I arranged to go back the next day and sign the contracts.

Sure enough, the next afternoon it was all set up. Harry was now my agent, the reality TV deal was signed, but more importantly, the book and album were also going out with the promise of some promo dollars to give them a rocket boost as well. Yippee! I'd managed to break the feedback loop of the Matthew Effect. What better way to celebrate than go out and hit the nightclubs again?

I went to the huge shopping mall in Bondi. Might as well buy some new clothes - there'd be no problems with money from now on. As soon as I walked into the shopping centre, peoples' eyes were on me. Girls checking me out, guys coming up and high fiving me, and little kids shouting 'Chica Boom' in my face. It was a riot! I walked past a group of teenagers. As soon as they noticed me, they started pointing and laughing. 'Come on, dude, say it,' one of them ordered. OK, just the once, if you insist. I did my silly, sarcastic little dance, gave them the double horns, and blessed them with a hearty Chica Boom!

So this is what it's like to be a star? It was great... I suppose. But if I was a star, why did I feel like a clown? Oh well, wait til the book and album came out, then everyone would forget this Chica Boom crap. In the meantime, might as well enjoy it. A couple of trendy clothes boutiques were side by side in the mall. I started browsing outside one, and a beautiful young shop assistant came up and touched my hand. 'Hey Chica Boom guy, ten percent off everything in the store for you.' The pretty young girl from the other store heard, and upped the ante. She grabbed my hand and whispered 'Fifteen percent off everything in *our* store.'

I walked out with several bags of new clothes. After changing back at home into the coolest of them, I hit the nightclubs. Not just the dodgy ones, this time I was A list. I was about tenth back in the line to get into one of the trendiest A-list nightclubs in town, when the doorman spotted me. 'Hey Chica Boom guy, get in here,' he said. I smiled coolly as I waltzed past a couple of lesser known soapie stars and pop wannabes. Chica Boom, baby!

Before long, I was being offered free cocktails from the bar, as well as some less legal substances. I headed to the dance floor, surrounded by women, who for some reason wanted to share their phone numbers. A pretty blonde said, 'Hey babe, would you go out with me, or do you only like Latinas?' I assured her there was no discrimination on the basis of race or religion, and I'd be prepared to go out with her if my schedule permitted.

Inevitably, the you-know-what song got played in my honour, and I was obliged to perform my silly little dance and mouth the words. Wow, everybody loved me. It was great... I suppose. It was a helluva night, that's for sure. I didn't get up til two the next afternoon, and it turned out someone called Harry had left a lot of messages on the answering machine. Harry? Oh yeah, my new agent. I called him back at once.

'Hey Jimmy, superhero. Where've you been?'

'Sorry, Harry, didn't get your messages. Is everything sweet?'

'You've got to get over to Channel Nine, fast. The current affairs show has offered $5,000 for an interview.'

'Five grand? Really?'

'OK, it's $6,000 less my commission.'

'Hey, that's twenty percent. You said you were taking ten.'

'They weren't going to pay at all until I insisted. Take it and be grateful.'

'I'll get dressed and get right over there.'

The traffic was bad, and after wasting time trying on the new clothes, I only just made it in time. Even so, not having been on TV before, I was a tad nervous, so darted into a nearby pub and downed a double scotch. That did the trick of relaxing me, but just to be on the safe side, I had another one before going into the studio.

The current affairs host - let's call her Sally - had already started the show, so I was rushed into the waiting area by her producer.

'Where've you been? We've already started.'

'The traffic was shocking.'

'We'll have to do it live. Quick, get into makeup.'

After a two minute makeup job, I was sitting in the interview chair next to Sally. The producer counted her in, and we were on air.

'And now for something a little different,' she said. 'Here's the guy you've all been waiting to see. We broke this story just three days ago, and we've finally tracked him down. It's Australia's newest internet sensation, Jimmy Brandt.'

'Thanks, Sally.'

'So, Jimmy, your video's had over five million views in just three days. You're a viral sensation. How did you do it?'

'It was nothing, really. That's just the way the internet works. You can be a global smash in no time, for doing bugger all.'

'You've certainly put the Chk Chk Boom girl in the shade.'

'Heh heh,' I laughed uneasily. 'Looks like I've out-Boomed her.'

'You sure have. What's the Jimmy Brandt story, anyhow? What's your background to coming up with this YouTube smash?'

'To be perfectly honest, Sally, the Chica Boom thing was just a one off. I'm actually an author and a songwriter. I've got a book coming out soon.'

'A book. You mean with words.'

'That's right, and also a CD.'

'A CD? Oh, one of those round silver things. I'm a Spotify girl myself.'

I frowned.

'Maybe I shouldn't reveal my age, but when I was a boy we had these things called records. They were like big black shiny CDs. Beautiful, they were. Each one was wrapped in a big, square flat box with brilliant artwork, and there was loads of space for photos and lyrics or whatever they wanted to put there.'

'Really? So you're a historian too. How fascinating. But what our audience really wants to know is how you managed to come up with the Chica Boom thing. It's quite a brilliant piece of performance art. Did it take you long to think of it? How on Earth did you come up with the concept?'

'Well, Sally, I don't want to downplay the magnitude of my achievement, but it's really very simple. I went out to a nightclub and starting dancing with this hot Brazilian girl. To be quite honest, I'm not normally such a fan of Brazilians. I'd rather see some bush back in the Whitehouse, if you know what I mean. You know what they say - Laura's got one, George is one. Uh... anyhow, to answer your question, I'm dancing with this gorgeous Brazilian girl to that incredible Dan Balan song. Surely one of the best songs ever made, it should be sent out into space on the next Voyager. We're dancing away like mad. Anyhow, I used to think Asian girls were hot, but you know what they say - once you've had black you don't turn back. So I walk outside the club, and it just hit me like a bolt of lightning. I think it was God speaking through me with inspiration. The whole performance piece just came to me - the dance, the hand signs, and the slogan - and next thing you know, here I am, an international star.'

Uh oh. Somehow I had the feeling my answer had gone a tiny bit wrong. Sally's face was pale and her smile seemed to have frozen. She quickly ended the interview. I collected my appearance fee, waited for the scotch to wear off, and drove home. Now what did I say again? You know how it is when you say one thing that's a little bit wrong, so you try to correct it and it goes worse, then you try to fix that one and the whole thing falls in a heap. Oh no, why did I mention the Brazilian thing... and what was it I said about the Whitehouse? Something about ex-president Bush. Hopefully nothing too bad. Better check it later on YouTube.

The next morning, I went online to check the news headlines and see how famous I was today. There was a headline alright, but not the kind you want. 'Chica Boom guy in racist, sexist rant,' it said. Eh? What was this all about?

I rang my agent, Harry. His voice seemed strangely cooler today.

'Oh, hi Jimmy, how you doing?'

'Fine, thanks Harry. I just want to check about the music and book deals we were setting up yesterday. Is there any progress?'

'Not yet. Look, Jimmy, we need to talk.'

'I don't like the sound of that. Is there a problem?'

'There's a very *big* problem. Have you seen the news today?'

'Yeah. Some rubbish about the interview last night. Did you see it? The interview, I mean.'

'I sure did. What the hell were you thinking?'

'Oh come on, I didn't say anything that bad, did I?'

'All you had to do was go on, do your little dance, and say Chica Boom. But for reasons best known to yourself, you decided to discuss female genitalia. You also likened the ex-president of America to one in a derogatory way, and said there's nothing you like better than shagging African-American women. Nice going, pal - you're a PR disaster!'

'Oh come on, a couple of silly little jokes. They didn't mean anything.'

'People are calling you a racist.'

'A racist? What for?'

'You said, once you've had black, you don't turn back.'

'So? I said dark skinned women are attractive. How does that make me a racist, for God's sake?'

'It's racist towards Asian and Caucasian women. You're implying that once you've had sexual relations with a dark skinned woman, you'd never look at a white or Asian woman again. That's offensive. The suggestion that you like shagging black women is *also* offensive, given some of the historical issues you should be aware of.'

'Oh come on. Aren't you reading a bit much into this? It's just a joke, and I've heard it said by black people themselves.'

'Yes, but they're allowed to say it. You shouldn't even say *black* really. You should say Indian, African-American, or Aboriginal.'

'Maybe I should've said "once you've had African-American you don't turn back," but it doesn't quite have the same ring.'

'This is no joke, Jimmy. You sound like a racist.'

'Oh yeah? Well answer me this, Harry. Why wasn't the whole Chica Boom thing racist in the first place? It's all about Latina women. How come that was cool, and this new thing isn't? This is all totally random and arbitrary.'

'I'm sorry, that's just the way people see it.'

'I'm not even interested in the topic of racism. It's a non-issue and totally bores me. This is crazy. For Christ's sake, how much PC arse do I have to kiss before you can spin it back the other way? How about this: I'll turn Mormon and have a harem of seven wives, one for each day of the week: black, blonde, redhead, Asian, Indian, Arabic, Eskimo, whatever you like. Will that prove I'm not a racist?'

'Now you just sound like a sleaze and a patriarchal abuser of women. For that matter, what business is it of yours if women choose to wax their genital hair or not? Why don't you mind your own business?'

'You're right, I shouldn't have said it. My preferences are neither here nor there - but what the hell does it matter what I think? Why does everyone care about some stupid throwaway line I said in an interview about my stupid Chica Boom dance?'

'A lot of people do care, Jimmy. You've hurt them very deeply.'

'You have got to be kidding me, mate. Anyone who is hurt by my dumb antics needs to get a life. Look, this is all bullshit, and so was the Chica Boom thing in the first place. All I care about is getting my book and album out there.'

'Sorry, pal, you're on your own. Our contract is null and void. It's all off - *Master Dancer*, *Big Brother*, the sponsorships. You can just forget it. You're officially cancelled.'

'What? But yesterday everyone loved me.'

'Come in, Jimmy Brandt, your fifteen minutes is up. Look on the bright side. You made five grand off your interview, and I made fifteen. The real appearance fee was twenty thousand.'

'Elijinx!'

'Ha ha ha ha ha ha ha ha ha...' Click.

I hung up in a state of shock, chilled by the laugh, the realisation he'd fooled me again, and a new insight into the depths of insanity to which our world had sunk. I went outside and walked to the shop in search of a coffee. The black dog began barking at me, and this time it didn't back away. The Indonesian shopkeeper looked at me with cold, accusing eyes, while his wife scolded her daughter into going upstairs and, presumably, away from me.

Perhaps from a sense of masochism, and to test the public mood, I headed back to the shopping mall in Bondi. I boarded the bus with my sunglasses on and a hat pulled down over my eyes. It may have been my imagination, but everyone seemed to be looking at me. Back in the shopping mall, I felt about as popular as a Buddhist at a BBQ. I sat in a far corner of the food court and ordered some lunch. Hundreds of eyes seemed to be burning a hole in my face, like I'd done to poor old Bill Steer at the BB King show, except this time I was copping it tenfold. Karma baby.

A little boy of about seven came to my table, laughing, and shouting 'Chica Boom.' Immediately, his mother, a young blonde, rushed over and grabbed him. I smiled feebly, and offered up a weak and hopeful 'Chica Boom?' of my own.

'I'll Chica Boom you, you fucking racist!' she replied.

'Please, I'm not a racist,' I answered, 'and it's probably not the best idea to swear like that in front of your child.'

'Don't tell me how to fucking speak to my own kid. And don't tell me how to wear my pubic hair either!'

'Look, you can dye it purple and wear it in plaits if you like. I couldn't care less.'

What a debacle. Aside from the prison, this was without doubt the lowest point of my adventures so far. I happened to have the Vortex Winder with me, and almost without thinking, muttered in exasperation, 'I wish I was invisible.'

And mercifully, I was.

Part Four

11

Darkness

Turning invisible was like stepping into an air conditioned room on a hot summer day. The fiery rays of accusing eyes ceased their assault on my skin, and I could breathe freely once more.

At first I didn't know what had happened, but simply felt a change in the atmosphere. The sense of being burned by dozens of hostile stares receded. I noticed the confused expressions of a few onlookers, who must have seen me vanish. Some of them left their tables in the food court and came over to see where I'd gone - but as they advanced, not one of them was looking straight at me. They were gazing to my left or right, or over my shoulder, and from this I deduced that they could no longer see me. Remembering my muttered wish for invisibility, it seemed I had now squandered my third wish in the hope of fixing the disastrous consequences of the second.

As several people blundered towards my unfinished lunch on the table, I darted sideways to escape their clutches. Not a single eye followed me. It was clear that the wish was operational. Yet as I looked down at my own body, I could still see my arms and legs. My face was also reflected in a silver panel at one of the food court shops. I was not invisible to myself, at any rate. As I edged through the dense lunchtime crowd, however, a series of collisions and gasps of surprise showed that I was invisible to everyone else.

The first priority was to escape the hordes of hungry humanity. With some footwork worthy of Nureyev, I dodged my way through the crowd and escaped into a Myer department store. The relative space was a relief, and I headed for the furniture section and sank into a velvety armchair.

My next concern was to experiment and try to gauge the extent of this new power. I conjured memories of the old *Invisible Man* movies about Griffin, the mad scientist who made himself invisible. Although Griffin's body had been unseen, any clothes he was wearing were visible. That was clearly not the case for me, as my fully clothed body seemed to be outside the perceptive range of anyone around me. With a sudden intuition, I speculated that perhaps my 'invisibility' was not the result of a literal rendering of my body into nothingness, but rather some kind of perceptive trick in which I no longer registered in the minds of other people. That would explain why they couldn't see my clothes, or what I was doing.

Seeking to test this theory, I went to the men's wear section and changed into some expensive pants, a shirt, and a jacket. Rather than entering the change room, I found a quiet corner of the store in which to undress. While admiring myself in the full length mirror, I was startled by one of the shop assistants. Yet he paid me no heed, merely muttering to himself at the sight of my discarded old clothes heaped on the floor. After looking left and right for their owner, he picked them up and departed, presumably to dump them in lost property.

So much for clothes, what about other external objects? Moving to the sports department, I picked up a golf club and lined up a drive right in front of the sales desk. Now, if it had been old Griffin from the movie, the golf club would have been seen moving spookily through the air by itself. Yet as I lined up my shot a few feet in front of the salesman at the desk, he seemed unfazed by any such phantom golf club. Thus, I reasoned that as soon as an external object was connected to me, it entered into my personal realm of darkness beyond the ken of mortal man.

In that case, I'd now be able to finish the lunch that had been so rudely interrupted downstairs. I found the Myer cafeteria, and helped myself to a few items from the buffet. No one batted an eyelid, and I sat down at a nearby table. This was all turning out to be very easy, and as long as I kept an eye out that no one else came to sit at my table, I'd finally be able to finish my meal.

The lunch was decent. I'd taken a small serve of everything on offer, and soon became lost in the comfort of eating. I began daydreaming and only woke up when a waitress appeared and thrust a wet dishcloth into my lasagne. The poor girl cried out at the strange tactile sensation, and I darted away to the next table.

That was close. I'd better be careful. After a few more minutes, I was halfway through my meal and spotted the same waitress bearing down on me again. This time, I'd checked that the table was spotless so she had no reason to wipe it. Even so, I stopped eating and sat up in my chair to wait until she had passed. To my further annoyance, she picked up the plate holding my unfinished lunch. 'What a waste,' she muttered, before walking off with it.

Of course! It seems I needed physical contact with an object for it to be invisible. When I'd let go of the plate, it was no longer under my protective aura and had re-entered the world of the seen. That was a point worth remembering. I returned to the buffet for seconds and, keeping a firm hold of the plate this time, finally managed to finish my lunch.

What now? Maybe a short break at the movies. At least I wouldn't have to pay to get in. I wandered down to the nearby cinema complex and walked straight past the door guy at cinema one. I had no clue what was on, and decided to take pot luck. A rom com, as it turned out. After about fifteen minutes, I changed cinemas to take in an action flick, then moved on to a French film with subtitles.

The novelty soon wore off. I'd gotten into the movies for free - big deal. Surely a better use could be found for the power of invisibility. The theatre would be much more interesting. There was bound to be something on at the Opera House. I'd have a short nap upstairs in the closed off part of the cinema, then bus it down to Circular Quay.

The bus ride posed a challenge. I'd have to wait until a fairly empty one came along. In a crowded bus it would be too hard to avoid the other passengers. After finding such a bus, this turned out to be quite easy. I merely had to keep a sharp eye out for people getting on and off, and heading for where I was sitting.

It was by now nearly 6pm but still light, so I had a casual stroll around the harbour. No one paid me the slightest attention, of course, but that's pretty much how it is in the city at the best of times. It was only when I ventured right up close to someone - which I did a couple of times as a test - that the person seemed to become vaguely aware of me. I could see them frown and do a little double take, as if sensing something just at the edge of their vision. Then they'd dismiss the idea and go on with what they were doing. Again, I had the impression I wasn't physically invisible, but under the protection of some kind of perceptive shield. I once saw a stage show where people were hypnotised into perceiving things that weren't there, and not perceiving other things that *were* there. In my current state, it was as if the whole human race was in a state of hypnosis where my presence was erased from their perceptual range.

Making my way up the steps of the Opera House, I took the time to appreciate this beautiful and world famous building. Tonight, I would have full access to its splendours, both architectural and theatrical. It turned out *Madam Butterfly* was being staged, a work with which I was unfamiliar, but could now experience up close under my cloak of darkness.

Taking a glass of champagne from a passing waiter's tray, I mingled with the well dressed patrons in attendance. Thanks to Myer, I was stylishly attired myself - it was only a pity no one could see it. Never mind. I'd just commandeer a couple more of those champagnes, then make my way backstage. Yet try as I might, the backstage entrance was nowhere to be found. There was nothing for it but to enter the theatre and go there via the stage itself. I snuck past the usher on Door Nine, dodged my way up the aisles, then strolled onstage and out the back.

Backstage was a hive of activity. Production crew were fiddling with the set, the director was giving orders, chorus singers were milling about, and the higher cast members could be heard warming up behind their dressing room doors. The buzz rose in intensity as show time approached, then stopped abruptly when the opera was about to begin.

The moment arrived. The orchestra began to play, the curtains parted, and I made my way onstage to rapturous applause. I proceeded to turn in a captivating mimed performance for the rest of the first act. Unfortunately, there was a selfish diva or two who tried to steal my limelight by prancing around the stage singing arias, but I supposed they'd put in the hours at rehearsal and had earned the right.

One thing I'd not reckoned with was the volume at which opera singers perform. These divas sure knew how to blast it out. I couldn't get too close, having left the old earplugs at home. With all the lyrics in Italian, I couldn't quite follow the story either, but the performers were certainly fired up about *something*. That histrionic vocal style gets you going alright, and I made a point of swanning around the stage over-acting like it was going out of style. Truth be told, I turned into the most dreadful old ham. Why, in the first act alone, I died three tragic deaths, each more heart rending than the last.

At interval, I went offstage with my supporting cast members and tried to score a drink from the head soprano, Patricia Racette. Surely these opera divas must have a pretty decent rider backstage, one would think. Sadly, she was too damned professional and her dressing room offered nothing stronger than water. Lame! I had to steal some booze from one of the orchestra members instead.

I returned to play a starring role for the second half, then finally took my bows before that adoring audience. Some romantic in the front row tossed up a few roses, and must have been confused to see them vanish into thin air when I caught them just in front of Patricia. No doubt she was startled as well - but she showed no sign of it, the old pro.

It was easy to find an empty bus home at that time of night, and I caught a 378 to Bronte. I got off just before the cemetery, which to be honest wasn't the best choice of stop. I felt like a ghost myself at the moment. Having joined the ranks of the invisible hordes, if there *were* such things as ghosts, now would be the perfect time for one to appear. Crossing my fingers, my walk through the graveyard was both quick and uncomfortable, but I made it through without being bothered.

The next day, I checked my messages. There were a few from journalists yesterday morning, but they seemed to have petered out by lunchtime. Looks like my fifteen minutes of fame were up. By now, the whole Chica Boom craze was 'so last week' that I'd have been fully invisible to journos regardless of any magical powers. The public is certainly a fickle bitch. Today, however, I had higher aspirations. I was going to fulfil a boyhood dream and take part in a cricket test match at the Sydney Cricket Ground. The sold out Ashes test between Australia and England was due to start today.

On the cricket field, Australia had been at war with its old imperial master, England, since 1877. They'd been playing test cricket for the best part of 150 years. I'm not sure why they call it a 'test.' Perhaps because, in sporting terms, that's what it is - the ultimate test of skill and character. Cricket is a bizarre sport in which a single match can go for five consecutive days, and sometimes still not establish a winner. It is incomprehensible to most Americans and Europeans. They don't understand that cricket was one of the best products of British imperialism, and that it had taken a firm hold in many of the old colonies - India, Sri Lanka, South Africa, the West Indies, Australia and New Zealand.

Australia had been winning the war with England for most of the last twenty years, thanks to some of the all time greats of the game - Warne, McGrath, Gilchrist, Ponting, and the Waugh brothers - but the tide had turned, and the old enemy had gotten the upper hand. England was one win away from clinching the 'Ashes,' the fabled prize in this contest. Australia's position in the series was dire, so I had resolved to get along to the ground and witness the battle up close, maybe lending them an invisible helping 'hand of God' if the chance arose.

The buses would be too full today, so I'd have to cycle down. I had a test ride along the footpath aiming straight at a couple of pedestrians, turning aside only at the last moment. As neither of them batted an eyelid, the bike was obviously invisible to them. It would be dangerous riding under those conditions, but really it was nothing new. A few times I'd ridden at night without lights, and the basic assumption to make at such times is that you're fully invisible to all other traffic. The ride down to the ground today would be exactly the same, only in broad daylight.

Another conundrum was whether to take sunburn cream. It was a question of whether I was literally, or only psychologically, invisible. If I literally had no visible presence, the sun's rays would not burn me. But if I was merely hiding behind some mass hypnotic shield, I could end up as red as one of the Poms you see walking round Coogee Beach with their shirts off. To be safe, the sunburn cream had better come, along with a good hat. For those who don't know, 'Pom' is an Australian slang name for the English. An affectionate one, really, though masked by friendly aggression, as in *You Pommy bastard.* Maybe you have to be Australian to understand.

I made my way to the Sydney Cricket Ground, riding on the footpaths and in the gutters for safety. After locking up the bike, I slipped through the gates of the ground, and ducked and weaved my way through the buzzing crowd. As it was empty of people, the safest place to be was on the field itself, so I hurdled the fence and landed on the grassy surface of the famous old ground.

It was a thrill to make my way onto the 'hallowed turf' which was the scene of so many battles in the past. As I made my way out to the centre of the arena, I performed a slow pirouette to take in all 360 degrees of the stands circling the field. The old stands were the best. The Bradman and Members' stands were still pretty much untouched. Less impressive were the arrays of plastic seating in the newer stands. It was a bit tacky, really, and it was criminal what they'd done to the old Hill. Back in the good old days, the Hill was a wide, grassy, unseated area where anyone could take a picnic rug, a basket of food, and an esky full of beer. Now, it had been demolished, replaced by a boring stand, and violated with plastic seating.

Those were the days! That golden era of the 1970s will never be topped. I was just a boy then, but I know it by reputation. It was like the Wild West. Fun, but not for the faint of heart. Anyone could walk through the turnstiles with an esky full of ice and beer cans, then sit in the summer sun and drink from noon til night, while watching the most charismatic bunch of cricketers ever assembled in one era. Thomson and Lillee terrorising the Poms with 90 mile an hour thunderbolts; the Chappell brothers all class with the bat; Marshy and Gary Gilmour despatching balls into the stands; and Doug Walters sneaking a sly smoke in the gully, still half pissed from the night before. And all the while, the drunken crew on the Hill cheering them on.

Nowadays, it was all sanitised, family fun. You had as much chance of taking beer into the ground as you would a samurai sword onto an aeroplane. Instead, you lined up for the privilege of paying six bucks for a plastic cup of low alcohol beer. The only place you could get a decent drink was in the Members' stand, which was where I was heading now. I made for the stand, climbed the fence, and walked past the fat security guard at the entrance. He was wearing mirrored sunglasses and for a moment I flashed back to the prison guards at Bang Kwang. I shuddered and, as if to banish a demon, I walked back and gave him the middle finger, six inches in front of his nose. Childish, but satisfying.

It was still only 9.30am, so perhaps the bar wouldn't be open yet. However, the Members' stand knew its clientele, and already had a barman up to service the early starters. I helped myself to a double rum and coke, for I needed a stern drink for what was coming next - a visit to the Aussie dressing room.

I made my way through the stand, past the media boxes and the English dressing room, and finally into the inner sanctum where the Aussie boys were getting ready to go out and bat. The current team was nowhere near that side of the 1970s, but it was still a thrill to be in among them. There was the captain, Ricky Ponting, nursing his broken finger, sidelined for this game, giving new boy Khawaja a few quiet words. Not far away was Michael Clarke, his deputy, running through the game plan. There were the fast bowlers Siddle, Johnson, and Hilfenhaus looking frustrated at not being able to bowl first. It wasn't quite clear how Hilfenhaus had made the cut. Only five wickets for the series, and no wonder Bollinger was looking rather flat at being named 12th man on his home ground. The only action he was going to see was carrying the damned drinks. Bolly looked like he wanted to go out and bowl a few bouncers at whoever picked the team.

Before long, the Pommy side began walking out onto the ground, with the Aussie opening pair, Hughes and Watson, not far behind. Hughes, fired up for a big knock, was fidgeting like a man on his way to court, while Watson was more relaxed, knowing that his bowling and golden tresses would keep him in the side for a while yet no matter what happened today. There was no doubt Watson could bat, though. He had a classical technique, and could usually be counted on for a solid 40 or 90 runs before unfathomably throwing his wicket away in sight of a half century or a century. Enigmatic, my dear Watson.

It looked like old Watto was all set for a big game at his 'home ground.' Watto, of course, was such a gypsy that he had about three home grounds to his name so far. The IPL would probably bestow upon him a fourth. Now, as he took strike against Jimmy 'Job' Anderson, I could see the steely resolve in his eyes from my vantage point at mid off. Even when Anderson sent a couple of balls whistling past his bat, Watson, in a Stalinesque re-writing of history, tried to imply that his misses were deliberate 'leaves.' That is, that he had missed them on purpose. The English slip fielders behind the bat weren't buying it, and made a couple of comments to that effect. But their exaggerated gasps at Watson's near misses were over the top, and got my dander up as an Aussie and a colleague of Watson.

For the next ball, I moved a bit closer to the stumps at the bowler's end, and just as Job Anderson was running in to bowl the next one, I gave him a firm slap on the bum. Anderson stumbled, bowled a rank long hop just outside off stump, and Watson pulled it to the mid-wicket fence for four!

Anderson's bowling became a bit erratic at that point, and he was replaced by the tall, skinny freak, Tremlett. I mean nothing personal by that, for freakish height and long limbs are a natural asset for a fast bowler. Same as Glenn McGrath and the like. At any rate, I wasn't game to give Tremlett the same treatment as Anderson, because those flailing limbs could go anywhere within a six foot radius. Instead, I wandered up and took my place among the English slips cordon, behind the stumps. There they all were. Prior, the wicketkeeper, Strauss, the skipper, then Swann, Collingwood, and of course Pieterson poncing around in the gully ready to drop another catch.

With each ball, they'd bend down, eyes peeled, ready to apprehend any stray ball that came their way. Yet their overdone gasps of disappointment every time Hughes played another lofted shot to the boundary began to get on my nerves. So I decided to have a little chirp myself, to square the ledger for the sly remarks they were directing at Hughes and Watson.

'Darby McGraw. Darby McGraw. Fetch aft the rum, Darby,' I croaked in a hoarse whisper as Tremlett blundered in to bowl another ball.

Now this line, of course, is from the old classic, *Treasure Island*, which I am wont to quote from at any chance. Just as I called Anderson 'Job' after one of the pirates from that same book. As to whether the England captain, Strauss, appreciated the literary allusion is a matter for grave doubt. He looked round, but couldn't see anything, so I said it again next ball.

'Darby McGraw. Fetch aft the rum, Darby!'

Again, Strauss glanced round angrily. 'Was that you, Colly?' he said to Paul Collingwood, standing at third slip.

'Not me, Johann,' Collingwood replied, using one of the captain's old nicknames.

'Right then Swannee, stop mucking about, or you can piss off to backward point and you won't get a bowl til tea time. The Ashes are on the line here.'

'I didn't say a word!' Swann protested.

I fell about on the grass, laughing quietly to myself. But not for long, because I had to have my wits about me. Those bowlers look fast on TV, but believe me they are three times faster live and up close. If one of Tremlett's fast balls had hit me, not even the Vortex Winder could have saved me. In fact, the slips cordon was too dangerous a place for an invisible man, so I wandered off behind point, some ten or fifteen metres further away.

It wasn't long before Hughes rode his luck once too often, and was on his way back to the change rooms. Young Khawaja replaced him, and thrilled the crowd by pulling his second ball to the boundary. Meanwhile Watson was making a steady start, building his innings, and was still there at lunchtime. I walked back with him and Khawaja to the dressing rooms, and we had lunch together with the team. All the boys were happy with the start, although Hughes was disappointed and Bollinger was still far from bubbly.

After lunch, Watson continued to build his innings and looked good for a century. But with his score on forty-eight, and for reasons best known to himself, he took a wild swing at one of Swann's tempting off spinners and heaved the ball straight up in the air. It was another promising innings thrown away, and Watson dropped his head and began walking off even before Anderson had taken the catch at mid wicket.

It was time for a little divine intervention from the 'hand of God.' In a flash, I jumped up from where I'd been lying down at square leg, a few metres away, and sprinted in the direction of Anderson. His face seemed strangely poised, like Schrodinger's cat, between the expressions of smugness and fear. I launched myself in a flying leap like that of a soccer goalkeeper, and tipped the ball out of his grasp just as he was about to catch it. Watching the TV replays later on, it looked very odd indeed. The ball seemed to drop down from the sky, then make a little loop in the air as it bobbed out of Anderson's hands. The fielder looked shocked and mortified as he picked the ball off the ground and angrily threw it in to the keeper. Funny game, cricket!

I'd done my bit for the side and felt I deserved a drink. I headed back to the Members' bar and helped myself to an unopened bottle of Jack Daniels, which I took onto the field for a few quiet sips. As I took in the unfolding game, I can't deny I got rather drunk, and felt I had rarely had a better day at the cricket. To be honest, I didn't quite go the distance, and there was an awkward incident where I fell asleep late in the day and let go of the bottle of Jack Daniels. The English fielder, Alistair Cook, noticed the bottle, which was visible now that I was no longer holding it. He handed it to one of the umpires, who looked completely mystified as to how it had got there. I woke up in a hurry when Cook came near, and I decided it might be wise to scarper before the crowd left and started to make its way home. With a heavy head and blurry vision, I dodged my way out of the ground, unlocked the bike, and rode unsteadily home.

The next day I woke with a bad hangover. It came with a dose of depression, as the events of the last few weeks started to catch up with me. Still, I had better do something with this day while still invisible. I'd done the opera, the cricket, what would be next? Breakfast first, at any rate. I caught the bus to Bondi Beach to see if there was anything good to steal.

The beach was already crowded, thronged with tourists at the cafes and shops. As I wove my way through them, I was overwhelmed by a profound sense of loneliness. I was not a human being like those around me, but a mere phantom, unseen and unknown, with no place in this world. Then another realisation hit, more devastating than the first, that this was exactly the way I felt in my normal life anyway.

It was a bleak revelation, and in my weakened, hungover state, the futility and emptiness of my life became clear. I was suddenly sick of it all. Was there really any point going on in such an absurd world where fame was as shallow as a YouTube video, and fate as arbitrary as a win on the Black Art? A world in which I, personally, could not hold down a job, a relationship, or find any recognition at all for my artistic endeavours. Perhaps I should just cast myself into the ocean, and let the waves wash my invisible corpse into oblivion.

Taking an orange juice and a roll from a cafe, I sat down on the grass above the beach and had breakfast, if you could call it that, considering it was nearly midday. Feeling a little better, I wandered around the cafe area, dodging my way through the crowd. There were certainly a lot of bikini clad girls around, and it was tempting to stare at them. Yet it felt wrong to take advantage of my current position, so I abstained.

However, I could not help looking at one young woman, who was busking near one of the cafes. She was a strikingly pretty girl about five feet tall, with long raven hair, a pale complexion, and some stylish glasses. She was just my type. Or rather one of my types, to be honest. There's more than one perfect type. The stunning young woman was playing a classical guitar to which she'd fastened a strap so she could play standing up. The guitar was amplified, which allowed it to cut through the crowd noise.

Most surprising of all was her choice of material. On approach, I was startled by the strains of an old song I'd not heard for twenty years or more. After a while, I placed it as 'Killer of Giants,' an obscure Ozzy Osbourne song from the eighties It was the last thing you'd expect to hear from a 21ˢᵗ century busker at Bondi Beach.

The girl whacked a capo onto the fourth fret and played Radiohead's 'No Surprises,' a more recent song, but still an amusing choice. Then, removing the capo, she followed with a medley of Black Sabbath's 'Children of the Sea' and 'Sign of the Southern Cross.' Here was a woman after my own heart, and no mistake.

The next one was the showstopper. 'Spanish Fly,' Eddie Van Halen's virtuoso acoustic piece off *Van Halen 2*. I was by now very much in love, and stared in wonder at this astonishing woman. Yet none of the onlookers were paying her any heed. It was unfathomable. People were walking past, ignoring her, or standing around staring at their phones. What was wrong with them? This girl was a genius. Fortunately, I was invisible, so she couldn't see me gawping at her.

She tuned down to D and played a Spanish piece called 'Torre Bermeja,' one of the best pieces in the classical repertoire, before segueing into an old David Lee Roth tune named 'Damn Good.' Wow. Tuning back to E, she played the intro to 'Seasons in the Abyss.' And then she played something that chilled me to my very bones - a song called 'Spark.' A song which had been heard by only three people in this world - my drummer, my producer, and myself. This was impossible, completely out of the question.

The girl turned to look at me, and smiled.

'Hi Jimmy.'

12

The Renaissance

The impact was shocking. After two days of invisibility, the gaze from a pair of clear blue eyes struck me like a physical force. I'd been wandering in darkness, and was suddenly skewered in the pincers of a twin spotlight. I began gabbling to cover my confusion.

'Hey, how'd you learn my song? Bet you can't play the solo anyhow. Then again, you probably can. You'd better give me some royalties out of your tips.'

I looked down and saw that the girl didn't have any tips. Then I noticed an odd pattern of movement in the passersby. No one was looking at the girl. They were walking near her, but rather than blundering into her as they would have done with me, they were being subtly deflected past as if by a hidden force, much as a magnet repels another magnet of the same polarity. None of the passersby could see her. Like me, the busker was invisible.

'It's you again, is it, Iolango?' I said.

'Who else?'

'You're looking a lot better than last time. What a letdown. I knew it was too good to be true, a girl like that.'

Iolango, in the guise of the girl, flashed a radiant smile. My heart leapt into the heavens before plummeting to Earth in sorrow.

'I can't really handle you looking like that,' I said. 'Can you change back to the way you were?'

Iolango morphed from the stunning girl back to the handsome man he'd been when we first met. I shut my eyes and shook my head. Then opened my eyes again.

'Let's go for a walk round the coast,' I suggested. 'Can you make me visible? I'm sick of dodging pedestrians.'

Within moments, both of us were visible, and we began walking towards the southern end of Bondi Beach in the direction of Bronte, Clovelly, and Coogee.

'Your wishes didn't quite work out, eh Jim.'

'The singing was great, and the invisibility was fun at first - but the fame was pretty much a farce. Come to think of it, all three of them started well and finished badly.'

'You weren't precise enough. A classic rookie mistake. People are granted wishes and they're too excited to think. They blurt out the first thing that enters their head. Then they try to use the second wish to undo the effects of the first, and the third to fix the disasters of the second. It's the usual sequence. If people would only take five minutes to think first.'

'Any chance of a re-run?'

'Too late. It was a mistake to set the new Vortex Winder to manual control. I should have let it tune into your psyche again and come up with the right magical powers.'

'It certainly worked out better before. You should have left it on auto.'

'Yes, the earlier powers worked out best. The waking dream, the foreign language - and the thug repellent came in handy, didn't it?'

'Sure - but what is the Vortex Winder anyway, and how does it all work? How does it know what powers to grant?'

'It's rather complicated, and if I were to explain it, we'd have walked all the way to Melbourne by the time I finished.'

We were only just past Tamarama. Melbourne was another thousand kilometres away.

'The world you experience is not the only one,' Iolango began. 'You live in a sea of possibilities. There are many alternate versions of the world you think you know - each one as real or unreal as the next. Heavens, hells, and a thousand gradations in between. The best of those worlds exist as ideals for which the human race strives. The Vortex Winder points you in that direction. The so-called magic powers, the talents, the knowledge - all exist in the realm of possibilities and are available to you.'

'Where did the Vortex Winder come from?'

'My people built it.'

'Your people. What, you and Elijinx?'

'There are others, but never mind that now. Our job, if you like, is to use the Vortex Winders to inspire people and point them down the right road.'

'What do you mean *winders*?'

'Well, you lost one over in Thailand, didn't you, so I gave you a replacement. You've got a portable version, remotely connected to the main one. Your device is a receiver. It taps into those ideal worlds I mentioned, and the highest potentials for each person. Most of the magic powers are abilities you haven't awakened yet. The power to speak a foreign language, to be wise or fearless. The ability to sing, or whatever talent you crave. There are a thousand latent talents you haven't yet used. The Vortex Winder gives them a short term boost, and puts you in touch with abilities that could be yours if developed.'

'I suppose once we get a taste of it, we can follow through afterwards. I don't understand why you bother, though. What do your people care about us humans?'

'The human species could be brilliant. We're trying to help.'

'You should just give us all a Vortex Winder and make everyone perfect.'

'There's such a thing as subtlety. We'll give you a nudge in the right direction, without taking away your independence. I'm no puppet master. Think of me as a kind of patron saint. A mentor.'

'What about Elijinx?'

'He's more of a tormentor.'

'Why? He's one of your people, isn't he?'

'There's always one. Someone who's got to be contrary and pull everything the other way. We try to lift humanity up. Elijinx wants to drag it down.'

'So this is some kind of good and evil equation. Elijinx is in the service of the dark side, or something like that.'

Iolango paused for a moment, as if deciding how to reply.

'Not exactly,' he said at last. 'It's complicated, but call it that if you like.'

'He wouldn't have much to do with the Vortex Winder then,' I said.

Iolango shook his head.

'He has his own power source. Calls it the Maelstrom. He named it that just to annoy me, because I was the one who came up with the name Vortex Winder.'

'You two just don't get on, I see. What does the Maelstrom do then?'

'It's a reverse Vortex Winder. The Vortex Winder reaches into the heavenly versions of this world, but the Maelstrom taps into the hellish ones. It accesses the lowest trenches of the human mind and amplifies all the meanness for which your species is sadly known. It stifles kindness, but radiates fear and hatred. It works on the individual and the species as a whole.'

'That bad, eh.'

'It's a waste. The ideal realms which the Vortex Winder amplifies, that's how life should be. But the Maelstrom taps into the dark prisons of the soul. While I try to lift the race up with the Vortex Winder, Elijinx does his best to drag it down with the Maelstrom.'

'Wow. I'd sure hate to imagine what the world would look like with the Maelstrom in control.'

'What do you mean, *imagine* it? That's the way the world already is.'

'You mean the Maelstrom is in the ascendency?

'Look around you, man. When we were fleeing through the sewers of Bang Kwang, did you think that was any kind of world made by benevolent forces? And since then, you've had to contend with other prisons of a different nature. Not as severe, but all prisons bear the stamp of Elijinx.'

'Like the artistic world, the Matthew Effect.'

'Yes, I've been following your adventures. That's all standard Maelstrom material. Look, I'll give you a demonstration. Rest here for a while.'

By now, we'd made it past Bronte Beach, through the cemetery, and to Clovelly Bowling Club on the cliff top where you see nothing but ocean views left and right. We walked on and came to a rock platform built into the cliff-face, which I visited from time to time. There, we sat with our backs to the rocky wall and looked out to the Pacific ocean in all its turbulent, azure glory. It continued to rise and fall, just as it had for millions of years.

'Close your eyes,' said Iolango. 'We will join our minds for a while. If you'll allow me to look at your recent memories, I'll make some changes and show you what the world would be like without the influence of the Maelstrom. Observe.'

I closed my eyes and let my mind relax. For a while, there was nothing but the sound of the ocean's rise and fall. Then a light appeared inside the darkness of my mind. It grew into a picture, and I was watching a scene as if on a theatre stage. It was set in a room I'd visited just once, and that quite recently. It was Barbara's office in that publishing house I'd gatecrashed. I saw myself standing in front of her, about to speak.

'Forgive me barging in on you, Barbara, but I'm in Sydney for the day and it seemed a perfect chance to meet you.'

'And you are?'

'Jimmy Brandt, at your service. Did you get the book I sent, *Harness and Heath*? No? Doesn't matter, I've a copy right here.'

I handed Barbara the book. She read the back blurb and flicked through a few pages.

'Yes, we already have this. We get hundreds of manuscripts a month, but as you took the trouble to print your book up properly, I asked one of my best readers to have a look at it. I'm sorry, Mr Brandt, I don't see people without an appointment.'

'Can I make an appointment then?'

'Really, it would be better to wait until your book's been read.'

'Please, Barbara, I'd prefer you take a look at it yourself.'

'That's confidence! Well, I've got a minute - tell me about your book.'

I saw myself begin a short, fast talking spiel about how *Harness and Heath* was a good book, full of wit, pathos, and potential mass appeal. I assured her that given a chance and just a little promo, it was a guaranteed hit. Furthermore, the short story genre was coming back into vogue, thanks to everyone's appreciation of concise, pithy storytelling, and the high standards of education in our schools.

Just as Barbara seemed to be considering the idea, there was an interruption, and one of Australia's most well known authors burst into the room. Barbara greeted him warmly.

'Hi Larry. Great to see you. This is Jimmy Brandt.'

I saw myself shake hands with him.

'I don't have much time,' said Larry. 'Got a lunch date. Do you mind if we get started?'

'Sorry, Larry, you'll have to wait. Jimmy's come in especially to show me his book, and it looks most intriguing. Why don't you take a look at it yourself?'

Larry looked annoyed, but controlled himself.

'Fair enough. Maybe I'll buy a copy when it comes out.'

'Why don't you come back after lunch?'

'That's OK. I'll wait outside.'

Larry left the room, and Barbara sat back down behind her desk.

'Alright, Jimmy, you've got a chance. I'll flick through your book in my lunch break and if it makes me laugh, I might just take a punt on it.'

'Thanks, Barbara. I appreciate your time. I hate to barge in on you, but it's not easy getting a start in this business.'

'Of course not, but everyone's got to start somewhere. Now, let me tell you something in confidence, but make sure you don't repeat it. Larry's come here today to discuss promo for his new novel. But he's been coasting lately, taking his audience for granted. Why should we blow our ad budget on him? His book will sell to his existing fan base without any press. I'd rather help someone who really needs it, a newcomer no one's ever heard of. I'm not promising anything, right, but if your book really is good, how'd you like a bus stop ad?'

'That would be brilliant!'

'No promises, but everyone deserves a chance. Larry's had a fair crack at it already. If he still wants it enough, he can stop resting on his laurels and write something as good as he used to. Keep that to yourself.'

'My lips are sealed, Barbara. Thanks so much for your help.'

The scene faded, and a new location appeared in this theatre of the mind. This time, I was talking to Baz, the rock manager.

'Hi Jimmy. So you're the guy on the album.'

'Have you heard it yet?'

'Sure, it's not bad at all. There's something different about your music.'

'So you think you can help us?'

'Maybe, but if you don't mind me saying, you look a bit different to the average rocker.'

'I don't look like your typical hard rock guy - but that's good isn't it? Bit of a cliché buster.'

'Agreed. I'm bored with the long hair and tatts things, it's been done to death. Rock's supposed to be about non-conformity, not wearing a uniform. Anyhow, music is about sound, not look. So, why haven't I heard of you before? Where've you been hiding?'

'I was around a while back, then I took a fifteen year break.'

'Now that's what I call a holiday.'

'So what do you think, Baz, can you get us a record deal?'

'If you'd asked a couple of years back, it would have been out of the question. The whole industry was dying. Bands had been getting screwed for years by the big record companies, and then they got screwed by their own fans too when the free downloading thing started. But since the Renaissance, everyone got a conscience - a miracle if ever there was one. I still can't believe it. Anyhow, since then, some of the record labels are back in business, and this time the artist is getting a fair cut. For the fans who are downloading or streaming, at least most of them are paying for it now. Everybody wins - the bands, the fans, and the labels. So let's put out your record.'

'Awesome! If I can see a sample contract, I'll get it checked out. Still need lawyers, even after the Renaissance, eh Baz?'

'No problem, Jimmy, but I think you'll find everything's above board.'

'Thanks for your help, mate. To level with you, I was a bit worried I was too old, and not your typical rock star. People can be superficial about such things.'

'That was the bad old days. Everything was about looks, image, marketing, or else flogging the artist to death on the road. Not anymore. The bottom line is the music. Your music is good, so it's going out there. Simple as that.'

'Thanks, Baz, you've made my day.'

The picture faded, and I came out of my trance to find myself sitting on the rocky ledge at Clovelly, looking out on the wild blue ocean.

'That's not how I remember it at all. Was that real, or something you made up?'

'I looked at your memories, then took a little poetic license and rearranged them - but it wasn't entirely fiction. The scenes you witnessed more closely resemble the world as it would be without the influence of the Maelstrom.'

'It seems too good to be true. Could the world really be like that?'

'That is the way it *should* be. As a young man, that's how you thought it would work, didn't you?'

'Until my spirit was slowly crushed by a thousand disappointments.'

'It doesn't have to be like that. Cynicism and self interest need not be the default modes of humanity. The Maelstrom has held sway for so long people assume that's how human nature is. It doesn't have to be that way.'

'I'd like to believe you, Iolango.'

'And that's just the beginning. You can't imagine how good the world could be without the Maelstrom. Politicians, for example. Instead of nearly all their actions being driven by personal or party ambitions, politicians from both sides would put aside self interest and work together for the greater good of all.'

'Now, that really is Utopian.'

'Is it such an implausible concept?'

'It seems very naive to think that could ever happen. How old did you say you were?'

'I'm older than any castle or cathedral. Older than the pyramids. I've seen empires rise from villages then fall back into the dust. I'm ancient enough to have seen what the world was like before the Maelstrom. That's how it was once, and can be again. Wouldn't you like to see the world as it really should be?'

'Of course, if it was really possible. You know when Baz talked about 'the Renaissance' - what did he mean? Some kind of post-Maelstrom world?'

'Exactly. The demise of the Maelstrom would bring about a new Renaissance.'

'I'd love to live in a world like that.'

'Then help me destroy the chains that bind you and your world. We can erase the Maelstrom and its tyranny. In fact, I can't do it without you. Only a human can end the Maelstrom, and destiny seems to have chosen you. Do you remember back to the time of your waking dream? You read that wrongly, you know. It was nothing to do with BB King.'

'Eh? It most certainly was. That's what's led me on all these months with my music.'

'Remember when that shopkeeper called you by the wrong name - do you know what he called you?'

'What shopkeeper?'

'The one in the corner store near your place. He called you Mael-Stormer.'

'What's he got to do with it? How would he know about any of this?'

'Never mind how. The fact is he called you Mael-Stormer. It's you who can bring down the Maelstrom and usher in the new era of the Renaissance.'

'I'm a musician, not a revolutionary. Surely you can find someone else to be this Mael-Stormer. I'd rather play guitar.'

'You can do both. With the Maelstrom dismantled and the Renaissance begun, all things become possible. Your music could be anything then. First fulfil your destiny, and the world is yours.'

'Let's say I humour you, how exactly am I supposed to bring down the Maelstrom? It can't be easy.'

'There is a way, but to achieve it, we have to go to the very heart of the blackness. To the domain of Elijinx himself.'

'And where's that exactly?'

'Let me give you a broad outline. The tentacles of Elijinx extend deep into the mass human psyche, yet the source of his power does have an external, physical location in the Maelstrom itself. Unfortunately, the Maelstrom isn't based at just one address. It operates from three separate locations around the world, and with this three pronged trident, Elijinx holds humanity in his thrall. One base is in Norway. The second is somewhere near India. The third is here close to Sydney. The three bases are far enough apart to allow the Maelstrom to radiate as an orchestrated force, and the separation makes it less vulnerable to attack.'

'What's your plan?'

'If we can sabotage the Sydney base, one prong of the trident will be no longer operational. It won't bring the Maelstrom to a stop, but it might undermine it enough that the balance of power moves in favour of the Vortex Winder. The grip of the Maelstrom's iron fist may loosen enough for your race to move towards a better world. If that happens, we'd only have to knock out one of the other two bases to dismantle the Maelstrom almost entirely. Then nothing would stand in the way of the Renaissance.'

'I still don't understand what it's got to do with me. Can't your people and Elijinx fight it out between you? I'm just a mortal man. You people are shape shifters, far more powerful than I could ever be. What chance would I have against Elijinx or the Maelstrom?'

'In understanding the composition of the Maelstrom, you must know its origins. It was formed as a result of human action. As I'll explain, it is mainly a psychic phenomenon rather than a physical force. Now, Elijinx and I are not of your world. We are visitors. We can exert an influence behind the scenes. We can help sway the course of events. Yet humanity itself must be the principal actor in this drama. While we can direct them to some degree, the Maelstrom and the Vortex Winder are chiefly composed of human energies. We, on our own, do not have the capacity to destroy either of them. It was a human who began the Maelstrom and only a human can stop it.'

'And that's me, is it?'

'You appear to be, for want of a better description, *the chosen one*. Whether you were chosen by destiny or simply by luck, you seem to have fallen into the role. You saved my life, and I returned the favour. You thwarted the plans of Elijinx, and he repaid you in kind. You are inextricably involved, and it seems only right you should follow your destiny through.'

'It hardly makes sense to say it's my destiny if I've a choice in the matter. Perhaps I'll decline.'

'As I said, your world exists in a state of potential. It can go many ways. When I say you are destined to be the one to bring down the Maelstrom, I mean that's one course history could take, and a very noble one. You could help bring in a new Renaissance.'

'So you keep saying. I can't say I'm fully convinced yet, but keep going. So you want me to somehow find Elijinx's Sydney base, infiltrate it, and sabotage the Maelstrom.'

'No need to find it. We know where it is. Elijinx made a mistake, which allowed us to track him. His Sydney base lies on an island off the eastern coast of Australia. The island is a facade. It's a barren outpost which gives no clue to what it conceals, so it can't be just stumbled across accidently. That's one reason it was so hard to find.'

'If his base contains the Maelstrom, surely it is detectable by radar. This is the 21st century.'

'The Maelstrom is a psychic force. Although there's a physical component to that force, it's not of a type your instruments are geared to detect. The vast power of the Maelstrom emanates freely right under the nose, so to speak, of your instruments.'

'I see. If the Maelstrom's immune to modern technology, I'll make sure I bring a pair of pliers or something old school like that to dismantle it.'

Iolango chuckled.

'That won't be necessary. As I said, the Maelstrom is a psychic phenomenon. The means of its destruction are within your own consciousness. You'll see.'

'Alright, I'll fulfil my so called destiny if I really must. How do we reach this island?'

'The usual way. I've a boat ready to depart.'

'Right. So we just sail out to Elijinx's island and knock over the Maelstrom. It all sounds very easy - but surely his base is well defended.'

'As I said, we've only recently learned the location of the Sydney base. Elijinx made a mistake, which I'll explain to you later. He has no reason to suspect that we know, so he won't be on guard against us. Apart from that, invisibility is his best defence. There is no actual trace of his base on the island. Why bother defending something that doesn't seem to be there? What's more, we've found out Elijinx isn't around at the moment. Apparently he's in Indonesia, no doubt fermenting some nefarious scheme or other.'

'He certainly gets around. I only met him in Sydney a few days ago. Even if he's away, I'm thinking his island has automatic detections systems of some kind. He's bound to know it if a couple of people cruise up on a boat.'

'We can cloak the boat. He won't know a thing. But these are mere details. What matters is to seize the opportunity while we can. Are we agreed?'

'I suppose so. When do we start?'

'The sooner the better. Elijinx is supposed to be away for a few days, but why waste time? We should begin at once.'

'How about tomorrow morning? I had a late one last night. I'm not at my best now.'

'First thing tomorrow, then. Let's meet at Coogee Beach at 9am.'

'Agreed. Should I bring anything special?'

'Just turn up, Mael-Stormer. That's all.'

Iolango gave a small bow, then turned and walked away. I watched him go, slowly shaking my head. Mael-Stormer indeed! I cursed the day I ever fished a cockroach out of a hotel urinal. It was probably me who was going to end up in the drink this time, halfway between here and Elijinx's island. Oh well, there was no getting out of it now. This insane chain of events would have to run its course, one way or the other. I set off for home to settle down for a quiet night. It could well be my last.

13
The Island

At home that night, I put my affairs in order. I made a will and left a note for my family in case of disaster. In the spirit of a 'last request,' I listened to my album one more time, the version with the all-star voices. That had been the pinnacle. When the final notes had died away, I packed a few things in a bag for the next day, tossed in the Vortex Winder, and went to bed.

I woke the next morning with a sense of foreboding. What had I done? Apparently all sense of reason had been swept away by the onslaught of recent events, and Iolango had convinced me to mount a raid on the very lair of our tormentor. I'd agreed to confront the fiend who tried to drown him in a Surry Hills urinal, had me locked up in a Thai jail, then for an encore helped to make me a joke on national TV. And if Iolango was right, I was merely one among millions under the thrall of his pervasive malice. Elijinx was the architect of torments from the trivial to the epic, yet I was about to attack his own fortress. It was daunting to ponder what such a mission would entail, and if it were not for the good Iolango by my side I would never have had the courage to go through with it.

The kitchen clock said it was only 7am, so there was time for a last blast on the old Gibson Explorer. Keeping the volume fairly low, I unleashed a barrage of riffs and solos. There were still a couple of spots left on the album for songs, though it was more doubtful than ever that the album would see the light of day or the black of night.

Halfway through playing 'Z Club,' there was a knock at the door. Someone must have left the downstairs security door open, because normally guests had to be buzzed in. A visitor was the last thing I needed. Who would have chosen today of all days to make a call?

I stopped playing, hoping the visitor hadn't heard me. The knocking became louder, and a vaguely familiar female voice called out, 'Jimmy, I heard you playing already. Let me in.'

I opened the door to be faced by the girl from the day before, the beautiful busker from Bondi Beach. She was wearing a short black skirt, and a skimpy white top. She was also wearing sandals, those sexy glasses I liked, and an enigmatic smile. I was too surprised to say anything as she brushed past me.

'What are you doing, Iolango?' I protested. 'I told you not to come near me looking like that. You're two hours early anyway. We said nine o'clock at the beach.'

'Change of plan. With Elijinx away, we have to hurry. Make me a cup of tea, will you.'

'You drink tea?'

'Why shouldn't I?'

'It seems so mundane.'

'I've got to drink *something*. You can make me a mango daiquiri if you prefer.'

Iolango, as the girl, sprawled herself loosely in an armchair, and stretched her arms up above her head, yawning extravagantly. I felt myself flushing red. The whole scene was quite unexpected and disconcerting.

'You know, Iolango, I think your shape shifting powers are a little off. Your breasts weren't that big yesterday.'

Iolango arched her eyebrows.

'Why Jimmy, fancy you noticing that.'

'I can hardly avoid it, with the amount of cleavage on display. Is that really an appropriate way for an ancient soul to dress?'

'We're not one of those types who look down on the physical world. Why not enjoy it? It's such a sensual sphere of existence.'

'If you want me to help you,' I said, 'you'd better change into a respectable body, or I'm going back to bed.'

'Sure. I'll join you.'

The girl stood up, and in a few fluid movements lifted the white top over her head and at the same time let her skirt sink to the floor. She was now standing before me wearing nothing but a red bikini two piece.

'Iolango, what are you doing? Have you gone mad?'

'What's the matter, Jim? You seem tense. I'm just trying to relax you a little before we start the mission.'

'For God's sake, I wake up this morning to confront Armageddon, and you come over here acting like an extra in a hip hop video. Apart from that, and forgive me for being so straight, but I'm not in the habit of having relations with non-human shape shifting entities.'

The girl puckered her ruby lips in a sulky look, and untied the clasp at the back of her bikini top.

'Come on, I saw you staring at me yesterday.'

'I was enthralled by your guitar playing.'

'Of course you were.'

The bikini top landed on the floor.

'Stop it! This is too weird. I can't help remembering what you looked like before as a man, not to mention as an insect.'

'We're all the same inside. The form is incidental. Bodies for us are nothing more than a vehicle. When you've been around as long as I have, you'll learn to change your body as you would a set of clothes.'

'Sorry, this is too much. It's totally out of left field.'

'Oh all right, Jim, if you're going to be a bore.'

The girl began to get dressed. She turned her back on me and bent down languidly to retrieve her bikini top from the floor. In that moment, I nearly capitulated, but by the time the girl had stood up, she had transformed herself back into Iolango's familiar male form.

'Excellent work, Jim, you passed the test. Just wanted to see if your mind was on the job. Elijinx's island may contain all manner of illusions, so you've got to be on your guard at all times. Nothing can be allowed to distract you from our task.'

'Oh, I see. What would you have done if I hadn't... passed the test, as you put it?'

'You would've copped a fair old slap in the face to wake you up. This is no time for frivolity. The future of the world is at stake. Now, we've got to leave.'

I followed the male Iolango out the door, shaking my head in bemusement, and we walked down to a little bay to the right of Coogee Beach where his boat was waiting. We climbed aboard, and he started the engine.

'Right, Jim, It's all business now. Everything we do is to one end – destroying the Maelstrom and moving this world one step closer to the Renaissance.'

'Can you let me in on your actual plan?'

'Wait until we get there. On a day like this, you may as well enjoy the trip first.'

It was a classic Sydney summer day. Coogee Beach was thick with sun-bathers and swimmers; either tourists who couldn't believe their luck in being here, or locals who'd grown up with it and took it for granted. The air shimmered with a heat haze, and the aqua blues and greens of the sea were fresher than daybreak. Family-friendly waves spread a curl of white foam wide across the sea as they reached the shore. It was hard to believe any kind of threat lurked anywhere near such an idyllic scene.

The boat cruised calmly out to sea. It passed Wedding Cake Island, a small rocky outcrop just off the coast. I had never been a strong enough swimmer to investigate it firsthand. Now, over the side of the boat, I gazed lazily at the submerged rocks and the lurid corals attached to them just beneath the water's surface.

After passing the island, the boat continued towards the horizon until Coogee Beach began to fade from sight behind us. As it receded, the contours of the greater shoreline came into view, with Clovelly, Bronte, and the wide expanse of Bondi to our right, and Maroubra and Botany Bay to our left. After a while longer the coast line began to disappear altogether.

The regular yet irregular lapping of the waves had a lulling effect. Their poly-rhythms conspired with the baking warmth of the sun to send me into a light and dreamy doze. This dreamtime was without measure, and at some unknown point I roused myself from my stupor and woke to an awareness that the scene had changed. The entire eastern coast of Australia had now vanished. Swivelling in my seat, I was awestruck to find there was no land in sight at any point of the compass, and our tiny boat was surrounded by the majestic might of the ocean. The size of the waves had increased since our departure, and I turned to Iolango for reassurance.

'I trust you know how to sail this boat?'

'Relax, friend. I paddled this sea when it was a salty lagoon in the backwaters of Pangaea. I've crossed every ocean on the globe more times than I can remember. I've sailed with Napoleon, I've sailed with the Vikings. Oceanus holds no terrors for me.'

'Napoleon and the Vikings? I thought you were one of the good guys.'

'So did they. There's two sides to every story.'

'As long as you keep us afloat. I suppose if it comes to an emergency, you can always transform us into fishes or birds.'

Iolango smiled, but said nothing.

'I really hope you do,' I continued. 'What would we change into for the approach to the island? It had better be birds, not fish. The water looks divine, but there are hordes of predators down there.'

'There's no need to transform. The boat can take us all the way.'

'It seems a bit risky. Surely we can't just sail onto the island.'

'You were invisible yesterday. You can be again. A cloak of darkness over the boat will cover us. Transformation takes too much energy. We'll hold it in reserve for a crisis.'

'Are you sure? We're not dealing with humans this time. Surely Elijinx is more formidable.'

'Trust me, shipmate. The boat is already cloaked. Neither man nor beast will see us arrive. We'll be there in half an hour, so relax. Now, get me an apple, Jim. There's some in that barrel over there.'

'Right you are, cap'n. If the island's so close, I'm surprised we can't see it yet.'

'You can probably spot it through the telescope.'

Sure enough, there was some kind of narrow landmass in the distance, and after a few more minutes, the island came clearly into sight. It looked to be a barren and unsheltered body of rocky earth, only a couple of kilometres long. A wild, inhospitable place on first impression and, as I observed a series of breakers assaulting the bleak shores, I wondered how Iolango intended to dock the boat.

The most striking feature of the island was a jutting vertical structure of rock at its centre. It wasn't wide enough to be called a mountain. It was more like a tower, broad at its base and slanting slightly inwards as it rose higher. The structure was composed of a sheer cliff face that would have daunted the most ambitious mountaineer. As we got closer, I estimated it to be perhaps a couple of hundred metres tall. In its isolation amidst the barren landscape, it resembled some kind of perverted lighthouse. Yet it appeared to be an entirely natural rocky outgrowth extending from the centre of the island itself. It was a daunting sight, rising imperiously above the sea as if in dominion over it.

To the left of the structure was a grassy, windswept plain stretching away to the rocky shore. I could make out a few seagulls alighting on the plain, before even they found it more restful to rise again into the supportive air currents above the land, rather than being buffeted by the winds at ground level. To the right of the structure was what looked to be the only area of respite from the elements on the whole island. It was a wooded area, scrubby at its perimeter, but surprisingly well forested at its centre.

Iolango slowed the boat and ran it carefully around to the far side of the island. As we rounded the corner, a narrow inlet came into view. This seemed to be the only conceivable entry point to the island, yet the turbulence of the water as we approached did not fill me with confidence. Iolango, however, seemed quite unruffled as he guided us towards the inlet. Soon I was clambering barefoot into knee high water, helping him pull the boat onto the beach beyond the reach of the waves.

The boat was still plainly visible to myself, but remembering my escapades of recent days, it was presumably invisible to others, and to any detection devices Elijinx may have employed in defence of his realm.

After pulling it up onto the beach, Iolango moored the boat by tying it to the thick trunk of a tree at the edge of the woods. The tree looked to have been there for decades, and could surely be expected to survive another day or two.

In considerable relief at being back on dry land, I began a survey of the island. After putting my shoes back on, I walked over a wide rocky platform at the ocean's edge. It was pockmarked with many crevices which had been turned into tiny pools by the rise and fall of the sea. Various sea creatures had found homes there, clearly unfazed by the proximity of Elijinx or the Maelstrom. Every few seconds, a breaker would expend itself just beyond the edge of the platform, sending a shallow current of water across its surface. As each ripple reached me, I stepped onto a higher rock to keep my shoes dry, all the while keeping a wary eye out to sea in case of the random rogue wave which might be waiting in the wings.

After tiring of this pastime I wandered inland across the beach, through the scrubby bushland at its edge, up a slope, and into the forested area. This was relatively shielded from the elements, and at once the atmosphere changed. In contrast with the roar of the wind and waves on the beach, an eerie silence filled the forest. With the sight and sounds of the beach having receded, I could briefly forget I was visiting an infinitesimal pinprick of land in a vast ocean.

I made my way through the wood, taking care not to blunder into any of the spider webs with which several of the trees were festooned. I wondered how the spiders had arrived at such a remote spot to begin with. Had they always been there or had strands of web, by some freak of nature, drifted there on air currents from a neighbouring island? One or more spiders were perched around the centre of each web. I had often seen such webs on the mainland, without much concern, but here, so isolated from the world of man, the webs had a more menacing aspect. For all I knew, these spiders had never laid any of their eight eyes upon human kind and I fancied that they maintained an aloof indifference to my presence. I trod slowly, keeping a careful watch and my hands just in front of my face.

Little other native fauna could be seen, although there was a steady hum of insects blending into the heat haze in a bi-sensory fusion. Elsewhere, a lizard perched on a rock, monitoring me with a sidelong reptilian gaze. I was glad to have put my shoes on again after going ashore, in case snakes were also part of the local ecosystem.

'Jim, where are you?' came a shout from somewhere back towards the beach.

'Over here,' I called, moving to the perimeter of the forest towards the voice. Iolango sounded uncharacteristically angry. Perhaps his sensitivity to what was all around us contributed to the edge in his voice.

'What's the idea of wandering off like that? Not very smart.'

'Just having a look around.'

'This is no tourist trip. Don't wander off again.'

From a few feet away, a large blowfly appeared and performed a circular flight of homage around Iolango's head, finally alighting on his neck. With a cry of exasperation, Iolango smote the insect into oblivion with a violent snap of his wrist. The blowfly fell onto the floor of the forest and expired. The incident struck a jarring note. I could not help remembering a random act of kindness in a Surry Hills hotel one night long ago, and could not reconcile the memory with what had just occurred. After a few moments, I reminded myself that blowflies have a painful sting and if they attack you, you're entitled to defend yourself.

'Come on, Jim, I think I've found the entrance.'

'Already?'

Iolango led the way along the beach, down a left hand path, up an embankment, and through a glade of trees. We came to the base of the rocky tower at the centre of the island. It was not quite the featureless shaft it had appeared from the boat. The base of the structure was dotted with plants, though the foliage became more sparse as it ascended.

'Here's the entrance,' said Iolango, pointing to an unremarkable section of the cliff.

'How's that an entrance?' I asked, approaching the rock and tapping it firmly with my right hand.

'Never mind what it looks like. It's a camouflage.'

'An effective one, then. Elijinx is cleverly hiding the entrance by disguising it as solid rock.'

'It's a perceptual illusion. It seems solid to you and any other creature on the island, but there's nothing really there. Take my hand and look again.'

I took Iolango's hand, and a door sized opening appeared in the rock. Surprised, I dropped his hand, and the cliff face reappeared. I repeated the sequence. It was like flicking a light switch. As soon as I took Iolango's hand, the opening reappeared, only to be replaced by the rock wall the moment I let go.

'Remember when you were invisible?' said Iolango. 'You hadn't really vanished, it was only that people could no longer perceive you. Or rather, they could hear and feel you, but couldn't see you. Here, the illusion is more substantial, if that's not a contradiction in terms. The rock looks and feels completely solid. It's only when you're in contact with me that you can see through the illusion. Elijinx's base is therefore impregnable to mortal beings.'

'But not to your people. Why couldn't you have found it yourselves before now?'

'Why would we come out here in the middle of nowhere? We'd have to venture very close to become aware of an illusion like this. It was only down to luck that we found out at all. Let's go inside.'

I took Iolango's hand and we walked through the opening into a circular cavern which made up the basement level of the tower. Once inside, it was strange to look back through the doorway and see the ocean outside. When I let go of Iolango's

hand, the entrance was gone. The ocean disappeared, and the waves faded to a distant roar.

We were in a cavernous chamber which seemed to be mostly empty. The walls were composed of rock and gave off a phosphorescent glow sufficient for us to see by.

'You're certain Elijinx isn't here?' I whispered.

'Don't worry yourself on that score.'

'What now then?'

'We'll search until we find the Maelstrom, and disable it. This is only the basement. It could be anywhere. May as well take the lift.'

Iolango crossed towards a vertical shaft by one of the walls and stepped onto the floor of what turned out to be the lift. The lift took minimalism to extremes. It had no doors, walls, or ceiling! I craned my neck and saw that the lift shaft stretched high above us to the very top of the tower. Apparently a movable floor was all Elijinx needed.

'Fine,' I said, when Iolango had explained this. 'I'm always impatient waiting for the doors to open and close, anyway. I've got to admit, by the way, I'm dying to see how you people live. Can we have a look around?'

'If you like. I'm a little curious myself. It's been a few centuries since Elijinx and I were on social terms. But make it fast. We shouldn't linger any longer than necessary.'

According to the lift controls, the tower had ten levels. If we were going to search, we had better do it a floor at a time, so we made a short ascent to the next level. As it turned out, the first floor seemed to contain nothing more than a series of stalagmites and faintly phosphorescent gems.

'What's this?' I asked.

'A rejuvenation chamber. In our most basic form, we find sustenance here. We can rest here for hours or days, if the need arises. You'll find some of the other rooms a little more human.'

Iolango's comment was not borne out until the fourth level. The second and third floors contained no human elements at all. Instead, they were home to a series of enclosed glass chambers, each about the size of a large bedroom. They were filled, however, with various types of natural environments. I opened the door to one and stepped inside, emerging soon after a little wetter for the experience. The chamber was lush with foliage and the air humid as a rainforest in high summer. In contrast, the glass chamber next to it housed a desert landscape with the dry, arid heat typical of such a locale. Nearby, another chamber was entirely filled with water, corals, and other undersea flora.

'What's all this, Iolango?'

'A little recreation. Your basic set of natural environments for home relaxation. If we want a change of scene, it's all there at our disposal.'

'Bit small, aren't they?'

'For a human, yes, but we can shrink. To an insect or a microbe, this chamber is giant sized. If we feel like the tropics, we fly right in for an hour or two.'

'It's weird.'

'You've been to a pool with a sauna, haven't you? What do you do there? Have a swim, take a steam bath in the wet sauna, then sweat it out in the dry one. Same thing here - we'll swim like a fish, have a spell in the tropics, and dry off in the desert.'

'I see.'

'Let's not waste any more time here. We'd better keep going.'

The fourth floor must have been the one where Elijinx hung out when he felt like being human. The suite was decorated like a sultan's palace, with a fine array of tapestries and opulent furnishings of one kind and another. Still, this wasn't the time to sit there staring at them.

When we reached the next level, it was clear his sensibilities weren't limited to interior decoration. The fifth floor was an art gallery of sorts, featuring a wide range of styles from all periods of art history.

'For someone who claims to hate us,' I said, 'Elijinx has an uncanny interest in our artistic work.'

'He's quite the aesthete - although I'd hate to think how he acquired this collection. Most of it ill-gotten, no doubt. I mean, look at that one. Raphael's 'Portrait of a Young Man.' That went missing in World War Two and was presumed looted by the Nazis.'

'Is that so?' I said. 'He must have taken it off their hands when the Reich went down.'

'And look at these Chinese paintings and vases,' said Iolango. 'A lot of work like this was destroyed in the Cultural Revolution.'

I shrugged.

'If they were going to be smashed up by angry Chinese teenagers, Elijinx may as well have them.'

'I suppose so.'

'Hey, look at these, Iolango. They're a bit risqué! Who'd have thought Elijinx had such an eye for the female form?'

'Well, the old goat!'

'They're pretty hardcore. You won't be seeing them in the Louvre anytime soon.'

'Look at the text, Jimmy. It's in old Latin. Wait, I'm getting something, an impression. Yes... I see. These paintings are from the erotic art collection of the Roman emperor Tiberius when he lived on the island of Capri. He was known for his debauchery.'

'That was two thousand years ago. How can they be so well preserved?'

'Nothing physical will decay inside these walls. It could have been yesterday.'

We moved to the sixth floor to find the art gallery had given way to a museum housing some infamous items from history. A showcase given to weaponry, for example, contained an Aztec sacrificial knife, a prototype for one of the earliest guns, and some scientific papers that looked like plans for the atomic bomb.

Another glass showcase contained first editions of some controversial books from history. Among them were Marx's *Das Kapital*, Darwin's *On the Origin of Species*, Hitler's *Mein Kampf*, the witch hunting guide *Malleus Maleficarum*, and several religious books. Prominent first edition novels included *Lord of the Flies*, *1984*, and *Day of the Triffids*. There were also a number of books in languages other than English, which I didn't recognise. Each book looked to have rolled off the presses just moments before, and if the collection were to be auctioned, a small fortune would be required even to open the bidding.

Elijinx also seemed to have an ear for music, as a number of LP covers were attached to one of the museum walls in a collage. Of those I knew, I spotted Stravinsky's *Rite of Spring*, and some Bartok String Quartets. I was taken aback, and somewhat pleased, to see the record sleeve for Slayer's *Reign in Blood*, one of the most evil recordings ever made. When I spotted *Blessed Are the Sick* by Morbid Angel, and *This Godless Endeavor* by Nevermore, it was clear that Elijinx had an ear for the extreme.

The contents of the seventh floor were so foreign to my understanding I could not discern their meaning. I pressed

Iolango for an explanation, but he said we were wasting time and should concentrate on finding the Maelstrom.

By the time we reached the eighth floor, we were getting warm. Any sense of recreation or aesthetics had gone, and the room looked more like a military control centre. There were banks of strange looking equipment whose purpose I could not guess, but there was one object which was wholly familiar. A large holographic three dimensional map of the Earth was projected in the centre of the room. It was the Earth seen from space, the familiar shapes of the continents easy to recognise.

'You can see our present location here,' Iolango said, pointing out an area east of Australia. 'But this is only one part of the Maelstrom. There are two others. One's near India, the other's further north.'

'I know. You told me that yesterday. Is the Maelstrom here in this room?'

'I don't think so.'

'Then what's all this equipment?'

'Who knows? Leave it. We'll go to the last level, then come back if we have to.'

At last we reached the top level of Elijinx's base. We must now be just below the summit of the black mountain I'd first seen through the telescope from the boat. The mountain had been slanting inwards in a cone shape, so that each level we reached was slightly smaller than the one below. The room we entered was circular and about the size of an old style merry-go-round. It was sparsely furnished, containing little more than a couple of chairs, a table, and some kind of computer.

At first glance, the single circular wall and the ceiling seemed to be painted black, but that wasn't quite right. I looked again. There was something strange about the wall. I walked forward, trying to draw it into clear focus, but the perception confounded me. It was not that the wall was black - it didn't seem to exist at all. It was like staring into nothing. The rest of the room seemed solid, yet when I stood two inches from the wall, it was as if space had ended and I was gazing into pitch black night unlit by a single star.

'Don't touch it,' Iolango said quickly. 'You don't know what might happen.'

'Why can't I see it properly?'

'We're close to the Maelstrom now. The boundaries between illusion and reality become ever more tenuous.'

Iolango sat down at the table with his back to me and switched on the computer. At this, a number of strange occult symbols appeared in the walls around the perimeter of the room. They were the colour of fire which made them stand out against the dark background. It was almost a relief to have the walls given a more tangible structure by these symbols. I queried Iolango as to their meaning, but he did not answer. He continued to operate the computer. At that, a large section of the wall in front of us began to serve as the computer's screen. Iolango seemed unsurprised by this, and kept typing in some language which wasn't English.

To our left, another 'screen' appeared, this time as a sort of window. It was as if a portion of the wall had turned transparent, much as when we'd first entered the base. As we were now high above sea level, however, this was rather alarming. I stepped towards this 'window' and got a glimpse of the island forest a long way below, and beyond that nothing but ocean as far as the eye could see. In some alarm, I looked at Iolango. He was still banging away at the computer. All I could see was his back from behind, and a glimpse of his fingers flying over the keyboard and other controls.

'What's going on?' I asked. 'Have you found the Maelstrom yet?'

'Of course,' he replied. 'It was here all the time, ever since we came inside.'

'You found it? Great. You certainly seem to know your way around that computer. How can that be, anyway?'

'Well, you see, Jimmy, it's my computer.'

Slowly, as if revelling in the dramatic effect, the figure in front of me swivelled the chair round to face me, and continued to speak.

'And never mind the computer. It's about time you gave me back my guitar.'

14

Nemesis

In a flash I knew him. The decadent angel face with its young-old oscillation, the blue and bloodshot eyes, the shards of blonde hair. There had been a lot of slaughter under the bridge since that winter night in Amsterdam. Now, on an island unknown, in an ancient sea, our paths were rejoined. The shock of recognition gave instant illumination to the last twenty-four hours. Rather than being guided by my mentor, it was my nemesis who had led me by the hand into the very depths of his lair.

'So how about that guitar?' said 'Jonathon.'

Although dazed, I was able to muster a reply. 'The Les Paul? We both know what happened to that - and the deal was to return it in ten years if you made a comeback. You're nine years early.'

'In that case...'

The face of Elijinx began to change as if in a time lapse film sped up. The hairline receded, the skin began subtly to line and to loosen, and the eyes seemed to become a little deeper set. More disturbing was the sense of moral dissolution. That night in the Amsterdam cafe, I had likened his face to the portrait of Dorian Gray after a couple of years in the attic. Still angelically handsome, yet starting to fray around the edges and corrupt from within. That face now looked to have been smouldering in the attic a good while longer. What before had been implied was now overt, the hinted decadence brazenly on display.

'That's about ten years, wouldn't you say, Jimmy? Which is just about when you should have been getting out of that prison. I heard about your escape. Is that the best Iolango could come up with?'

Elijinx laughed.

'I suppose the old boy is still waiting for you to turn up at the beach.'

'So that was really him at Bondi yesterday... but not today.'

'As you can see.'

'I wondered why you were early and came to my place when we'd agreed to meet at the beach. Not to mention the way you carried on when you got there. Iolango wouldn't have done that.'

'Get off your high horse, Jimmy, I saw you wavering. Why be so uptight about your desires? You should give them full reign.'

To illustrate his pun, an image of the *Reign in Blood* LP cover appeared on the black wall, as if projected onto it. It flickered there for a few seconds, then faded away.

'How did you know what we were planning?' I asked.

'I knew Iolango had learned the location of this island. When I leaked false information about my absence, I guessed he'd try to contact you and bring you here. I monitored you until he did. Your invisibility was nothing to me. I was tracking you from the outset, right up until his pathetic attempt to charm you with that girl. I hitched a ride as a sand fly during your walk and sat in on your conference. Then all I had to do was copy the same body he'd used and intercept you.'

'Is what Iolango said true? That the Vortex Winder taps into ideal possible worlds to draw out the best in people, and the Maelstrom taps into the hell realms to bring out their worst?'

'It's technically true.'

'He also said the Maelstrom is controlled by you. I don't understand what would motivate someone to such bastardry.'

'Well, kid, let me put it this way.'

Elijinx stood up and transformed himself into Harry, the manager from the time of my Chica Boom fame, wearing the suave attire of a nightclub singer. Adopting a Sinatra pose, he winked, and began crooning a paraphrase of the old hit song.

'That's life, and as crazy as it sounds, some folks get a buzz just knocking people down.'

Retaining his present form as Harry, Elijinx reached into the empty void at the edge of the room and pulled out a couple of liquor bottles. He mixed a martini and handed it to me genially.

'Now Jim, there's no need to look so judgmental. I'm just doing my job in nature, acting as the yin to Iolango's yang. Every force must have its opposite, and every good its evil. All must be kept in balance.'

'I don't believe that. A system of balanced opposites is one of the dumbest ideas I've heard. If every good must be balanced by an evil, all our efforts would be futile.'

Elijinx raised his eyebrows.

'I just thought I'd throw it out there and see if you bought it. It seemed about your intellectual level, given that you've taken Iolango's simplistic worldview at face value. This whole Vortex Winder - Maelstrom idea is a standard good and evil schema, wouldn't you say?'

'But is it true?'

'Must we deal in absolutes? The world is a lot more complex than this childish division into good and evil. But even in your simple terms, what makes you so sure Iolango's the hero and I'm the villain?'

'Your appearance is a clue.'

'My appearance is a mirror of your projections. I pick up on your concepts and change my appearance to match them. You, in turn, finetune your perceptions until the illusion is complete. Therefore, you judge nothing but your own concepts. If I were in the mood for parody, I'd grow horns and a tail.'

'If your face is an illusion, I can still judge you by your actions. You cheated me and made me a laughing stock.'

'It was not I who wished for fame, or induced your drunken public antics.'

'You had me sent to a Thai prison, and if not for Iolango's compassion, I'd still be rotting there.'

'Granted. That was, in your terms, an evil deed. I make no denial. Yet when you become aware of the bigger picture, you may understand my motives. Now, take another example. Go back to the night we first met, when you sabotaged my rightful execution of the criminal, Iolango.'

'Criminal?'

'That's right. You know nothing about him. He buys you off with a cheap Vortex Winder, and you swallow his every pompous utterance without a thought. What do you really understand about him and his motivations?'

'Was he lying then about the Vortex Winder and the Maelstrom?'

'What he said is true enough at face value. What your noble friend failed to explain was the larger context which gives these concepts their meaning. When I've corrected his omissions, you'll have a different view of the matter. But first, I'll play along with your simplistic schema and give you what you expect. If you insist I perform in character, I'll humour you for the time being.'

With those words, Elijinx reverted to the appearance of Jonathon after ten years in the attic. This time, he held nothing back, and the sense of moral dissolution was now complete.

'Am I evil, human? If that's what you want, you will have it. Look inside, deep into my eyes, and see your reflection. Face your nemesis. Face yourself, and the true spirit of all your kind. I am the one who sold you into oblivion in that prison, and far more than that. I'm the prison guard that caned welts into your flesh, and the airport cop that laughed at your arrest. In the eternal tyrannies of humanity, I am the one and the many

- from the schoolyard bully to the third world despot and everything in between. All bear the mark of the Maelstrom.'

'The Maelstrom that you created.'

'No. The human race gave birth to the Maelstrom. I merely act to maintain it. All the properties of the Maelstrom are inherent in the human psyche. The Maelstrom is a self sustaining system, which draws its vigour from that endless well, the tears of humanity. I am only its guardian. You could think of me as a patron saint, but I'm barely even an instigator. There's no need for me to corrupt a heart that's born tainted. I offer a nudge from time to time, and that is enough. It takes only a little nurture for nature to bear fruit.'

'What do you have against humanity? We're not all evil.'

'Do I have to catalogue the litany of sins for which your race is infamous? Let us bypass the obvious – your endless appetite for war, your dominion over all other species, and damage to the planet itself. Look further and behold a race infinitely divided, waging war among all of its parts.

Of course, you have your high ideals, your principle of equality. Yet what a fine dance that principle has led you. On the one hand, some inequalities are scandalous. On the other, some are inevitable and should be left alone.'

'What do you mean?' I said.

'Take your four most populated nations of the last century. In one, the inequality was institutionalised in a system of castes. In the second, the government tried to fix it by terrorising its own people, and imprisoning them to use as slave labour. In the third, free speech was banned, its dear leader ran policies by which millions died, and violent anarchy was promoted as a national virtue. The revolutionary cures were worse than the disease, producing a new crop of regimes that live in historical infamy. The golden palace is always built on a graveyard of bones.'

'What about the fourth nation? You said there were four.'

'Ah yes. That farce is still in progress. There, the ideal of equality, poorly understood and wrongly applied, creates scenes of pure comedy. Some inequalities should be left alone. You can turn your country upside down trying to reverse them, and the results are plain to see. But do carry on. It's all terribly amusing.'

'What are we supposed to do then? You denounce inequality, then say it's inevitable.'

'The devil's in the details. The trouble is all your endeavours, your noble reforms, are sabotaged by the Maelstrom. It's a lead weight round your neck whenever you try to climb out of mediocrity and chaos. No matter how good your intentions, your efforts are damned. So how did the Maelstrom begin? I will tell you, and that will put a different light on the matter.'

As Elijinx delivered his long dissertation, I stared in fascination at his face, which seemed to flicker in firelight as if warmed by the embers of an internal hearth. Although still frightening to behold, his features had acquired a certain morbid nobility. There was a grave and austere beauty within the evil visage. I could not, however, ascertain his motives, and queried him thus.

'I would say you have two faces, Elijinx, but that much is already clear. You sit in judgment on humanity's evil. At the same time, by your own admission, you tend to the Maelstrom, the very device leading us on. Are you not then responsible for that which you condemn?'

'I am humanity's dark spirit, its soul and shadow. I lead the race on to its destiny, but the Maelstrom itself comes from the dark side of the human psyche. It is not the other way round. Now, it simply urges and insinuates. It amplifies and exacerbates those traits that are already there. It will guide the race to its ultimate destruction, and in that act the circle will be complete. Let me tell you about the origin of the Maelstrom, then you may understand. Iolango has told you a child's tale, yet he did not begin at the beginning, nor did he correctly explain the end.

To begin this story we must go back in time - before the Romans, the Egyptians, or the Sumerians. Before the annuls of recorded history as you know it. In those ancient times, two great incipient civilisations shared the Earth. One has been all but erased. Only fragments remain that hint of its existence. The other was the civilisation from which your own race began. You are the descendents of this second group.

It fell to Iolango and myself to act as guardians, to help the two great civilisations work together for the full flowering of your planet. Iolango was to guide your forefathers and I was to guide the civilisation that is now gone.

Had the two peoples succeeded in working together, a world would have been formed which was the very jewel of creation. Yet there was an act of betrayal. An act of self interest and petty ambition leading to a war in which ultimately, the people I was to guide were destroyed.

In that act of evil, the Maelstrom was formed, and Man began the interminable era of dominion over all others. Even with every other species subjugated, the lust for conquest was unsated, and he turned on his own brethren, waging war upon his own kind.

Iolango was as dismayed as anyone at the turn of events. It was never intended. Yet in achieving its victory, humanity became its own tormentor. It was now under the thrall of the Maelstrom, the psychic entity to which it gave birth. Ever since, Iolango has dreamt of a way to overcome it, to break free of the prison inadvertently formed.

He came to me for help. He reasoned with me, he tried to bargain, finally almost pleading with me to help him. Yet I scorned his entreaties. Instead of helping him dismantle the Maelstrom, I became its guardian. He has never forgiven me that - but why should I save a species which damned itself by destroying the world as it could have been?

Now, here is where Iolango and myself differ in our interpretations. He's a foolish idealist who believes humanity is redeemable, can rise above its sins, and fulfil the destiny that was once possible. I say that the race has damned itself many times over and is more akin to a disease on the face of the planet. This cancer is terminal, and the sooner the disease speeds to a conclusion, the better for all concerned. Thus, I do all I can to hasten the species' demise. There's no man who can outrun time, and the species itself will learn this and face the judgments of posterity. The sooner humanity drives itself to extinction, the better for all other species and the planet itself. So, I do everything I can to protect the Maelstrom and help it eradicate its creator.

In those terms, then, your evil is my good. Every act of destruction works towards the greater good, which is the demise of humanity and ultimately - I believe there is a way - the resurrection of that great rival civilisation I once guided.'

All the while, I gazed at Elijinx's face, mesmerised by the gravity of his words. Ever since Elijinx had revealed himself, I'd known things would never be the same. Yet now, listening to his long dissertation, I had undergone a surprising change. I experienced what some call a 'paradigm shift,' in which my worldview changed profoundly.

There are some well-known psychological pictures which reveal the partial nature of perception. One is the duck / rabbit illusion. On a first viewing, you see the image of a duck, but when prompted, you see the rabbit which was previously hidden. Even more striking is the old woman / young woman illusion in which a simple line drawing can be perceived two ways. At first, you see a beautiful young woman then, if your gaze is redirected, the face of an old crone comes into view. Nothing in the picture has changed, only your perception.

This had now happened to me. At first, under Iolango's direction, I'd accepted a picture in which Elijinx was a wholly evil being and the Maelstrom his tool for malicious sabotage. That perception had now changed. I saw that Elijinx was not the villain he had been depicted. On the contrary, he was a moral being who acted under the direction of good ideals. Thus, I could also infer that Iolango may not be the flawless force for moral good I had assumed him to be. Even the Maelstrom, while still an agent of destruction, was not necessarily evil but an instrument of justice, a means of defeating the real enemy - humanity itself.

Not everything in my worldview had changed. Elijinx's depiction of humanity as a corrupt species was not a foreign concept. It had been there in my mind all the time. Elijinx had simply given it a rationale and brought it into focus. I saw now I had been greatly mistaken about Elijinx. He was not a force of pure evil, but a moral being waging war in a just cause. The profundity of this change, and a sense of shame at my former prejudice, made me receptive to the extreme proposal Elijinx was about to suggest.

My proximity to the Maelstrom must also have played its part. All the while, I had listened to Elijinx's tale with a mixture of fear, wonder, and exhilaration. The atmosphere in the chamber was like no other I had known. It was as if I stood atop the Earth's highest mountain looking down on the world in awe, a witness to its creation and destruction. I had been foolish enough to drink the martini Elijinx had offered at the start of our conversation. Had he slipped me some intoxicant, or was it simply the overwhelming presence of the Maelstrom itself which had bewitched me? Either way, I felt a sickly exhilaration as Elijinx delivered his speech.

'Now, Jim, we have moved beyond Iolango's simple tale and you know the truth. The immediate question is what I am to do with you. We have three options. The easy one is that I could dispose of you now. Yet I can see into your heart and know that you secretly crave such a fate, and I am not in the business of granting wishes. You have thought about ending it all, have you not?'

'I would never do that. I'll survive, and keep on fighting no matter what happens.'

'It is pointless lying to me. I can feel your disillusionment, the sickness of your spirit. You can conceal it out in the world. Here, in such intimate proximity to the Maelstrom, your every thought and emotion is amplified a thousandfold. I can taste your hatred and your urge for vengeance against those you believe have wronged you. These emotions frighten you, and you wonder what you are capable of. You almost yearn for your own destruction as an escape, yet fear the moral damnation surrounding such an act. Well, we can open the doors and step onto the summit of this island, and if you have the courage, you can hurl yourself into the abyss below. But don't think I will extend even the tip of my little finger to assist you and absolve you of your guilt. If you want to play the victim, be it by your own hand.

Our second option is a far more fitting punishment for your act of opposing me. I could allow you to go back to your world in all its insanity, and to your life with its forlorn dreams. You can live out the rest of your days until the Maelstrom completes its work. It's only a matter of time, and you wouldn't have long to wait. It would only be a stay of execution.

There is a third option and I'll put it to you plainly. You can join me and help in my quest. You can help to bring down a species which has done nothing but betray you. Together, we can move past the era of humanity's bloody reign, and begin a new age of peace and justice. To do that, we must eliminate what currently exists. Only by erasing the present can we move into the golden future. You have the power to deliver this blow, and in so doing, history will revere you as a revolutionary. Jimmy Brandt, the Liberator. That will be your epithet.'

'What are you planning to do?'

'As I said, I intend to allow the Maelstrom to finish its work and erase the human cancer from this planet. You will assist me.'

'You want me to betray my own kind?'

'Have they not betrayed you? Not once or twice, but a thousand times. You owe them nothing but the firm hand of your judgment.'

'Even if that were true, I can't do anything about it. I have no power in this world.'

'Then listen, and I will explain. You have a unique chance to strike a blow for justice. This entails nothing less than the destruction of your tormentors and the evil world they created. The means of their destruction is in the Maelstrom.'

'Where exactly is the Maelstrom? Can I see it?'

'It is all around us. You cannot see it directly, but you can see its effects. I would say that the Maelstrom is a psychic entity, but then you would not understand its magnitude as a physical force. In truth, there is no real division between the mental and the physical. They are one. The Earth is not some lump of dead rock upon which life grows. It is itself a living entity, connected to the beings it supports. Its physical matter, its seasons, and even its weather patterns are linked to the minds of all its creatures. There are psychic storms and physical storms, and they are more closely linked than you realise.

Now, there are certain locations in the world prone to natural turbulence. We are in the region of one such point, as we speak. I have guided the Maelstrom here to take advantage of this turbulence, to further agitate it.

In similar fashion, there are certain moments in history which are pivotal, in which rival destinies balance upon the slenderest of tipping points. We are approaching such a point now. There is a great volatility at this juncture, and as you will see, this is reflected in the natural world.

There is a convergence, if you like, between physical forces and historic potential. A climactic event is just within reach. To use one of your human proverbs, you can say that the present moment is a camel that bears the weight of future time on its back, and it would take the merest straw to break it. You, / Jimmy, are that straw.'

'What are you talking about, Elijinx? You've lost me.'

'Let me get to the point. When was the last time Sydney had a tsunami?'

'A tsunami? There's never been a tsunami in Sydney.'

'Not in recorded history, at any rate. My memory stretches further. Of course, your country, Australia, has a long and intimate relationship with the ocean. It has seen many changes. Tasmania, for example, was at one point part of the mainland. But that is the past. We will look to the future.

I have hinted, if not explained, that the mass human psyche has a direct link to the natural world. There is a great volatility which has the potential to erupt, and in this I am not speaking metaphorically. There is, at this moment, an instability in these very parts around us. It would take the barest prod for this instability to tip over and lead to an undersea earthquake of some magnitude, and a resulting tsunami the likes of which have not been seen in your history. It would devastate much of the east coast of Australia.'

'You can't be serious.'

'Why not? It was only a few years ago the Asian tsunami killed hundreds of thousands of humans. Whole towns were simply erased. Who remembers those people now? And let me tell you, Jim, the wave to come will make the Asian tsunami look like a surf carnival.'

'That's a terrible thing to imagine.'

'Terrible it may be, but it is a necessary evil. As awful as the short term effects would be, in the long run, such a wave would act for the greater good. It would devastate your nation, yet at the same time offer the means to start afresh. Much as I regret the suffering, the end justifies the means. In the longer term, history will view this event as the clean break which birthed a new era.'

'One wave wouldn't end the country. They would rebuild.'

Elijinx laughed.

'We'll rebuild alright - build back better.'

'For all their faults,' I said, 'Australians are tough and resilient. They would prevail. But even if you were right and the wave destroyed this country, Australia is only one nation. Humanity would survive in the other six continents.'

Elijinx raised his eyebrows.

'You know what they say, Jimmy. Think global, act local. There will be ripples. There are other such events in place, lined up like a series of dominos, waiting to be triggered by this first event. This wave is the first domino.'

'So, if I hear you right, I'm the straw that breaks the camel's back to set off the first ripple of the domino effect. You're jumbling your proverbs there, wouldn't you say?'

'Words don't matter. Actions will make them redundant.'

'Even if this is all true, I don't understand why you're telling me. If you're determined to set off such a wave, it's nothing to do with me. Unless, for some reason, you can't do it on your own.'

'You're right. Iolango and I are visitors to your world. We can work behind the scenes to incite others to action, but we cannot act directly. We can exert profound historical influence, but only through human agents. The Maelstrom itself is a human creation, as well as the means of the species' destruction. Just as it took a human to create it, only a human can bring the process full circle. You are the one. It falls to you, Jimmy the Liberator, to complete the cycle of history. It's your destiny.'

'I could never dare commit an act of that magnitude. It's far too extreme - and no matter my personal grievances, I'd never betray my own species.'

'You can and you will. The weight of this destiny is too heavy to resist. In one sense, you are incidental, simply acting out a role that was set long ago. It could just as well have been someone else playing this part, and indeed I have been grooming several other candidates all the while in case they were required. Yet ultimately, it is you fate has chosen. The moment you meddled with history by your ridiculous act of fishing Iolango out of that toilet, you became a candidate for the role! Your escape from the prison put you in the box seat, and subsequent events have confirmed you as the winner. As for a 'betrayal,' I have already said that history will see you as a liberator, not a traitor.'

'I still don't understand my connection with this tsunami. These forces are far beyond my control.'

'Of course they are. I have said that you are simply the straw. The proverbial straw to activate the tipping point.'

'What do you mean?'

'You asked me where the Maelstrom was. It is all around us and its effects are plain to see. Take a look out the window.'

Elijinx activated the window in the wall to my left and his right, so that we could see a view of the ocean from the cliff top behind which we were hidden. It was a daunting sight. Conditions had changed since our entry into Elijinx's base.

The sea was far more turbulent. The breakers were bigger, and seemed to be buffeting the island in a violent and chaotic assault.

'The Maelstrom is all around us,' Elijinx repeated. 'You can see its effects already, and we are at its very centre. Strange as it may be for you to understand, the effects you see on that screen emanate from this very room in which we sit. More to the point, they emanate from you. All this time we have been in dialogue, the Maelstrom has been becoming part of you. It has fused with you - body, mind, and soul. You and the Maelstrom are now linked, and you stand poised, ready to deal humanity the judgment it deserves.

As I told you, the Maelstrom is a psychic entity, yet so powerful that its effects manifest in the physical world. It has joined with the subterranean depths that surround us, and also fused with your own consciousness. You now have the capacity to activate the wave.'

'You're telling me that all that out there is influenced by what I do here in this room.'

'That's right, but don't flatter yourself too much. As I said, you are the straw to break this camel's back. The conditions were set up long ago, and you are only here to trigger them. The undersea environment is now so unstable that the merest jolt can tip the balance and set it off. The key now is your mind and emotions. And of those emotions, it is anger that will do the job for us.

Of course, anger is the most volatile of the emotions, and it is anger which will give us the desired result. You are at the very heart of the Maelstrom, and at such proximity your every thought and emotion is amplified a thousand fold. All you have to do is give expression to the grievances you rightly feel. The balance will tip and the sea will boil over. From that point, the Maelstrom will finish its work.'

I was overwhelmed by several intoxicating forces – the presence of Elijinx and the Maelstrom, the terrifying images outside the window, and the strange tale he had told me. Yet I was not so intoxicated that I could go along with what he was suggesting.

'No, Elijinx. Even though I harbour resentments against my own kind, I could never have a hand in their destruction, and I would never join with forces of such magnitude. I want no part in this. Release me.'

'It is too late. You have fused with the Maelstrom. What's done cannot be undone. You will not leave this room until you have played your part in history.'

15

Oceanus

'Now that you have fused with the Maelstrom, your emotions are amplified and poised to trigger the undersea fault. Thus, I have only to incite in you a little anger and the job will be done. I will proceed to present the evidence of humanity's sins. That should be enough to provoke you.'

Elijinx paused, before beginning to make his case in the manner of a courtroom prosecutor.

'The seeds of your species' demise were in the first act of betrayal that gave birth to the Maelstrom. You and the Maelstrom have been locked in a feedback loop, each increasing the power of the other. The world has been a disaster ever since.

The Maelstrom stems from the dark side of the human psyche. It offers a license for a litany of sins. All the greed, the self interest, and the enslavement of others comes in answer to the Maelstrom's song. Yet the Maelstrom alone cannot be blamed. Each human has the power to think and act independently. Even I would admit many have passed the test and proven themselves worthy.

It is not enough to save you. On balance, the human experiment has failed. How could it not, considering its roots? The world was seized by duplicity and conquest, and millennia later, little moral progress has been made.

At this time of wealth and technological advance, many of the world's citizens live in dire poverty. Even in the richer countries, the economic divide is extreme. The power struggles never end. In a hierarchy of slaves, each level dominates the rank below and kowtows to the one above. Power is given to those who are already strong and taken away from those who are weak.

There are factory farms in which animals are kept in terrible conditions, and abattoirs that practise cruelty beyond the needs of the profession. The natural environment itself has suffered from excess plunder.'

As he spoke, I watched the screen to see pictures supporting Elijinx's case. A procession of sins paraded before me, as Elijinx unveiled case after case of man's inhumanity to man and beast alike. Instances of murder, corruption, cruelty and deceit. Yet my mood was not so much one of anger as of horror, and sorrow for the victims. Elijinx seemed to sense that he was not eliciting the anger he'd been looking for, and rebuked me.

'What is wrong with you? The evil of this world is plain to see, yet you cannot muster the necessary anger. Have you no heart?'

'They're still my people. Many of them are good and kind. You show only the dark side of us, the minority who are evil.'

'Minority! What naivety is this?'

Elijinx stopped and thought for a minute.

'I see the problem. The case I've made is too abstract, too removed from your own life. It's one thing to hear about the wars, poverty, and regimes, but until you experience them yourself, you can't fully understand them.'

'In some ways, I've had a fortunate life.'

'But you experienced the prison. That helped you see what the race is capable of.'

'I understand it, but that's not enough to make me turn against them. I feel for the victims as much as hating the perpetrators. The victims are human too.'

'Then what is the source of this darkness inside you? It radiates like a beacon. I must look deeper to find the fatal weakness, this stone of night pulling you down.'

'What's this - you're quoting Dickinson now? Bruce that is, not Emily. So you do listen to metal. I thought as much after seeing your record collection downstairs.'

'You expect me to listen to jazz like that poseur, Iolango? If you could just see the visions, Jimmy, you'd let go of your restraint and allow Oceanus his way. What is your stone of night? The Maelstrom will magnify it and bring it to me. Give me a moment.'

Elijinx closed his eyes for a considerable while as if listening to some internal sound only he could perceive. This went on for so long that I wondered if I should make some kind of rash attempt at making a break and escaping in the boat. Eventually Elijinx opened his eyes with a triumphant smile.

'I see. So it's your creative work. I've just read your book - very droll. Why was it never published?'

'No comment.'

'Your music is excellent too. Why has no one heard of it?'

'Maybe because I've got no contacts, no money, no one's ever helped me, and the whole industry's a cesspit of evil.'

'Aha - here comes the anger! So these are the books and albums you were talking about when you came to my office last week.'

'You could have helped me promote them, instead of offering me a spot on Big Brother.'

'All is now clear. They betrayed you, Jim! You, a talented artist, never had any support for your work. Meanwhile, far lesser beings got the recognition and reward that should have been yours. Yes, this is the stone of night weighing you down. I can feel your resentment, your hate. All that's required is to bring it to boiling point to trigger the undersea fault, and thus the tsunami.'

I had fallen easily into Elijinx's trap. Yet if he'd somehow been able to access my books and music in minutes by an act of will, it was hard to see how I could have resisted him anyway. I resolved to keep my emotions in check and give a deadpan response to any further attempts to bait me. Elijinx, however, seemed to read my thoughts. He gestured at the window, showing the looming sea around the island.

'See how it simmers and bubbles, Jim. Your rage will set it aboil. All I have to do is goad you sufficiently to ensure its eruption. Don't even think of concealing your true feelings. It is futile to deny them. You're fused with the Maelstrom. Your inner life is laid bare, and you are bound to truth.'

Elijinx returned to his computer and called up a familiar website.

'Isn't YouTube great? Such a rich resource. We should check your Chica Boom video and see how many hits you've had. Then again, that was last week, wasn't it? How about some music instead?'

Elijinx played a video of a young girl dancing provocatively while singing a simple pop tune over an electronic beat. There was even the clichéd cameo from a rapper after the second chorus. It was formulaic stuff indeed. The song seemed familiar, but such songs are so alike I may only have seen one of its infinite clone siblings.

'Would you look at that, Jim. How many views has this song had on YouTube? Fifty-two million! That equates to a million views a week for a whole year. It's heartening to see such quality art finding an audience.'

Elijinx began singing the chorus, but I interrupted him.

'And now it's had fifty-two million and one. Big deal. You'll have to do better than that.'

'Here's another then,' said Elijinx, calling up a new video. 'Your own hard rock genre this time. Boring, forgettable riffs, weak and uninteresting lyrics. But the right look, and underground media darlings for some reason you never could understand.'

'So what? That's the music world for you - it's a matter of luck, timing, and personal taste. It doesn't mean anything.'

Elijinx laughed and looked out the window at the angry sea.

'You're not much of a liar, Jim. This feigned indifference doesn't fool me, and it won't fool the Maelstrom. The Maelstrom's inside your soul now, and the effects are out there for all to see.'

'Why don't you pick out one of the bands I love like Sabbath or Priest? I'm glad they made it big. Good on them.'

'That wouldn't serve our purpose. We want to tap into your envy and resentment. You'll love this next one. Axis of Awesome's Four Chord Song.'

'Don't bother, I've already seen it. That's the comedy clip where those guys play the same four chords for ten minutes, and sing a load of hit songs that all use that chord progression.'

'That's the one.'

'Put it on - it's a laugh. It's funny because it's true, but the joke's on them, not me. I wouldn't even write a song using that corny old chord progression.'

I forced a chuckle. It sounded like a maniac's cackle. Elijinx looked out the window.

'Your face is smiling but the ocean shows your true feelings - and the joke's on you. Since rock music began, we've had thousands of bands and millions of songs. Yet there are still only twelve notes in an octave. If there's one commodity in music which should be at a premium, it's originality - which is one quality you do have. How galling, then, that your music is unknown, while these 'four chord songs' are hits.'

'Pop music has always been like that, it's nothing new. It's a little irritating, sure.'

'A little?'

'So it's annoying - so what? There's not much I can do about it.'

'But you can, Jimmy. This next one's a beauty though. Have a look at this poll of the 'Five Hundred Best Songs Of All Time' from *Rolling Stone* magazine a few years ago. See what came in at number two. 'Satisfaction' by the Rolling Stones. The band that is, not the magazine.'

'What - you mean 'Can't Get No Satisfaction,' that one? I don't believe you. That's a three chord song that I used to teach on guitar to six year old kids at school. It's not even one of the Stones' best songs. 'Time Waits for No One' is fifty times better, and they've got plenty of others.'

'There are the poll results in black and white. 'Satisfaction' - the second best song of all time. It's in print, so it's a fact.'

'Are you sure it's not the five hundred worst songs of all time?'

'No, it's the best, and this poll was organised by one of the leading authorities on popular music. How do you feel when you read such an article? Do you feel that the world is in sane hands?'

'Look, it's only some stupid magazine poll.'

'It galls you nonetheless. Ever since the sixties, the Stones had a big machine of managers and publicists to help them succeed. Who in the world of music ever helped you? What manager or record label ever lifted a finger to support your cause?'

'I already know this.'

'You made a good album and had to fund it yourself at great expense. Then you were locked out of the system of distribution, promotion, and airplay, so no one ever heard it. Even your own friends didn't buy it, they wanted freebies. Then you couldn't afford to make another record, there were no funds left. Meanwhile, out in the real world, you can see how money is spent these days on things that really matter.'

On screen, a new sequence of images appeared, for which Elijinx gave a running commentary.

'Look how the rich waste their money. An ivory toilet seat made from elephant tusks bought by a rich family who live in your own suburb. A million dollar engagement ring for a celebrity airhead in the US. An English Premier League footballer getting paid more in a week than you could earn in three years. And a successful rock band who made it, and then blew their fortune and several years making the follow up to their hit album. Meanwhile, you had to retire from music because you were broke.

But you know what? Even if you *had* made it in music, you'd still have been doomed. Every bloodsucker in a business suit would have sought to feed on your labours and inspiration. Then the fans would have downloaded your music for free, and justified it any which way that suited them. You'd have been plundered from above by the biz, and screwed from below from your own fans. The whole enterprise was doomed from the start by the evil of human nature.'

'Where are you getting this stuff, Elijinx? How do you know all this?'

'The Maelstrom is amplifying your thoughts to be read, and the rest is common knowledge.'

'It's obvious what you're trying to do. Bombarding me with negativity, trying to break my self control. Why not look at the positive side? I had fun recording my music. It's one the best things I've done. I'm happy about it.'

'Still the pretence, the denial? And I haven't even started on the writing. All those bookstores with the beautiful shelves and the shiny book covers. You wanted to be part of that world, but never made it past the gatekeepers. The publishers and agents didn't give you a shot. They only worked with people who were already successful. Your work was unproven - but how could it be a success if it was never given a chance?'

'That's the Matthew Effect for you.'

'Then that so called award for unpublished novels which was hijacked by the judges' tedious political agenda. Your book was beaten by lesser works which sucked up to the boring, obvious politics of the judges. Remember that?'

'I've been trying to forget it ever since.'

'The arts world is just another prison, Jim. Another caste system run by gangs and cliques. The haves and have-nots, same as always. Same as everywhere else in the human world. You'll die alone as a pauper with your music unheard and your books unread. That's the way it was always going to be in the human world. Did you really think you had a chance?'

'Yes, because my music was good, my books were good. I believed they would succeed on merit.'

'Artistic merit may come into it later, but it won't get you a start in the arts world. If you want to make that first breakthrough, it's all about politics, sucking up, and networking.'

'I hate all that stuff. What's networking got to do with art? Why should I have to do any of that?'

Elijinx transformed into Barbara the publisher.

'To finally answer your question, Jimmy, because *that's* how it works.'

At the sight of Barbara's smug, stupid face, I lost control and succumbed to the fury Elijinx had been trying to elicit. At that moment, Barbara wasn't just one gatekeeper denying me entry, she was every gatekeeper in the world. This mean-girl-supreme ruling the arts scene, with all its cliques and petty thuggery. To hell with the whole damn lot of them. I let out a wordless cry of rage that seemed to endure longer than any law of nature should have allowed.

The change in the atmosphere was palpable. Elijinx resumed his previous form and smiled, for he knew that the tipping point had been reached.

'That's done it, Jimmy. The Maelstrom has heard your call, and Oceanus approaches. The end has begun.'

An opening appeared in the ceiling of the room, a winding staircase dropping down from it to the floor. Elijinx climbed the staircase and I followed, until we emerged onto a rocky platform at the very summit of the island. There, we looked out on a scene of latent apocalypse.

The sea was aboil. Far below us, great torrents of water surged onto the island in a deadly ebb and flow. It was the scale of the spectacle which terrified me most. To the north, the south, the east and the west, there was nothing in sight but a writhing blue canvas, scarred by jagged lines of white foam. Awestruck and aghast at the terrible majesty of Oceanus, I cowered as I saw Titanic-sized hollows of water fade into the abyss, before rising again in horrific resurrection to almost seem to threaten our perch on the island summit.

The cliffs upon which we stood suffered a terrible assault. Looking giddily down, I saw no trace of the boat we had left tethered on the beach. The island itself was being repeatedly engulfed by monster waves, which made their charge before retreating from whence they'd come. My thoughts went briefly to the forest below where I had walked. Only those creatures who could fly high above the torrent or burrow deep into the earth would survive. For the rest, doomsday had arrived. From high on the summit, I looked down once more to see the waters fading back into the body of the ocean, perhaps drawing numerous tiny victims with them.

When each wave had fully receded from the island, the devastation was clear. The forest below had been flattened as if by the swat of an almighty fist. I looked out to the boundless sea with its fearful rise and fall. Vertigo struck me a blow and I cowered upon the rock platform, crouching low for fear of being blown from my perch by the howling gale and dashed upon the rocks below, or swallowed in the depths of the watery abyss.

Elijinx strode across the platform and hauled me to my feet, his face radiant. There was no trace of fear, merely exhilaration at the realisation of a long awaited dream. He clapped me on the back as if we were co-conspirators.

'Was that it? The tsunami?' I asked.

'That was only the *beginning* of our vengeance. Oceanus will rise in waves upon waves upon waves!'

'Let's go back inside. This is insane. Make it stop, Elijinx!'

I looked to my right, but could see no trace of the opening in the rock through which we had climbed. There was nothing but bare stone from one edge of the summit to another. Elijinx's face was exultant.

'Too late. There is no reverse to this resurrection. Hail to Thanatos riding home on the wings of his brother Oceanus. The great wave is coming, and no power in this world or the next can stop it.'

The ocean stretched as far as the eye could see around the island. Not a shred of land was in sight amidst that world of water, bar the island and the column of rock upon which we perched. The great bowl of water frothed and bubbled below us.

Once again, that bowl seemed to empty, as if some giant plug had been pulled from the ocean floor. Collages of rocks, which had been hidden, formed a momentary archipelago of small islands. Then the recession of water stopped with an ominous pause, and surged upwards with startling speed. As the tide rushed up towards us, I was sure it would swallow the column of rock upon which we perched, before hurling us into watery oblivion. With a roar, the tide thrust upwards until it was almost upon us, then fell back at the last moment. If I had lain and reached down, my finger tips could nearly have brushed the foam. The surge, denied its prey, fell back to the surface of the frothing ocean far below.

'Behold, the might of Oceanus!' cried Elijinx in rapture.

'Let's get inside!' I screamed against the wind.

'No, Jim. This is a moment of history. Only a fool would miss it. The climax is almost upon us. Look to the horizon. See the glory!'

I looked out to sea but could detect no change in the conditions. Then astonishingly, the wind died down, the waves calmed, and the surface of the ocean seemed to sink.

'What now?' I asked Elijinx in relief and hope. In the sudden eerie quiet, I no longer had to raise my voice and could speak at a normal level. 'Is it over?'

'Yes, it is over. This is the beginning of the end for you and your kind. Yet I will go on into eternity.'

With those words, Elijinx began to change form in front of my eyes. The face and body transformed, the feet became talons, and the arms turned to wings. A black eagle perched on the edge of the rock. It rose slowly into the air to a vantage point high over the ocean, looking down at me as I cowered alone on the rock platform.

The giant plug had again been pulled, causing the waters to recede even further than before. I almost fancied that the ocean floor itself was laid bare, although this may have been a terror-induced hallucination. Then, the lost waters began to rise once again. The eerie quiet gave way to a murmur, then a growing roar. I looked to the horizon to behold a horrifying wall of water stretching as far as the eye could see. That horizon continued to rise and approach in a relentless surge.

I glanced up to see Elijinx's eagle circling the air currents high above me. Then I returned my awestruck gaze out to sea and the apocalyptic wall of water rushing closer. The end was at hand.

The wave rose up and up, until it was even higher than my platform at the summit of the island. It loomed high above me and swept forward to deliver the crushing blow. With a silent prayer and a cry of desperation, I seized the Vortex Winder from my pocket and raised it skyward.

16
Lighthouse XIII

The wall of water loomed far above me, a blue-black mountain of destruction. I closed my eyes, grasped the Vortex Winder, and prayed to the gods and powers for a merciful death.

If the wave had broken at that point, I would have been smashed to smithereens. Yet as it was still building towards a pending apocalypse on shores to come, I was spared its full wrath. Instead, the wave swept me up like so much plankton, before continuing on its way. As it plucked me from the summit of Elijinx's island, I took the deepest possible breath and bowed my head before the might of Oceanus.

I could not have survived without the Vortex Winder. In some manner which I don't understand, it must have protected me. Whether it extended my lung capacity underwater, or helped me float after I'd surfaced, it surely helped prolong my life. But not even the Vortex Winder could save me indefinitely.

At this stage still engulfed by water, I was truly helpless, with no more control of my destiny than a gnat in a hurricane. With the roaring tide in my ears, my body was tossed this way and that by forces beyond my comprehension. Finally, I reached a point of relative calm. Yet having been thrown in all directions, I could not tell up from down. With my lung capacity stretching thin, I opened my eyes. There was a light somewhere to my right. Reckoning this to be the water's surface, I thrust towards it as the last air in my lungs threatened to expire.

I surfaced, a tiny cork bobbing on the water. The ocean had lost none of its turbulence. It was still in the process of landscape oscillation, forming a sequence of watery hills and valleys, with myself an unwilling traveller across them. Surely only the Vortex Winder was keeping me afloat by now, and without it I would have already given up the ghost.

I spied Elijinx's island some distance away and was amazed how far I'd come since being plucked from the summit. There was, of course, no other land in sight, so there was nowhere else to go. I was surprised to be still alive at all, yet when I began to see shadowy images in the water nearby, I began to question even that. It occurred to me I might be hallucinating, and on which side of the valley of death this was occurring was far from clear.

I raised my arms above the water and stared at the Vortex Winder, which I'd tied to my left wrist. But far from helping me, the Vortex Winder began to melt like a Picasso wristwatch. At this further hallucination, I sank beneath the surface and swallowed some water. I spluttered upwards once more, but couldn't regain a normal breathing rhythm. Through my panic and pain, it was clear that the end was nigh. I sank again and in my desperation sensed something just above the surface of the water. I reached for it, and felt a hand pulling me upward. The hand was cold, but its grip was firm as it lifted me above the water.

I opened my eyes to a most unexpected sight. An old school friend, Michael Quant, was standing astride the water as if surfing, smiling down at me. I was now in a dream-like state of mind where anything seemed possible.

' Quanty!' I said with relief. 'You've saved me. But what are you doing here when you've been dead these fifteen years?'

Michael didn't reply, just continued to smile. He hadn't aged at all since his death in that car accident all those years ago. I glanced down at Michael's feet and saw them hovering just above the water. When I looked back, his face had been replaced by the blank features of Thanatos, the death spirit. As a child, I could name every Greek god. Perhaps this was why the reaper chose to appear to me in this form. A small kindness? Yet the face offered neither punishment nor pity, only cold deliverance. I dropped the hand and slipped once more beneath the waves. When I resurfaced, the Vortex Winder had regained its form and was once more strapped to my wrist. I thrust it skyward in a last call for help.

I was damned, floating in a sea of foam, floundering desperately as I faced my liquid doom. Even if I could somehow escape from my watery peril and swim back to Elijinx's island, I would still be trapped in the stark surrounds of that stony island prison untold miles from home.

Another monster wave was approaching. It was a baby compared to the tsunami wave, yet still a formidable sight as it loomed above. As it approached, two human forms were visible astride the wave, looking down at me. One was Thanatos, the suitor I had rejected. The impassive mask now bore a look of faint amusement, as a cat may look at a mouse which has run a few inches from its claws. The other was his fellow deity, Poseidon himself, the guardian of Oceanus. The supercilious gaze of the two gods was the last thing I saw before the wave broke. I went down for the last time. The Vortex Winder was no longer strapped to my wrist. It was over. I stopped struggling and accepted defeat.

In the moments that followed, I began to hallucinate a new sensation. I felt my body seized and wrapped in some kind of soft fabric. Whether it was a tissue, a cloth, or a burial shroud, I did not know. Whatever it was, I felt myself lifted and flying through the air. The violent thrashing of the ocean receded until its angry roar was far beneath me. After a while, I sensed my body descend until it was placed gently down on a flat surface.

I opened my eyes to find myself back at sea level, but with conditions much changed. The ocean was becalmed, the wind had died down, and Elijinx's island had vanished entirely. I was lying on a raft, drifting on gentle tides. Although it was still dark, all signs of threat or malice had disappeared.

It was then it appeared, a radiant beacon of ethereal light rising in the distance. A lighthouse, shining like the Grail. On the shore of a new island its outline glowed, ghostly and luminescent against the darkening sky. Though the raft had neither engine nor oars, it drifted without effort towards the light, and the closer I came, the stranger the lighthouse appeared. As I neared the shore, it soared above me, a shining, white tower marked only by some windows at its top and a carved Roman XIII at its centre.

The lighthouse gave off an unearthly silence, all the more noticeable after the ocean's apocalyptic roar. There was no question of whether to approach. The tower had an otherworldly shimmer which drew me to step onto the land and walk towards it. My clothes were completely sodden as I moved towards the great doors, yet when I stepped over the threshold, they had become bone dry. All sense of pain or discomfort vanished, and there was instead an air of unshakeable calm.

I was alone in a ground floor room of quiet opulence, but did not linger there. A spiral staircase led upwards, and I ascended through a succession of circular rooms at various levels of the shaft. About halfway up the tower, I looked out the window to see the blue ocean stretch endlessly out from the island in bright sunshine. This was odd, as night had been falling as I sailed towards the lighthouse. In the tranquil and rather surreal atmosphere of the moment, it did not seem to matter. I continued to climb the winding staircase, ascending at last to the top section with the light, where it was no great surprise to find Iolango waiting.

'So it was you who plucked me out of the water. I suppose it had to be.'

'Consider it an act of symmetry, Jim. Now the circle is complete.'

'You saved me from certain death. Unless this is some kind of afterlife. Where are we?'

'Lighthouse XIII. It's not quite an afterlife. It exists on the cusp of your world. It does not occupy any physical space in your universe, nor does it take up time. It's outside of time altogether. Hence the thirteen.'

'What do you mean, thirteen?'

'A whimsy. Clock time is divided into recurring lots of twelve hours, thus the thirteenth hour is outside of time.'

'I see. Although when I was in Germany, thirteen hundred hours was one o'clock in the afternoon. The twenty-four system, you know.'

'Call it Lighthouse XXV if you like. I prefer the Roman system - and Lighthouse XIII has more of a ring to it.'

'And what is Lighthouse XIII?'

'A place of transition, and infinite potential.'

'Like the trade winds.'

'The trade winds are dwarfed by this. We're far beyond the trade winds now, beyond life and death and the struggles of mortal beings. Can you not sense its power?'

'If this is outside of time and space, as you say, I must surely be dead.'

'Not yet. We are on the threshold of your world, but the lines of transition go both ways. You can still return.'

'To a city destroyed by a tsunami which I helped create? No thanks.'

'The tsunami was an illusion. Elijinx misinterpreted an old prophecy which said Sydney would be destroyed by the ocean. These prophecies are cryptic, you know, and Elijinx's reading was far too literal.'

'What do you mean?'

'I am not omniscient either, but the prophecy he discovered was symbolic - and here's how I interpret the symbols. The ocean is time, plain and simple. It has been there, more or less unchanged, for millions of years. Man by contrast is ephemeral, a mere speck in the vastness of history. In that context, the tsunami represents a rapid acceleration of time, a reminder that brief mortal lives will be washed away. In that sense, Sydney will indeed by destroyed by Oceanus.'

'Why do you and Elijinx keep using that name?'

'It's a name from antiquity, and Elijinx and I are such classicists, of course. We call it Oceanus because it pleases us. Chronos is another name for you. Chronos was time. Yet Oceanus has taken Chronos's mantle on this occasion.'

'Why do you speak of symbols? This is not some intellectual puzzle. I was there. I saw the tsunami. It was real. Horribly real, I assure you.'

'It was a localised hallucination, a joint creation between you and Elijinx, induced by the mighty power of the Maelstrom. It was astonishingly vivid, no doubt, but an illusion all the same. There was no physical tsunami that devastated the east coast of Australia and left the country in ruins.

Yet symbolically at least, a tsunami may indeed destroy you. Oceanus will, of course, outlive your kind. That's a given - but whether the lifespan of your race will be measured in centuries, decades, or years is unknown. If only years, the tsunami will have destroyed you.

In your personal illusion, Elijinx induced the tsunami from your own anger. You didn't destroy your civilization, of course, but only your own participation in it. In a sense, you travelled into the future beyond your own lifespan, or out of time itself - and here you are.

In a way, your whole world is also undergoing a vivid mass 'hallucination,' fully believed in and experienced by your fellow humans. That is not to say it isn't real. Now, whether that 'hallucination' endures for centuries or for decades, we will see. There are certain disastrous trends of your time that threaten your survival. If you can solve those problems, the society will endure. If you continue on the current path, however, the civilisation may not last. It could fall quite suddenly from the present into the past. Instead of flourishing gracefully with a normal lifespan on the shores of Oceanus, it will be swept to a premature demise.

Anger was the trigger for you. So, look at the society overall. It's a society awash in anger. Some of it legitimate, but much of it artificially created and amplified by the Maelstrom. So much anger, so little time. You are all being manipulated. And that is how I interpret the prophecy, and the hallucination which you created.'

I waited for a moment, but Iolango's dissertation seemed to have come to an end.

'If what you say is true,' I said, 'I'm guessing Elijinx will be more than a little put out when he learns his so called tsunami didn't destroy Sydney after all. But if you knew all this, why didn't he?'

'I think he was too consumed with excitement at the events brought about when you went to his island and fused with the Maelstrom. The Maelstrom's power intensified at that point, and his mind may have been so addled he could no longer distinguish between illusion and reality. It won't take him long to come to his senses. When he realises his mistake and that I've rescued you, it will give him another reason to hate me. It's just another chapter in our ancient feud.'

'What about the Vortex Winder and the Maelstrom - is it true what you told me about them?'

'The struggle will continue between the Vortex Winder and the Maelstrom, just as it does between myself and Elijinx until the battle is won and lost.'

'There's something I still don't understand. If we are outside of time, surely you can see what will happen in the future, so you already know what will happen to the world.'

'As I said before, there are many ways your world can go. There are more worlds than are dreamt of by you, I, or Elijinx. It's all part of the overall struggle, and what happens to each individual is important to them, at least. So, I will continue to try to help people with the Vortex Winder, and Elijinx will use the Maelstrom to influence history to take the course he favours.'

'Why did you lie to me, Iolango? You didn't explain the true story of how the Maelstrom formed. Elijinx told me about the rival civilisation that was destroyed. Is that true too?'

'It didn't seem necessary to mention it at the time. It's true there was another great civilisation who suffered at your species' hands. The difference between Elijinx and myself is I have moved on. What's done is done. I look to the future, whereas Elijinx is so unable to forget the past it distorts his view of the present. I look at a newborn baby and see unlimited potential for good, but Elijinx sees only a latent tyrant.'

I stared at Iolango.

'I can't help feeling a little used. According to you, my name was Mael-Stormer and I was to bring in the Renaissance, but Elijinx said I was 'Jimmy the Liberator' whose destiny was to wipe out my own race. Sometimes I wish I'd never gotten involved in all this.'

'I must admit my people can be a touch manipulative. It's an occupational hazard. You see, we're not supposed to exert direct influence on history, but only operate through human agents.

We bend the truth at times to get what we want. Anyway, you've done more than enough. You've earned your own liberation.'

'To do what?'

'Return to your world. Or not. The choice is yours.'

'Where else would I go?'

'You can 'move on' if you like. The physical world is not the only realm of existence.'

'I'm not ready for that. You know, when I was drowning in the water, I felt afraid, but also a terrible sadness. I realised that, for all its flaws, I loved the world. It broke my heart to think I was leaving it all behind.'

'Then return - and by way of apology for getting you involved in all of this, I can take you right back to the beginning. Back to the beer garden of the Excelsior Hotel in Surry Hills the night you saved me. You can fish me out of the toilet - much obliged, thanks - but I'll return you to that point in time and never reveal myself to you. You can finish your cigarette in the beer garden, go in to watch Nevermore, and never know the difference. There'll be no Vortex Winder, no Maelstrom, and you can carry on your life as you would have done from that point.'

'What about Elijinx? Won't he still come after me?'

'He won't bother if I don't involve you by giving you the Vortex Winder.'

'Come on now, Iolango, that's a hell of a decision to make. It would mean none of this will have happened. My comeback to music, the Black Art, going to Germany to see Freya. Even the prison and the invisibility and the rest of it. Would I really want to erase all that? It would be a terrible thing to lose. As you said - what's done cannot be undone. Maybe I should let it be.'

'Wise words. From our current vantage point you can see the value of it, suffering and all. Where we are now, we're far beyond the petty struggles. Lighthouse XIII is transcendent.

Far beyond good and evil, beyond the victories and tragedies alike. It is creativity above all, for better or worse.'

'Speaking of creativity, that's what I want to do most of all. Get back to my music and my writing. Never mind that I can't get an audience. Just forget all that Maelstrom stuff. I'll do it for my own sake. Make new albums, write books purely for the pleasure of it, and to hell with the outside world and trying to reach others.'

'That's the spirit.'

'I mean, it is a bit depressing that a newcomer can't break into the mafia of the arts world, but what can you do?'

'Just keep going, things may change. They're not all as bad as you think.'

'As for the books, I've got an idea. How about this - instead of erasing my memory of what happened after we met, how about if I actually write down my adventures and communicate them to others? Is that OK with you? I suppose I'd be blowing your cover, talking about the Vortex Winder and the Maelstrom and the rest of it. I can change your name if you like. Elijinx's too.'

'Do what you want. No one will believe these events have any basis in fact. It'll be considered merely a whimsical fantasy. Then again, a part of them will know. They'll feel a stir of recognition. Perhaps it will occur to them to act as if there really is a Vortex Winder and a Maelstrom. In that way, you'll be continuing to work for the cause. So, write whatever you want.'

'I just might. No one will ever read it anyway.'

'Very well. The choice has been made. Let us return.'

'Is this goodbye, Iolango? Will I meet you or Elijinx again?'

'As I have said, there are more worlds that exist than could ever be dreamt of by you, I, or Elijinx, and I'm certain that in some of those worlds, we'll meet again. On the night we first met, a friendship was forged that will last a lifetime and beyond. A random, unnecessary act of kindness from a mortal man towards a lowly despised insect was enough to ensure that. In such acts lie the salvation of your world.'

With that, I took Iolango's hand and departed the ethereal lighthouse on the cusp of reality, and returned to the world of time.

17
Vortex Winder

And so, I returned to the ordinary world. I wrote the last two songs, 'Elijinx' and 'Oceanus,' and recorded them to finish the album. I've sometimes wondered what Elijinx would think of the song I wrote for him, using some of the phrases remembered from our dialogue, but there's been no sign of him since his flight from the island. If he really is into metal, he'll like the song. It's the heaviest one on the album. I've also imagined what it would sound like if he came to the studio and sang it. His voice is rather more 'evil' sounding than mine. Either him or Tom Araya, anyhow. The song does have a Slayer vibe in parts.

I say Elijinx hasn't appeared since that day, but nothing is certain. From time to time, strangers cross my path, as if by chance. It may be all in the imagination, but I wonder if one of them is Iolango keeping a watchful eye on my affairs. More disturbingly, I fear it may be yet another manifestation of Elijinx in all his infinite cunning. Time will tell if I've seen the last of them.

I don't regret my return here. This beautiful world won't last forever. We should make the best of it while we can.

I don't bother much trying to enter the arts scene nowadays. The humans have spoiled it with their politics, so I try to ignore them. Let them have their networks and their cliques and their petty tyrannies. They will all bow before the might of Oceanus in due course. Their politics carry no weight with him.

I finished recording my album, and writing this book. *The Vortex Winder*. It's a novel. A work of fiction. Of course it is.

In idle moments, I wonder if I really returned at all. Did I perhaps travel in the other direction from Lighthouse XIII, then dictate this work through the mediumship of a mortal man within your world? I speculate on that for a minute, then dismiss such thoughts as idle fancy.

Yet in a larger sense, this is indeed a book written by a ghost. I have but a few short years before returning to Lighthouse XIII and whatever lies beyond it. Perhaps this book will outlive the man. Knowing I will soon be gone, I wrote it to leave something of myself behind, to let people know I once lived.

I was one human, among billions. One man, who loved and laughed, who fought demons within and without; who battled the absurd follies of our world and the Maelstrom-cursed blackness of the human heart. That darkness did not defeat me. I had a good life, and thus the victory was mine.

One day I will succumb to the pitiless might of Oceanus and then there will be no return. In the meantime, there will be more books, more albums, more travels and adventures. And all the while, the magic journey will be lit by sparks of the Vortex Winder that lead the way. Unwind, unwind the spiral without end.

Afterword

If you liked this book, help spread the word. Tell a friend... or five friends. Your support is appreciated.

The music album that goes with this book is called *Vortex Winder*, by Lighthouse XIII. It is available on iTunes, Amazon, Spotify, and YouTube.

The sequel to *The Vortex Winder* is called *The Maelstrom Ascendant*, and it also comes with a music album - in fact, two albums – *Waves Upon Waves* and *The Maelstrom Ascendant*.

Website – www.vortexwinder.com

Contact - Alfadex Books can be contacted as follows:

By email:
matthew.alfadex@gmail.com.

By post:
PO Box 2150,
Clovelly, NSW, 2031

Song Lyrics

Vortex Winder

Come to life, begin again
Unwind the spiral without end

It spins, transforms
In the vortex born
It morphs, it grinds
Let the vortices unwind

Flowing, spinning,
Sparking

Winding spiral stairway, to Earth ascend
Into infinity, we live again
Ride the golden helix, to Earth ascend
Welcome to the new world

Come to life, we rise again
In time, the spiral has no end

It sparks, it shines
Illuminates free minds
It spins, it swirls
Unravelling this world

Flowing, spinning,
Sparking

Winding spiral stairway, to Earth ascend
Into infinity, we live again
Ride the golden helix, to Earth ascend
Welcome to the new world

Trade Winds

Dawn is bright and life is short
What we seek cannot be taught
Distant shores are beckoning
Deja voices echoing

When the trade winds blow, worlds collide
When the trade winds blow, dreams take flight.

Seeds will fly and worlds collide
I will ride the trade winds tonight
Cut the cards and roll the dice
I will ride the trade winds tonight

Seeds are scattered far and wide
Crossing through the great divide
Dynasties to make and break
Midwived by the winds of trade

When the trade winds blow, worlds collide
When the trade winds blow, dreams take flight.

Seeds will fly and worlds collide
I will ride the trade winds tonight
Cut the cards and roll the dice
I will ride the trade winds tonight

Black Art

Light the candles, light the fuse
Nothing but my chains to lose

Regicide, Justice rise

I call on the Powers that protect this world
Take the tyrant from its heart
Give me the keys to the kingdom
Black art

Matthew's reign stops my ascent
Spells bring down vile government

Regicide, Justice rise

I call on the Powers that protect this world
Take the tyrant from its heart
Give me the keys to the kingdom
Black art

I call on the Powers
I call on the Powers
I call on the Powers
I call on the Powers

Life Line

Destiny in my hands
Y shaped life line,
Long and straight or
Short and divine

My fate concealed
Only now is real

And if my life ends before its time
No regrets this choice was mine
Let the fruit not wither on the vine
Take a chance on my lifeline

Destiny in my hands
My true life line,
Long and safe or
Short and sublime

My fate concealed
Only now is real

And if my life ends before its time
No regrets this choice was mine
Let the fruit not wither on the vine
Take a chance on my lifeline

Spark

In the darkest place still hope lives
Resurrecting against all odds

In the depths of the dark
Burns the tiniest spark
Fan those flames
Higher

Curse this prison, I will live on to
See these walls all go
Up in flames

In the depths of the dark
Burns the tiniest spark
Fan those flames
Higher

Road Rage

I step into my car
I know I won't get far
Until the next fight in the endless war
There's too many humans, and too many laws
You sabotage my life every day
My sanity is starting to fray

Why are you the speed hump in my way?

Stop, go
Yes, no
Fast, slow, Stop

I trip over your mind
Reason so hard to find
My will slowly crushed by the daily grind
Obstruction is by you so well defined

Your job is to prevent and deny
You'd legislate the wings off a fly
Why do I bother to even try?

Stop, go
Yes, no
Fast, slow,
Stop

You sabotage my life every day
My sanity is starting to fray
Why are you the speed hump in my way?

Z Club

Fire up your ragged hearts tonight
Armies of nobodies on the rise
Fight for an illusionary prize

Z list, make a wish, iron fist
Just another fool who won't be missed

Is this fame or infamy?
Welcome into Club Fifteen
Feed poor bored humanity
Then you pay the exit fee

The beast is always hungry for fresh flesh
New blood sweet and easy to digest
When the bones are picked, bring on the next

Z list, make a wish, iron fist
Just another fool, you won't be missed

Is this fame or infamy?
Welcome into Club Fifteen
Feed poor bored humanity
Then you pay the exit fee

Epitaph

I was born a child in time
A simple life in rain and sunshine
All things must pass, now my story's been told
Only these words left say I once lived

Gone, my time is past
In these words, I live again

Old friends pass from light to shade
With each mind, my memory fades
I loved this world, yet we all must move on
My spirit lives on when my body is

Gone, my time is past
In these words, I live again

Elijinx

Human
Face your nemesis
Look inside, deep into my eyes
Spirit
Executioner
Sharpen the axe for your demise

There's no man can outrun time
None escape the scythe
Evil deeds sharpen the blade
Hear the laughter of the vanquished as you die

Destroyer
Accursed is your race
A living carcass rotting from inside
Seeds
Of your own downfall
Carnage that carved your bloody rise

Tyrant
Enslaving your own kind
Gorging in the face of starvation
Plunder
The booty that awaits
In the end only damnation

There's no man can outrun time
None escape the scythe
Evil deeds sharpen the blade
See the faces of your victims as you die

Rank
Hierarchy of slaves
Equality an idealistic myth
Freedom
The freedom to obey
Matthew wields his iron fist

Here's a salute to the victors
The rulers of this world
Your empire has its day in the sun
Your rise to the top was a nepotistic feast
Domination of the many by one

Animal cunning, and ruthless intent
An endless appetite for war
With no one left to subjugate
You'll turn on your own blood
And violate your own inner core

I am the dark spirit, the shadow of your soul
The memories you can never ignore
I gave you a license for a litany of sins
Do what thou wilt shall be the whole of the law

Feel it beating
The black heart pumps the blood,
Conquest is such intoxication
But when the vigour dissipates
Your destiny awaits
Your empire crumbles into the grave

Liar
Corruption to the core
Your golden palace hewn from blood and bone
Aspire
To grasp for always more, and
Hang another skull behind your throne

Wallow
In your mire of wealth
Chronos is waiting at the door
Hollow
Sockets of Thanatos
Return you to the dust for evermore

There's no man can outrun time
None escape the scythe
Evil deeds sharpen the blade
Hear the laughter of your victims as you die

Human
Face your nemesis
Look inside, deep into my eyes
Spirit
Executioner
Lower the axe for your demise

Oceanus

Bow to the one that can never be tamed
Vast as its terrible power breaks
Since time immemorial
Fear at the sight of the one that is named
Crashing, destroying, no mercy, no, no

Power, universal energy manifest as water
Bow to the might of Oceanus
Oceanus, Thanatos

Fear at the sight of the deity's power
Watching it build as you run in vain
Devastate, ruin, obliterate
Swallow a city and darkness devour
Beasts of the water in dwellings
Once held by men

Power, universal energy manifest as water
Bow to the might of Oceanus
Oceanus, Thanatos

Acknowledgments

The author would like to acknowledge the following as sources and inspirations. Song lyrics are alluded to, but not quoted.

Chapter 7: *The Needle and the Damage Done*, Warren Fellows, Pan Macmillan, Australia, 1991.

Chapter 9: 'The Matthew Effect' was a phrase coined by the philosopher of science Robert K. Merton in 1968.

Chapter 9 alludes to the Prong song 'Shouldn't Have Bothered' composed by Tommy Victor from the album *Prove You Wrong*, Epic, 1991.

Chapter 14 alludes to the Frank Sinatra song 'That's Life,' composed by Dean Kay and Kelly Gordon, from the *That's Life* album, Reprise, 1966.

Chapter 15 alludes to the Bruce Dickinson song 'King in Crimson,' composed by Bruce Dickinson and Roy Z, from *The Chemical Wedding* album, Air Raid Records, 1998.

Also Available

Books By Duncan Smith

The Vortex Winder
The Maelstrom Ascendant
Conquest By Concept
Cultown
The Vast and the Spurious
The Tightarse Tuesday Book Club

Albums By Lighthouse XIII

Waves Upon Waves
Vortex Winder
The Maelstrom Ascendant
Cultown

Contact

Website: www.vortexwinder.com.

Alfadex Books can be reached on matthew.alfadex@gmail.com.

Also available by this author

The Maelstrom Ascendant

Sequel to *The Vortex Winder*.

Rocker Jimmy Brandt has given up on his dreams. He's settled down in the suburbs with his girlfriend and cat... until strange forces tempt him back to his former life. Soon he faces a choice between good and evil - and life is so rewarding when you turn to the dark side.

Flying high again, Jimmy battles divas, despots, and most of all, himself. Yet the higher you fly, the further you can fall. Only an old, forgotten friend can save him. But does he want to be saved?

Conquest By Concept

A novel about the culture war.

John Gilbert loves Angie, his far-left Antifa girlfriend. Then he meets Edward Hall, a charismatic right wing figure. Hall makes John question Angie's political beliefs. Soon, John can no longer tell which side is good or evil.

John begins a journey through the culture war. Along the way, he has to navigate a 'whiteness' workshop, a Me-Too allegation, and the PC school system in his job as a trainee teacher. Caught in a political 'love triangle' between the far-left and right, John has to make a choice. Will he stay true to Angie's passionate progressive values, or can the seductive Edward Hall turn him to the dark side.

Wars are fought in the mind, not just on the battlefield. It's conquest by concept - but which side is telling the truth?

Reviews of *Conquest By Concept.*

- "Smith goes where more timid writers fear to tread... serious themes brought to life through brilliant characters and dialogue. Edward Hall is one of the best anti-heroes of our time." PW
- "I'm halfway through *Conquest by Concept* and I can hardly put it down. It's brill! A breath of fresh air ramped up to a gale force wind." MG

Cultown

Thomas Swan forms the Milinish, a cult with an odd mix of scientific and religious beliefs.

From humble beginnings in Sydney, the Milinish moves overseas to become the fastest growing cult in America. Yet Swan's mad reign spirals out of control. Finally, on the brink of disaster, he decides to tell all.

Here, in the ultimate inside story, Thomas Swan reveals the secrets and scandals inside the Milinish, the greatest cult of the 21st century.

'Exposes not just the cultishness of religion, but of science too. This is the best novel yet written on the trouble between science and religion.'

J. Williams, Fuse.

The Tightarse Tuesday Book Club

This new set of stories has some of Duncan Smith's best work. 'Hook Up Hell' is a comical Tinder farce, 'Badminton Boy' a superhero send-up, and 'Ghost Squad' a wry look at celebrities who pretend to write books. But it is 'Marla Okadigbo,' that is the most timely for its look at the hot topic of racism in modern America.

This is the story of a literary scam that takes America by storm. White male author, Winkler Jones, pens an online review of *The Handmaid's Tale*, Margaret Atwood's book about a world where women have no rights and exist only to serve men. Jones calls it a work of 'oppression porn' and says it's only a matter of time before a black American writes a novel where slavery is restored.

Jones' crooked agent tells him to delete the review and write the slavery book himself. Jones does so, publishing it under the pen name, 'Marla Okadigbo,' supposedly a black American woman. The book is a hit until the author's true identity is revealed. It then becomes a scandal, and perception of the book changes from a story of the struggle for black liberation to one of oppression by white supremacists.

Meanwhile, Jones is haunted by the spirit of the real Marla, a black slave from the early 1800s, and feuds with his girlfriend, Sonia, a white English teacher struggling to help school students in the poor neighbourhood where she works.

The Vast and the Spurious :

25 Problems For Feminism

Non-fiction

We live in the age of the gender wars, and there is probably more anger between men and women than ever before. Is there any hope for a harmonious future, or will these wars rage until doomsday?

A clear and incisive look at some of the main gender war issues of our time, with some surprising solutions.

"Whether for the uninitiated, the curious, or the indoctrinated, this book offers a witty rebuttal to popular claims and exaggerations. Grounded in common sense and empathy, it makes the rational case, too rarely heard, for harmony between the sexes and respect for men's contributions."

Janice Fiamengo, Professor of English, University of Ottawa, Canada, and editor of *Sons of Feminism: Men Have Their Say.*

Lighthouse XIII Albums

Waves Upon Waves

Songs: Mountain Gods, SMS: Save My Sanity, Between the Stairway and the Highway, Reaper Bones, Leuchtturm, LHXIII, Temporary Kingdom, Retro Stereo, Waves Upon Waves, New World Alchemy.

Vortex Winder

Vortex Winder, Road Rage, Trade Winds, Black Art, Life Line, Spark, Z Club, Epitaph, Elijinx, Oceanus.

The Maelstrom Ascendant

Black Phoenix, High and Mighty, The Price of Dominion, Moonlight Tiger, I for an Eye, Haunted, Death Bed Regrets, Extinction.Net, Quitter, The Maelstrom Ascendant, The Ephemeral and the Eternal.

Cultown

Amnesia, Skeptic Eclectic, Evil But Not Vile, In Nihilum, Cultown, Helix Eternal, Doom Pipers, Fallen to a Higher Place, The Scythe and the Scalpel, Triangle of Fire, Transcendence, The Cultimate Culminates.